PROTECTORS - BOOK ONE OF BEYOND THESE WALLS

A POST-APOCALYPTIC SURVIVAL THRILLER

MICHAEL ROBERTSON

Email: subscribers@michaelrobertson.co.uk

Edited by:

Terri King - http://terri-king.wix.com/editing
And
Pauline Nolet - http://www.paulinenolet.com

Cover Design by Dusty Crosley

Protectors - Book one of Beyond These Walls

Michael Robertson

MAILING LIST

Sign up for my spam-free mailing list for all of my latest releases and special offers. You'll also receive these four FREE books. You can unsubscribe at any time.

Go to www.michaelrobertson.co.uk

Michael Robertson
EDEN
A Short Story
About The Zombie Apocalypse

RAT RUN
A POST-APOCALYPTIC TALE
Michael Robertson

CHAPTER 1

Spike ruffled his nose against the stench coming from the chamber pot. No matter how many times he did this job, he'd never get used to carrying his family's waste. The liquid inside the large ceramic container swirled as he walked, forcing him to tense his upper body to counter the motion of it. Many people in Edin carried the pots by their rope handles. Because he'd seen one snap in the past, he didn't. As much as he hated the stinking things, the job had to be done and, like so many people in Edin, he did it at least once every two days. If they left it much longer, the smell became unbearable.

His dad walked beside him as they headed towards the large wall along the back of the city. They shimmied and weaved to negotiate the flow of people returning from dumping their waste. The foetid liquid inside the pots echoed their movements, constantly in opposition to the present moment.

They often made the journey in the evening. It gave his dad a chance to get out of the agricultural district after a long day working in the fields. In Edin, there were very few chances to get out of the place you lived and worked in, so the vile job ended up becoming an outing for his old man. Because Spike hadn't yet done his national service, he still had the freedom to roam the city. Minors, politicians, and protectors could go wherever they liked, whenever they liked.

As much as Spike hated carrying the pots, he loved the chance to chat with his dad. But tonight felt different. Tomorrow he turned eighteen; in two days, he'd be picked up and taken for national service. He'd not return for at least six months—if he returned at all.

The vast wall surrounding Edin got no lower than twenty feet at any point. The back section Spike and his dad currently headed towards stood the tallest at around thirty feet. A set of double gates at the bottom of the wall led outside. No more than about six feet tall and the same wide, they were once the main access to the city. Now they were used for something else entirely. While staring at them, Spike said, "Do you think they'll have an eviction tonight?"

"Who knows?" his dad said, grimacing while hugging the larger of the two chamber pots to his chest. A strong man with a thick frame, it made sense for him to carry the heavier container. "We normally come at a good time for it."

"Do you think those who empty their pots at different times of day never see one?"

"Maybe that's why they do it. For some, they probably don't want to see it."

"So why do we?"

The wall had wooden scaffolding attached to it. It had four levels, each one accessed via a ramp from the level below The path to the top involved climbing the first ramp before walking to the end of the first level in order to climb the second ramp, and then walking to the end of the second level to the third ramp, repeating the process until they finished their zigzagged ascent to the fourth level.

Spike and his dad joined the queue to get onto the first ramp, the scaffolding always busy at this time of night. The combined smell of many pots drove two hard fingers down the back of Spike's throat, locking him in a battle against his gag reflex.

"I think seeing people evicted is a good reminder of what the city does for us," his dad finally said when they started moving again. "What happens to those who choose not to abide by the rules."

In all the years they'd been emptying their chamber pots, Spike hadn't given it much thought. Evictions happened. They were part of being an Edin resident. If you did nothing wrong, then you had nothing to fear. And why would the city waste resources on those who didn't want to help it grow? Things were tight enough without having to keep criminals and anarchists alive.

By the time they'd walked the length of the first level and climbed the ramp to the second, they were about fifteen feet up and higher than most of the structures in the city. Materials being what they were, most residential buildings reached no taller than one storey. In the past, they'd tried to build taller houses, but many collapsed. Countless families had perished beneath the rubble of an ambitious home. His arms aching from the heavy pot, Spike sweated, the night unseasonably warm for March. With both of his hands in use, he blinked against the sting of it running into his eyes.

The only buildings taller than one storey were communal and government buildings. The mayor had a three-storey house, several warehouses were slightly taller, three or four monuments celebrating Edin's greatness, and of course, the Arena. Just looking at it gave Spike a boost, his arms hurting less than they had a few seconds ago. "I'll be there tomorrow. And when I'm the next protector, I'll be there most nights. I'll make sure you have front-row seats whenever you want them."

They usually chatted a lot on their trips to empty the pots, discussing everything from what existed far beyond their walls to how long it would be before the next section of Edin opened up to everyone. But as they moved up to the third wooden platform—the entire walkway shaking with the thud of Edin's citizens moving along it—Spike's dad didn't seem to have a reply in him.

On the fourth and final walkway, Spike now had the clearest view he'd get of the city. Ten thousand citizens divided into districts. Agriculture, ceramics, textiles … all of them standing in stark contrast to their neighbours. The ceramics sector was distinguished by the glorious mosaic of colour throughout. They had wind chimes outside nearly every house. Sheets of every possible shade and colour flapped in the gentle breeze of the textiles district as they dried in the open air. Large swathes of yellow and brown marked the agriculture area filled with its crops and ploughed fields. They all worked to make Edin greater and to support an ever-growing populace and infrastructure.

As wonderful as the patchwork looked, the clear demarcation lines reminded Spike why he had to be the next protector. If he failed, he'd be imprisoned in the agricultural district for life. He loved his mum and dad, but he didn't want their restricted existence. He wanted to move freely through the city. He wanted a job that made him feel alive. Most importantly, he wanted Matilda. She lived in ceramics, and if he wanted to be with someone from another district, he had to be a protector. There was a saying in Edin about falling in love with someone from another district. They said it was reserved for protectors, politicians, and fools. No way he'd be a fool. Even less of a chance of him becoming a politician.

Spike looked across to the opposite end of the city at the two large gates leading to the national service area. It was where the national service cadets stayed. He would be one of them in two days' time, spending evenings there and days outside the city's walls, extending Edin's boundaries so the city could grow.

"Just focus on national service before you think about becoming a protector," Spike's dad finally said, breaking him out of his daze.

Spike looked away from the gates and to his dad's sombre face. "What's wrong?"

His dad looked the other way, staring out over the wall, his deep frown set against the strong wind as he gazed at the wastelands and the vast lake beyond the city. A scratching sound from where he rested his ceramic chamber pot on the top of the rough stone. About five feet wide, the huge barrier had so far stood the test of time. "I love that you have the ambition to be the next protector, and I don't want to take that away from you."

"But?" Spike said.

"National service is brutal. You need to promise me you'll take every day a step at a time. Focus on what's in front of you so you remain alive. Don't go into it overconfident, because you won't get to the end of the six months."

"But you've always supported me in becoming a protector."

"And I still do. It's just, I don't want you to underestimate what's coming to you in two days' time. There's a reason why only fifty percent of cadets return from national service." He snorted an ironic laugh. "If you can call many of the broken shells who come back *returned.*"

"Why don't more people talk about it?"

Usually, whenever Spike had a question or wanted to pose a thought, his dad would always listen intently and offer the best heartfelt advice he could. Today, he had a glaze to his eyes that showed he had his attention elsewhere. "It's brutal," he said. "In national service, you're forced to make decisions. Life-and-death decisions. Sometimes you have to choose your own well-being over that of others. You might have to watch someone die to save yourself, and the chances are you know that person well because you've shared a dorm with them for however long you've been there. No one wants to relive that, and no one wants to be judged for the choices they made. For that reason, it's easier not to talk about it."

While letting go of a hard sigh, his cheeks puffing out, Spike too looked at the lake outside the back of the city. He felt the force of the strong wind without a wall to block it. He looked at the pulley system they used to retrieve water from it without having to go outside. The complex wooden framework had many of the characteristics of the scaffolding he currently stood on. It stretched across over two hundred feet of long grass before it reached the water.

Then he looked at *them.* Even now, on a seemingly quiet night, Spike saw the shambling forms of at least fifteen diseased. It reminded him of the walls keeping them safe from the creatures desperate to take chunks from them. Another reason to become a protector: he wanted to be part of the solution, culling them on a daily basis and showing them they wouldn't ever win, no matter how many of them there were.

A loud horn sounded. A Pavlovian response to it, Spike smiled at his dad. But his dad's face remained stoic. Not even an eviction could excite him tonight. "What do you think this one's done?" Spike said.

They often played the game, and Spike's dad did his part as best he could. "Maybe he robbed someone."

"I think he's a murderer." When Spike had been little, his dad would make the people being evicted the worst kind of people he could imagine. He'd make them scarier than the diseased so Spike felt safer to have them outside the city. At times, he even came close to feeling grateful to the diseased for dealing with them on Edin's behalf.

A few moments of silence always followed the horn, those on the wall watching, waiting for the evicted to emerge. The snap of the heavy bolt on the gate cracked through the air. The diseased in the long grass lifted their heads as one. Then the first scream. A hellish and broken wail of torment, it sounded somewhere between a hiss and a shriek. The sound of the long grass rubbed against legs as the creatures took off, sprinting at the gate. Even from where he stood, Spike's stomach clamped with the adrenaline rush. It didn't matter how thick the barrier between them, he always felt like this would be the time they got through. The time when one of them went for the gate rather than the evicted.

"There goes the rabbit," a woman farther down the wall shouted.

Spike saw the man. He couldn't have been much older than Spike himself. He looked fresh back from national service. After doing his bit for the city, he'd clearly then screwed them over in some way. Although, the younger they were, the better the chase. Maybe he'd make it to the water.

As the young man made his bid for freedom, the diseased closest to him screamed as if to call the others to its position. The pack altered their course, zeroing in on the young man and ignoring the gate completely. The bolt snapped home as someone locked it below.

Many of Edin's evicted knew if they went the wrong way, not only would they find the ground boggy underfoot, but they'd be coated in the contents of everyone's chamber pots as the residents emptied them from above. Like so many before him, the young man ran away from the full pots.

"He's fast," Spike said, bouncing on his toes while he glanced at his dad.

Although his dad smiled, his eyes didn't.

Spike looked back at the man in the grass, his path easy to follow because of the trail he left behind him. "He's seen a gap. I think he might make it!" The closest diseased lost distance to the man as he headed for the lake. Very few made it to the lake. If they did, and if they could swim, the diseased would follow them in, but they couldn't stay afloat. Every drop of water from the lake had to be boiled until it almost evaporated. God knew how many infected bodies rotted at the bottom of it.

The man had already halved the distance to the lake. "He's going to make it!" As much as Spike hated the criminals when he was a kid, he now saw them as the underdog. Besides, he knew what the diseased were and he couldn't bring himself to root for them. Not like he might have done as a younger boy.

Crack! A diseased exploded from nowhere and clattered into the man's side. Spike winced at what sounded like bones breaking on impact. Despite their withered appearance, the creatures were both fast and strong.

The diseased who'd taken the man down snarled as it bit into him. Another crunch, this time from where its teeth sank into flesh and bone. The bite turned the man limp.

The diseased who were running after the man just seconds before stopped as if he no longer existed. The one who'd taken him down got to its feet. Feral and with blood coating its maw, its eyes glistened a deep crimson and were spread wide on its wrinkled face. It walked away from the downed man, leaving him in the long grass. Now it had bitten him, it had done its job.

No matter how many times he'd watched it, Spike couldn't ever look away from someone who'd been taken down. They always started with a pulsing twitch. Violent in how it threw their limbs away from them. The man's right leg went first. Then an arm. Like many before him, the disease ripped through his frame, spasming and snapping his form. Seconds later, he jumped to his feet, blood coursing from his eyes like those of his diseased brethren. No more than fifty feet between him and the water's edge, as much as Spike knew the man to be a criminal in some way, his heart hurt for him. "He got so close."

The touch of his dad made Spike jump and turn to him. Where

his eyes had been glazed, some of the presence he knew his dad for had returned. "I'm sorry to be negative today."

Spike shrugged and emptied his chamber pot over the side. Every few weeks, they rotated where they could dump it from so the ground around the wall's foundations didn't get too boggy.

"I want you to enjoy your birthday tomorrow and your trip to the arena. Tomorrow is the last day of true freedom; you should celebrate that. Just promise me you'll stay focused when you go for national service. Worry about becoming a protector when the time comes. Just surviving will put you in a good position to try out for the apprenticeship." Tears glazed his eyes for a second and his features twisted as if they might buckle out of shape. "If I could go in your place tomorrow, I would." He tapped his own heart. "Know I'll be thinking about you every second of you being away." Once he'd emptied his pot over the side too, he said, "Come on, let's get home. You need some rest if you're going to the big event tomorrow."

His dad's sombre tone sank through Spike. As he looked at his hero's slumped shoulders, he drew a deep sigh. Surely national service wouldn't be that bad. And surely it would be worth it if it gave him a lifetime with the girl he loved.

CHAPTER 2

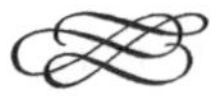

Just over two hundred spectators sat shoulder to shoulder on the stone benches encircling the fighting pit. Spike knew this because … well, there wasn't much he didn't know about the main event and the city's protectors. After all, he planned to win the apprenticeship to be the next one. He might not know the other cadets he'd be competing against in national service, but he doubted any of them wanted it more than him. He looked at Matilda on his right.

The fighting pit in the centre of the arena had bloodstains covering the stone ground. In the very middle, it had a metal sheet that lay flush, a trapdoor over a hole through which the protector emerged. Spike sat several rows back. The best seats in the house were lower down at the front. They were the closest to the action, but were still elevated at least fifteen feet from the pit. They were lifted high enough to make them a safe spot to watch from. In a lifetime, a resident of Edin might get five or six trips to the arena. No chance would they get one of the seats in the front row. Those seats were reserved for the more influential contingent in the city.

Despite there being over two hundred spectators, no one spoke. It was so quiet, Spike could hear the beating of his own giddy heart. Another look at Matilda on his right. She might not have had the same enthusiasm as him for the main event, but there was no one else he'd rather be there with.

After smiling at her, Spike looked down at those in the posh seats again. They wore finer clothes, had more space on either side of them, and didn't look behind them at those in the second row and beyond. To get there, he'd have to become a politician or protector. No way would he ever become a politician.

Like most of the structures in Edin, the arena had been built from stone and concrete. It made Spike's seat too hard to be comfortable. But he didn't care, he'd waited a lifetime to be amongst the crowd for the main event.

Although Spike leaned in to talk to Matilda, he stopped himself. The noise would carry and he had nothing to say that he hadn't said a thousand times already. She knew how excited he felt.

Despite it being Spike's first visit, he knew the experience well. He'd asked so many questions of those who'd been there before him. Inquisitive to the point of being irritating, but he'd had to know. The seats were as uncomfortable as they all said. The tension as thick in the air.

Having just turned eighteen, Spike got his invite to attend the main event that morning. And a good job too. Occasionally, some eighteen-year-olds were forgotten about and they had to appeal. He'd be in national service tomorrow. If they'd screwed his allocation up, he'd have had no chance of finding a councillor to rectify it with so little time.

Spike smiled at Matilda again and she smiled back. Despite her pallid hue, she'd said she wanted to come. She wanted to be with him on his eighteenth birthday, however he chose to celebrate it.

Then the sound they'd all been waiting for. It started as a series of clicks. Many of those in the crowd looked skyward in reaction to the shriek and grind of the old machinery. Despite its daily use and maintenance, the ancient crane groaned like it didn't have long left before it gave up completely. Spike looked up and behind him too. He took in the long neck of the mechanical beast. Red flaking paint, it wore its rust like psoriasis. It strained from the weight of its cargo, which currently remained hidden from view. A buzz of excitement broke the crowd's silence, and Spike leaned close to Matilda. "It's finally here."

Despite her nodding at him, her intelligent brown eyes taking him in, Spike couldn't ignore the slight strain to her features. She'd wanted to be here to share in this with him—she'd said that a thousand times over—but she couldn't share in the sadistic pleasure many got from the main event.

A reluctance in his muscles told him no, she'd reject him, but Spike reached across and held the back of Matilda's hand anyway. An already rapid heart, it beat quicker and harder at the contact of her warm skin. They'd spent their lives holding back from one another—led more by her than him—and would have to continue doing so until he became a protector. After a few seconds, he pulled away. If he hadn't, he'd hold on forever and she'd have to reject him. "Are you sure you're okay with being here? We can leave if you want to."

"*What?* That would break your heart."

"Not as much as making you suffer would."

It seemed to disarm Matilda, who stared at him for a few seconds before she said, "All summer you've made it your mission to pass this arena every chance you get."

Spike smiled.

"I've been with you so many times, it would be anticlimactic to miss it now. Even if it does mean sitting through a main event. I *want* to be here. I truly do."

The bright sun caught the shine of Matilda's long brown hair. When she tucked half of it behind her left ear, Spike took in her tanned face. Nowhere near as dark as him, she'd inherited the olive-skinned complexion of her parents. It didn't matter that he'd known her his entire life, just the sight of her still ripped the air from his lungs. His forbidden love from ceramics. He'd entered the realm of protectors, politicians, and fools. "Thank you," he finally said. "I know how coming here is bittersweet for you. With your dad and all." Not that he knew the truth of her dad, just that he made their life at home hard and it had something to do with the protectors. It prevented her from trying to be one herself. She'd tell him when she felt ready.

A slight steeling of her features, she turned to face the arena. A second later, tears glazed her deep brown eyes. Spike watched her throat bob with a hard gulp.

When Matilda looked back, she appeared to have regained her composure. "I'm sorry," she said, "I don't want to put a downer on your birthday by talking about my family. Let's just enjoy it, yeah? I'm honoured to be here with you. Happy birthday."

All the while, the clack of the crane called out. The neck of the thing continued to creak and groan. A permanent feature on Edin's skyline for as long as Spike had been alive, the crane could be mistaken for a wreck for those who didn't know. But at least two to three times a week, when the arena hosted a main event, it came to life like an old skeleton finding the motion it had once had when encased with muscles and flesh. Apparently, back in the old days, the crane operated on something called an *engine* that ran on a liquid called *diesel*. Not that he understood the magic of the olden days, but the end result meant the crane could move without manpower outside the arena. It seemed light years ahead of the pulleys and winches that shifted the large beast now.

The sun hurt Spike's eyes as he waited for the glass container to lift into view. A glance at the crowd showed him they all squinted up at it too. Only the front row remained facing forwards. They'd probably seen it hundreds of times before. The novelty had well and truly worn off for them.

The noise of the crowd rose when the glass prison appeared over the wall. A buzz of excited chatter, it lifted the hairs on Spike's arms and the back of his neck. He bounced where he sat.

About six feet long and three feet wide, the glass crate had been strengthened by the steel frame wrapped around it. The diseased inside had no chance of breaking out. Although, from the way it behaved, it looked to give it a good go. It slammed against either side as it sprayed bloody spittle from its furiously snapping mouth.

The crowd booed. The deep swell of their collective bass note ran a vibration through the stone structure. Where Spike had only ever heard it from outside the arena, the noise damn near blew the top of his skull off. "This is amazing," he shouted at Matilda.

The crate reached the tip of the crane. As high as it would go, it had a pendulous swing from where the diseased inside sprinted from one end to the other. It wore nothing but a pair of jeans, the thud of its bare feet beating against the glass floor of its prison. Almost white skin and covered in the wrinkles of an OAP, the thing looked weak. Atrophied and pale, it would be easy to underestimate its strength. But when he saw the way it moved the container … the deep *boom* of each contact with the walls at either end … the venom driving its screaming fury … Spike had also seen their power in what they did to people evicted from the city.

A man near to Spike shouted, "We've got a lively one."

Spike laughed with the rest of the crowd. Adrenaline tightened his stomach and made his skin electric. He'd waited his entire life for this moment.

Despite the noise inside the arena, the thud of the creature's movements could still be heard over the top of it. Every violent collision with one of the walls of its prison sounded like it could break through. If it did and the monster fell on the crowd, all two hundred of them would be turned in minutes. It could be enough to take the entire city down. But a diseased hadn't ever broken through and never could either.

The crane's neck pivoted, accompanied by the sound of a winch outside. It moved the transparent prison over the wall across the top of the crowd. The creature got closer as they lowered it. Tracks of blood stained its cheeks. A crimson maw, when it hissed and spat, it sprayed the air with a claret mist.

One of the taller spectators stood on their bench, reached up, and banged the bottom of the container. The loud thump silenced the crowd, and Spike joined everyone else in watching the monster inside. It halted for a moment, its jerking head movements snapping in the direction of the sound. The thick glass silenced its scream, its wrinkled face straining with the effort, its entire frame shaking with its release. The ex-human then charged, zeroing in on the man. It connected head first with the glass with a loud and resounding *tonk*. It turned the beast's legs bandy and it fell limp.

Spike expected the creature to jump back up again. The diseased were famed for their resilience, so why wouldn't it? But instead, it twitched and twisted before it fell completely still.

Another blanket of silence fell over the crowd. Spike's stomach dropped and he shook his head. "No. Please don't let it be over already. I've waited so long for this moment."

Unable to hold onto his panic, his breaths quickened as he turned to Matilda and grabbed her hands. "Do you think it's dead? Please don't say it's over already."

Matilda gave his hands a calming squeeze and her eyebrows rose in the middle. Her sad eyes spoke the apology her mouth couldn't.

CHAPTER 3

Silence descended on the crowd again, and Spike focused his attention on the bloodstained fighting area below. Easier than looking at Matilda. If he turned her way, he wouldn't be able to hide his disappointment. Since he'd known about the arena, he'd been waiting for his turn to see a main event, and now the dumb diseased had killed itself by running into a glass wall. From what he could see, everyone else looked up at the box behind him—even the front row—but there seemed little point in watching the now expired diseased.

Still focused on the arena, Spike reached across and held Matilda's hand. "You've been a great friend for coming with me today. Thank you. I know this isn't your kind of thing at all, but there's no one else I'd want here with me right now."

She acknowledged what he'd said to her with the gentlest squeeze of his hand before letting it go. The arena had fallen so quiet, he heard her whisper, "I'm sorry," but couldn't tell if she meant about letting go of his hand or because of what had happened with the diseased.

After pulling in a deep breath—the dirty funk of sweaty bodies around him—Spike steeled himself. He'd assume she meant the diseased. "The fact that you came means more to me than seeing the main event. I'm sure I'll get another chance at some point in the future. Hell, I'll probably be taking part in it soon."

Suddenly the crowd roared and Spike turned to face the box. But the diseased hadn't moved. The sounds around him quieted down again. A shake of his head, he muttered, "The thing's dead. There's no point in hoping for anything else." No one wanted to believe it, but they had to.

Still, Spike kept his attention on the glass crate. Closer than he'd ever been to a diseased, he looked at the shirtless creature. Wrinkled and saggy-skinned, it looked like it had had the life sucked from it. Then he saw it. He pointed for Matilda to look. She turned in time to see another spasm snap through one of the diseased's skinny arms.

Spike got to his feet, as did many around him. A more definitive twitch then kicked through the thing. The same arm as before, this time it came to life, rising from the floor of its prison before slamming down, palm first, against the glass with a slap.

Joining in with the crowd's shouting, they cheered so loud Spike's ears rang. Grinning, his breaths quickening, he watched the thing's arm twitch again. It looked to be coming back stronger than before.

The sound dropped again as if the two hundred people there held their breaths. Quiet enough for Spike to hear the withered hand hitting the glass floor of the container for a second, third, and fourth time. Padding and pawing, it played an irregular beat.

Spike's heart pounded in his throat to watch the diseased human get to its feet. Still dazed from the self-inflicted injury, it swayed where it stood. Wide and bloody unblinking eyes, it worked its loose jaw in a circular motion as if tasting consciousness again.

The message must have been passed to the people operating

the crane because the sound of the turning winch called from outside the arena. The container several feet above them, Spike reached up for it like he'd seen the man do earlier. He missed. As it moved away from him, it rocked and swung. The diseased inside pressed against the glass walls of its prison as it fought to remain upright.

Taking a moment to sit down, Spike turned to Matilda. "I want to follow it."

"You *what?*"

"I haven't had a chance to see it properly. When it was over us, it was dazed." He pointed across the arena. "Those on the other side will get to see it in all its glory. I've waited too long to miss out on that." As the container moved over to the crowd on the other side, Spike watched the creature regain its fury.

"I don't think you should."

The concrete steps would be easy enough to shimmy around on. "No one will begrudge me trying to have a closer look. This is my best chance to get near one."

As Spike moved to stand up, Matilda pulled him down by hooking her hand over the top of his shoulder. "It's an awful idea, Spike. You'll just annoy people. I get how desperate you are to see this, but at least the thing isn't dead. You'll still see the main event."

At that moment, Spike noticed a man get to his feet and shove his way past the other spectators. The faces of those he passed suggested they weren't happy, but he made progress, getting closer to the box.

The farther the man travelled, the more those close to him jeered and shouted. As the box made its slow journey across the arena, he moved around to meet it. Spike would take the abuse if he could get as close.

Then Spike saw movement down in the fighting pit. Four guards appeared in the middle. They all had whistles. One of them sounded a shrill peep, her face reddening from the effort of it. Many in the crowd looked at them rather than the diseased in the box. The guard with the whistle pointed at the man. Although he pretended he didn't see her, those around him didn't let him get away with it. The crowd turned on the man, shoving him down the steps towards the pit.

Even those in the front row saw him coming and moved aside so they didn't halt his momentum. He fell the fifteen feet and hit the concrete ground with a thud. It might have hurt, but not enough to keep him down. As he got up onto one knee, the guards went to work on him with a flurry of baton strikes.

It took them a matter of seconds to knock the man unconscious. Spike forgot about the diseased in the crate at that moment, his stomach turning over to watch the brief yet effective beating.

Three of the guards dragged the man from the arena while the woman with the whistle addressed everyone else. "You don't shove and push people out of the way. It's dangerous."

Matilda leaned close to Spike. "I told you it wasn't a good idea."

"Point taken." As he released a hard sigh, Spike deflated where he sat. He'd still get to see the main event. At least that hadn't passed them by.

CHAPTER 4

Now the man had been removed, Spike returned his attention to the diseased in the box. The crowd on the other side of the arena booed and hissed at the thing, many of them standing up to reach its glass prison.

Now it had gathered a little momentum, the glass case had increased its pendulous swing on the end of the large and rusty hook. The creature inside grew ever more agitated, thrown about by the motion of it.

An already hot day, sweat lifted beneath Spike's collar from close press of bodies around him. He tugged on it to beat the itch threatening to bite into his skin. God only knew what the diseased felt inside its thick glass walls—if it felt anything. No doubt the container stank. Just the thought of it turned his stomach. Sweat, excrement, rot, blood …

The glass box moved over the main part of the crowd directly opposite, and Spike watched it get lowered until it swayed no more than four feet above their heads. Were the old hook to fail, at least twenty of them would be crushed instantly.

The people around Spike were loud, but they had nothing on those directly opposite. Screaming and shouting at the beast in the box, the crowd directed pure venom at the thing. It represented everything that stank about their lives. Jobs and homes in the same district for life, they were no more than cogs in the larger Edin machine with just one mission: to grow large enough to take more of the world back from the things that kept them imprisoned inside the city's walls. The diseased deserved to be the focus of their hate, and as soon as Spike became a protector, he'd make it his mission to kill every single one of them.

Some of the crowd jumped up and banged against the bottom of the box. The onslaught against its prison sent the beast into a rage. A trapped animal robbed of its pride and power, it looked like it wanted to direct its fury at something but couldn't. Clearly overwhelmed, the creature then fell to the floor as if possessed. It clapped its hands to its ears and writhed around like it could squirm free from the torment. Spike's jaw fell loose to watch it turn backwards rolls before it fell flat again. It then jumped to its feet, screamed, and banged against the glass walls surrounding it. If only he could watch the spectacle from a closer angle.

Spike couldn't tell what age the man would have been when he turned. Mid-thirties maybe. Always hard to judge because of what the disease did to them. Half-naked in a pair of torn jeans and nothing else, it had the familiar sag of the creatures. Its skin looked like it would slough off it. It added years to its appearance.

The *knack, knack, knack* of the winch called from outside the arena again and the box moved back over to Spike and Matilda's side. Spike gasped. "It's coming back!"

When the container got to within about ten feet, Spike bounced where he sat. "They're bringing it around again."

As the glass box drew closer still, Spike stood on the step like many of those around him. So high up, the back of his legs tingled to look down at the pit. When he focused on the box again, the sensation left him.

Were it not for his six-foot-two-inch frame, Spike wouldn't

have had a chance of reaching the glass prison. Watching many before him miss when they stretched for it, he balled his right fist as it came closer, and banged against the thick base. He hit it so hard it stung his knuckles. Despite the noise around them, it grabbed the diseased's attention. In that moment, only Spike and the creature existed. The thing fixed him with its glossy red stare. Its cracked lips pulled back to reveal yellowed teeth.

Unlike all the other times, the creature didn't go wild. Maybe it finally accepted its limitations within its prison. Instead, it dropped to all fours—the sound of its knees slamming down against the glass—and it pressed its face to the transparent floor of its box. No more than twelve inches between Spike and the beast, Spike's heart ran away with him and his throat dried. He couldn't see any white in the creature's stare. Its eyes were swollen with the blood gathered in them.

The knacking sound continued outside the arena and the box passed over the top of Spike's head. He sat down again, adrenaline lighting him up. "Did you see that, Tilly?"

In spite of her distaste for the whole thing, she held no judgement in her eyes. The noise around them damn near deafening, Spike read her lips as she mouthed *happy birthday* at him before flashing him another broad smile.

CHAPTER 5

The glass box moved away from Spike across the crowd to his left. The pallid and wrinkled creature inside appeared to have settled down. "Do you think it's realised it can't get out?"

Matilda watched the glass box for a few seconds. "I'm not sure they're that smart. Do they even think?"

"Probably not. They seem more reactive than anything." The creature continued to pace, twitch, and look at those around it.

"Maybe it's exhausted. It must be hot in there," Matilda said, fanning her own face, a very slight glow of sweat to her tanned skin.

Movement down in the ring dragged Spike's focus away from the creature. A flutter ran through his heart to see who'd just entered. "That's Jake Biggs," he said as he watched him walk over to the centre of the arena and drag away the sheet of steel lying there. It revealed a hole about six feet long by about three feet wide. He then walked over to a winch attached to the wall.

When Matilda replied with a vacant look, Spike rolled his eyes. "Last season's winner of the protector apprenticeship. He'll be replaced soon by the new one. And then that one will be replaced by me."

The noise in the arena had grown louder. The novelty of the diseased in the box had passed for many of them, but the activity down below told them they were getting closer to the main event. Spike raised his voice so Matilda could hear him. "It's such an honour to introduce the protector to the crowd. A rite of passage on the journey to becoming one yourself." Pushing his hands together as if in prayer, he looked up at the sky. "I hope it's Magma today."

"It's not."

Spike turned to the woman next to him. Dark-skinned, she had deep brown eyes, her hair wrapped up in a colourful scarf on top of her head. Her vivid clothes marked her out as someone from the textiles district.

"Sorry to break the news, love," she said, "but everyone's saying Magma's outside the walls at the moment."

The only response Spike had in him would be laced with poison. He shouldn't take it out on her, so he directed his attention back to Jake and felt the gentle touch of Matilda's hand against his back.

As Jake wound the winch, Spike drew several breaths. So what if he didn't see Magma today? There would be other chances. He shook his head and continued his conversation with Matilda. "Jake's a big lad. I thought I was tall, but he's *huge.* He must have bossed the trials. I wonder if anyone even came close to challenging him. What do you reckon he is, six feet four? Six five?"

Matilda leaned forward in her seat as if those extra few inches would help her assessment of the apprentice. She squinted as she stared for several seconds. "I'd say six five at least." Looking up at the top of Spike's head as if it would give her some kind of reference for Jake's height, she raised her eyebrows. "What are you, six two?"

"Yep."

Another look at the protectors' apprentice, his arms bulging with the effort of turning the winch, she shrugged. "Yeah, six five."

The crowd's noise fell away again, the sound of Jake's winch rattling as he bobbed up and down, winding it with all he had. A cage slowly rose from the hole in the ground. It had a sheet covering it, hiding the protector inside. Leaning so close he could smell the floral scent of her perfume, Spike spoke so only Matilda could hear him. "I don't care what that woman just said, until I see it's not, I hope the protector in that cage is—"

"Magma, I know."

"Sorry, I'm repeating myself." His attention back on the covered cage, Spike said, "I know being a protector is all I ever go on about, but I want this *so* badly. More than anyone else who's going to be going for the apprenticeship. And to see it now. To see Jake and know that'll be me there soon."

"And you'll get it. I've never known anyone to want anything more. You'll be fine, I'm sure, but promise me one thing."

Spike looked at Matilda.

"Promise me you'll put all your focus on national service first. Only fifty percent of cadets survive it."

"You sound like my dad."

"You're being flippant, Spike. Don't let your arrogance kill you."

"I'll be fine."

"Statistically, only one of us will."

"Are you saying you don't trust me?"

The question made her wince, her reaction sending a sharp pain into Spike's heart. In all the time he'd known Matilda, she'd not trusted anyone but Artan. As a child, she'd trusted her parents and they'd let her down. "There's a reason people don't talk about national service. I'm saying you need to go in expecting it to be hard and harrowing. We all know plenty of people who have come back changed."

"We'll both be fine."

"How can you say that? How can you be so certain of something you know *nothing* about."

"And you do?"

For a second, Matilda looked like she wanted to say more. That second passed. She shook her head and folded her arms across her chest.

"Look," Spike said. "I'm not an idiot. I know national service is going to be hard."

"I'm not sure you do."

Tension made the muscles in Spike's back ache. Acid in his tone, he said, "Stop putting a downer on my day, yeah?"

Before Matilda could reply, Spike turned away from her and looked down into the fighting pit at Jake winding the handle. He'd come here to enjoy this, not to be made to feel like a child.

CHAPTER 6

After a few seconds of not speaking to one another, Matilda touched Spike's hand again. Brief, as always, she did it to get his attention before pulling away. "I'm sorry."

"Why do it, then?"

She waited for him to look at her. A glaze covered her eyes, magnifying her grief. "Because I worry about you. I worry about us. Tomorrow, we're going to do national service. Whether you feel scared about that or not, you should; it's a big deal. I expect it to be one of the most traumatic things we have to do in our lives, and I'm worried. I'm worried I won't make it. I'm worried you won't make it. I'm worried about leaving Artan, which means I can't even try to be the next protector because that'll mean leaving him alone with my dad for even longer than the six months we're away for. I'm worried that puts too much pressure on you to succeed."

"I can cope with the pressure."

"I'm worried it will change us. I'm worried something might happen that's out of our control, which means we won't get to see each other once it's all done. None of those worries are about you not being good enough."

"So what do we do? Run away together?"

For a second, she looked like she considered it, her eyes narrowing as she stared out across the noisy arena. "National service is going to happen. We both know it. All I ask is that you concentrate on that. Expect it to be a challenge so you're ready for it. Put all your energy into the next six months. Focus on being the next protector once that's done. So many things can go wrong between tomorrow and getting to the end of the apprentice trials. Even if we both survive national service, there's so much more to do beyond that."

"I need to focus on the end goal. I can't imagine a life without it." He wanted to say *without you.*

"Of course, but don't lose sight of the next step. And maybe it's just me, but I find it overwhelming to think too far into the future. Will Artan be okay while I'm away? Will the next six months screw with our heads like they have with my dad's?"

More than she'd ever said about her dad, Spike waited to give her the chance to elaborate.

"Will we end up as a lonely couple on one of the benches in the square?"

"That *won't* happen."

"How many of those who go there every night thought that?"

Spike shook his head. "It won't happen. Anyway, I thought we agreed we wouldn't be negative about the future?"

"I'm worried we won't have a future."

"Look, seeing as we're talking about it, you need to know that I don't want to be one of those lonely people in the square either. Of all of the reasons to become the next protector, that's the biggest. I want the freedom to live where I want, go where I want, and love whom I want."

Matilda flushed red. They'd not said it to one another before. Only fools in this city fell in love with people from other districts. Protectors, politicians, and fools.

After glancing at the glass box—the sound of the winch clacking from outside the arena—Matilda looked back at him. “So you understand why I’m petrified?”

“Of course.” Spike gulped. “I’m petrified too. I want this more than I’ve wanted anything in my life. The thought of failure is overwhelming. But if I don’t keep a positive mindset, I don’t stand a chance.”

A moment’s pause, Matilda said, “I believe in you, Spike.”

While filling his lungs with a deep breath, Spike nodded.

“I’m going to stop being negative now. Let’s focus on today. You’ve waited a long time to see the main event, the least you can do is enjoy it.”

When Matilda flashed him a tight-lipped smile, Spike smiled back. “I’ll make sure I put everything into getting through national service. I won’t underestimate it for a second. The price of failure’s too great.”

Matilda’s eyes glazed. “I lo—” She let her words trail off. They’d never said it to one another. “Happy birthday, Spike.”

And he wanted to say it back. He wanted to tell her exactly how he felt. But they’d promised they wouldn’t. Only fools fell in love with someone from another district. Protectors, politicians, and fools.

CHAPTER 7

Spike tried to put his conversation with Matilda to the back of his mind and focus on the main event. He'd waited too long to get here to be distracted by anything else. Besides, the fact he loved her wasn't anything new.

The crane had moved the diseased in the clear prison, so it now hovered over the centre of the arena. Suspended above the ring, the cage with the sheet over it continued to rise straight up from the ground. The suspended glass box swung gently from the creature inside pacing from end to end.

When Jake stepped away from the winch, Spike looked at the cage with the sheet. It had a protector inside. Jake walked over to it and looked at the glass box above him.

The diseased stopped and stared back. The crowd fell silent again.

While cupping his mouth with his hands, Jake turned outwards to face the onlookers and slowly spun on the spot. "Ladies and gentlemen, it's my pleasure to introduce this week's protector to you. First and foremost, I want to thank Edin council for continuing to put these games on." He nodded at the front row. "We think it's important you see what your champions do for you and what they face every day to help with the cause. Just like you all work hard in your districts to keep Edin productive so we can grow and reclaim our world, the protectors go outside the city's walls to fight on the front line. Because everyone does their part, Edin survives. It's a hard life, but we're all pulling in the same direction." He held up a clenched fist and shouted, "Praise be to Edin."

The two-hundred-strong response came back at him so loud Spike felt it in his seat. "Praise be to Edin!"

Jake gripped the sheet covering the cage, his face reddening as he shouted, "As a child, all he wanted to do was kill the diseased. As an adult, all he wants to do is kill the diseased. If he's not protecting this fine city, he's planning how he can do it better."

Spike twitched on the stone step, damn near ready to burst with the anticipation of it as Jake continued his introduction.

"The protector we all aspire to be like. The one. The only …"

"Magma," Spike said, throwing a sideways glance at the woman next to him. "Please be Magma."

Jake tore the fabric away as he shouted, "Mmmmmmmmmm-mmmmmmmmmagmaaaaaaaaaaaaaa."

His fuse lit, Spike jumped to his feet with the swell of the crowd. Hard to see the ring for the people in his way, but he joined in with their jubilation by whooping, yelling, and punching the air. He turned to Matilda and screamed, "Can you believe it?"

She smiled at him, any hangover from their previous conversation gone from her face.

The chant started and spread through the people until they were all shouting the same thing, "Mag-ma! Mag-ma! Mag-ma!" They stamped their feet to the rhythm—some people even danced. The collective thud of boots felt like it could shatter the foundations of the stone structure.

It took a few minutes for the crowd to sit down. Beginning with those at the front, it rippled outwards all the way to the back. It finally gave Spike a clear view of Magma. At only about five feet ten inches, the stocky protector stood as wide as he did tall. The shortest of all the male protectors, but the fiercest too. Naked from the waist up, his huge muscles bulged, stretch marks ran around his pecs, and scars lashed across his skin. The man looked to be chiseled from rock rather than made of flesh and bone. His double-headed battle-axe—Jezebel—over his shoulder, he stepped from the cage he'd been in. He spun a full circle, slowly taking in the crowd, his face sombre as if he might slaughter everyone there when he'd finished with the diseased.

A true professional, Magma milked the crowd by sneering at them while the winches both inside and outside the arena sounded. Jake lowered the cage Magma had been in, while the crane from outside the arena lowered the diseased to cover the hole Magma had emerged from.

Now he'd done his job, Jake made a quick exit through a reinforced door in the wall surrounding the ring.

The diseased's box made a crunching sound when it touched down on the stone ground.

Spike gulped against the dry itch in his throat, his leg bouncing in a bid to spend some of the energy running through him. The sun burned into the side of his face while he stared down at his hero, sweat lifting on his brow.

A flick of his flowing and dark hair, Magma continued to rest Jezebel's long handle against his shoulder while he stared at the diseased. The diseased stared back through the thick glass separating them.

For a moment, it looked to Spike like Magma and the dumb creature shared a moment. It had once been human and maybe Magma needed to acknowledge that before he removed its head from its shoulders.

Several slow and heavy steps—the crowd damn near taking

every one with him—Magma walked closer to the transparent box, held Jezebel with both of his strong hands, and tapped it against the glass. The ting of it rang through the near-silent arena. Spike had heard people say Jezebel sang. As he now listened to the axe holding onto the note, he now understood what they'd meant.

Then it started: the chant he knew he'd hear. The chant he'd heard many times from outside the arena. It lifted gooseflesh on Spike's skin as he joined in with the rest of the crowd. "Magma, bomaye, Magma, bomaye."

When Matilda tugged on Spike's sleeve, he kept his attention on the ring, but leaned closer so he could hear her.

"What does *bomaye* mean?"

Although the word wasn't in common use in the city, those with any interest in the arena fights knew it well. Unable to contain himself, Spike grinned. "It means *kill him.*"

Like a batter getting ready to swing, Magma adjusted his grip on Jezebel's handle, glanced across the arena at the door Jake had gone through, and nodded. It took for that moment for Spike to see the small window in it. He'd be the one on the other side of the door soon.

The sound of the winch started outside again, slackening the cable that had held the diseased's prison aloft. The hook loosened and unlatched before it lifted out of there. It would have taken Spike's attention with it were it not for the loud slap of the glass box's front falling outwards, exposing the creature for the first time.

Fury switched on and the diseased charged Magma.

Although it moved quickly, Magma moved quicker. Evading the diseased's lunge—its arms a flailing mess of uncoordinated chaos—he threw the flat side of his axe into the diseased's right cheek. A loud crack, the diseased stumbled for several steps before it fell forward and crashed face-first against the tall concrete wall surrounding the ring.

For the briefest of moments, Spike looked away from the action to Matilda. His grin stretched so wide it almost hurt. "He's *amazing*, isn't he?" Before she could reply, he looked into her dark eyes. "I'm so glad you're here with me."

Matilda nodded. "Me too."

Spike returned his focus to the action. The diseased got to its feet on bandy legs. It ran at Magma again. It might have given its run a wobble, but the collision with the wall hadn't done anything to dull its aggression. As it made its stumbling charge, its scream damn near shook the foundations of the arena.

Magma tried to evade it with a sidestep, but the creature followed his movement. It dropped its head and hit him with a shoulder barge. Spike and the rest of the crowd gasped and jumped to their feet as the two of them fell to the ground. Jezebel skittered away from the champion protector, who reached up and clamped a tight grip on the diseased's throat. He held it at the end of his thick and outstretched arms.

The wrinkly and pallid diseased snapped and hissed. Although it had arms and legs, their uncoordinated spasms proved ineffective. It directed all its aggression through its mouth as it tried to bite Magma. Teeth clicking, it snapped at the air between them, its thin lips peeled back with its ferocious snarl.

What had been composure on Magma's face had now locked into a scowl of concentration. He gritted his teeth as he fought against the skinny diseased. Although it looked like it shouldn't be able to, the diseased appeared to be putting up a good fight.

The diseased's scream had snapped Spike's back taut, but when Magma roared, it sounded like thunder. It stunned the diseased long enough for the protector to shove it away from him, launching it back across the fighting area.

Magma went for Jezebel while the diseased scrambled to its feet.

Unable to get to his axe before the creature reached him, Magma ducked its swinging arm and thrust out a leg. The creature tripped and crashed face first into another part of the wall. Despite the sweat glistening on the protector's face, he beamed a wicked grin.

Without giving the diseased a chance to get up, Magma grabbed one of its withered arms and pulled it to its feet. He punched it across the jaw.

The wet crack made Spike wince, the blow sending a spray of blood and teeth flying from the diseased's foetid mouth.

From where Spike stood, it looked like just blood, but on closer inspection, he saw torn flesh where Magma had punched the thing's bottom jaw clean off its face. While keeping his eyes on the fight, he shouted at Matilda, "This diseased is dangerous now. With its top row of teeth exposed, it only needs to trip and land on him and he's infected. The smallest amount of saliva in his blood and Magma's screwed. He'd best pick Jezebel back up again."

When Magma lifted the axe, Spike nodded. "Good call."

The diseased charged Magma again, arms windmilling, top jaw snapping. Magma ran Jezebel through the air in a wide arc. The precision of an artist, the weapon appeared to move in slow motion, removing the diseased's right arm.

Spike held his stomach to see the tacky mess where its limb had once been, but still laughed with many others in the crowd. He shouted, "Go for it, Magma. Rip its damn head off."

When the diseased circled back around, its one arm slashing at the fierce protector, Magma threw another swing at it, removing its remaining arm before dodging out of its path like a matador. The arm fell close to the other one, both withered appendages lying lifeless on the ground.

"It's not really bleeding because diseased blood congeals in their veins." Spike said while keeping his eyes on the fight. "It's why you can see some red, but not the gushing you would see if you cut off a real person's arms."

Stumbling now, dumb, exhausted, limbless, and without a jaw, the diseased leaned forward as it ran on the edge of its balance.

Evading it once again, Magma swung his axe and took the bottom of the thing's legs off just below the knees.

Joining in the chant, Spike jumped up on his seat to get a better view and clapped his hands. "Magma, bomaye. Magma, bomaye. Magma, bomaye."

Magma stood over the downed creature, the thing squirming on the concrete ground like a wretched grub. The protector lifted his axe high into the air, let out a feral cry that would have woken the gods, and brought Jezebel crashing down. He split the thing's head in two.

The wet crunch ran straight to Spike's stomach and he noticed Matilda cover her mouth as if she might vomit.

The crowd screamed so loudly, it made Spike's ears ring and threw him off balance. Too high up to be feeling dizzy, he sat down to find his legs again.

It took a few seconds before Spike stood back up. He watched Magma push his boot against the diseased's face, using it as leverage so he could remove his buried axe. Spitting on the remains of his victim, he wiped his sweating brow with his fore-arm, threw Jezebel over his shoulder, and strode towards the same door that Jake had exited through. Even his heavy gait seemed to shake the arena floor. The man moved like a god.

CHAPTER 8

Spike squinted against the bright sun when he stepped from the arena with the exiting crowd. Where he'd been shoulder to shoulder with the other people on the benches, he now had the added press of bodies both in front and behind him. He writhed as if he could somehow squirm free from his sweating body. Not that he should complain too much; nine times out of ten, his birthdays were characterised by dreary weather—usually cold, wet, and windy, even inside the walls of Edin. For his eighteenth, the gods truly were smiling on him. The adrenaline from watching the fight still pumping through him, he grinned and shouted over the excited chatter of those around them, "Did you see it in there? Magma's a legend! How he dispatched that diseased was awesome."

Although Matilda smiled back at him, her large brown eyes were flat. They shifted to those around them, many of the crowd shoving in their haste to get back to their districts. The guards hated those who dawdled.

But Spike knew how she'd be. Months before, when she'd agreed to come because she wanted to spend his birthday with him doing whatever he wanted, she said she'd never be able to enjoy the experience as much as him. Deep down, he thought she'd change her mind when she saw it. Apparently not.

She finally replied, "Did you see how that diseased nearly got Magma?"

Spike sent a dismissive shot of air from his mouth and shook his head. "Not a chance. He had it covered the whole time."

"My point is we're going to be around them in national service, and we just saw one nearly take down our most experienced protector."

"Another lesson to learn before tomorrow, eh? God, am I glad about having my birthday now. I know I've said it before—"

"About a thousand times before."

"Well, it matters to me. I want to be with you in national service. If I'd have been born a day later—"

"You'd have to wait six more months to go. I know."

"I just wanted to say it. It's good to be grateful."

The main street leading away from the arena had one-storey walls lining the cobblestone walkway. Spike's feet rolled and turned as he walked over the uneven ground. Most of Edin's main roads were paved in the same way.

Spike then stopped and turned around. Matilda did too. Many of the exiting spectators scowled at the pair for coming to such an abrupt halt in their path, but he didn't care. They were in national service tomorrow, so today they moved at their own pace.

Spike looked at the vast arena, the city's tall back wall behind it. "I've walked past this place a million times in my life."

"And I swear you've dragged me with you every time."

Smiling, Spike continued taking in the large circular stone structure. The crowd showed no sign of thinning, so he had to plant his feet to avoid getting dragged back with them. "It looks different now I've finally seen the inside. Smaller somehow. More attainable." As if showing Matilda an invisible banner on the side of the arena, he read it out to her, "Spike Johnson—Protector. I can already hear the crowds going wild."

The same smile as before, Matilda's eyes were still flat as she looked around them again. Guards lined either side of the street as a reminder to those who weren't in a hurry to get back to their district. But Spike and Matilda were exempt. They didn't have to stay in their district. Not until after national service.

"Come on," Matilda said. "I need to get home. I want to check on Artan to see if he's okay."

"He'll be fine. We've only been gone a few hours. We should make the most of the freedom we have in the city. This is our last day before it's taken away from us. It would be a shame not to enjoy this great weather."

"I'm sorry," Matilda said, shaking her head and looking at the ground before she turned her back on the arena and moved off with the rest of the crowd.

As much as he wanted to challenge her, it had been a big deal for her to come in the first place. She didn't like to leave Artan with her parents at the best of times. Her dad had started to lose his head like he always did around this time of year, although Spike didn't entirely understand why. She'd tell him when she felt ready. When she trusted him; *if* she ever trusted him. He knew it had something to do with national service coming up. From the way she'd been acting, her having to do it had hit him doubly hard this year. She'd been twitchy and on edge, and from the shadow of black rings beneath her eyes, it looked like she'd been losing sleep over it. At least she didn't have any bruising on her like she used to have as a kid. Spike wouldn't stand for it now. Hell, she wouldn't stand for it now.

"Can we at least slow the pace a little?" Spike said, tugging on Matilda's arm.

Although she continued in the direction of her district, Matilda slowed down.

"Thank you. It won't be long before we won't have this luxury. Once we've done our national service, we'll have to stay in our sectors."

"Not if you're a protector," Matilda said.

"True—which I will be—but that's a while away yet. I also want to make good use of the freedom our youth affords us while we still have it. It'll be different when I'm a protector. Better in a lot of ways, but the next time we walk freely through these streets, people will know who I am." As he said it, a middle-age couple barged past them.

While the couple continued walking, the woman shook a fist at Spike and Matilda. "You need to get a move on, girl."

After looking at Matilda, Spike turned to the woman. Although she'd already spun around again, he still called after her, "Hey, you! Watch your tongue, yeah? And if you want to be pissed off with anyone, be pissed off with me." But the woman never turned back around.

Before Spike could say anything else, Matilda dragged a sharp tug on his arm and nodded to the side of the road. His stomach did a backflip when he saw five guards heading straight for them, billy clubs raised.

CHAPTER 9

Where the crowd had been packed tightly before, Spike looked around to see the last of the people duck down a side street at the sight of the angry guards. Alone with Matilda in the middle of the grey cobblestone road, he shifted across so he stood in front of her. They were dawdling because of him, and he was the one who shouted at the woman.

"You," the lead guard said. A woman of no more than five and a half feet tall, she pointed her billy club at Matilda.

Spike held his ground.

Two male guards walked on either side of the woman. Two more walked close behind them. All four of them were slightly shorter than Spike. One of them—a man with cropped hair and thick stubble—raised his top lip in a sneer. "I suggest you get out of the way, son." The sparkle in his green eyes spoke of his lust for violence.

But Spike didn't move.

Another guard grabbed him by his lapels and shoved him away with such force he tripped and fell. He landed with most of his weight on his right hip, which sent a searing pain running down his leg. Still, when he saw the female guard raise her baton to Matilda, he jumped back up again and shoved her aside before she could swing.

A moment's silence as the female guard went down. Her face red and her jaw set, she looked up at him. "Who do you think you are, *boy*?"

"What's your problem with Matilda? You can't come over here swinging without at least telling us why."

"*Can't?*"

Spike held his ground, glaring at the woman as the other guards closed in around him and Matilda.

Maybe the mass exodus helped because the lead guard didn't have to put on an intimidating show for a crowd. She got to her feet and walked close to Spike. Although she spoke with a low voice, her words crackled with tethered fury. "You get a pass. *One* pass. Do that again and I'll beat you into a coma, you got me?"

"What do you want with Matilda?"

"She's holding people up."

"We're *both* holding people up."

"*You* have a scarf on."

The clap of Matilda slapping her hand across her mouth sounded behind him. "Oh, God." Her hands shook as she fumbled through her pockets. "I'm so sorry, Spike." A second later, she pulled her black scarf out and tied it around her neck.

The female guard stared at her and her eyes narrowed. Her jaw tensed and relaxed. Her nostrils flared. "Why didn't you have it on?"

Matilda sniffed, straightened her back, and stamped her foot. "I hate the way people look at me when I'm wearing it."

A second of silence, the female guard then released a long sigh as if letting go of her fury. "I wouldn't wish national service on my worst enemy. For that reason, you both get a pass." She looked at Spike. "You won't get another one, you understand?"

"Yes, ma'am," Spike and Matilda said in unison.

The lead guard hooked a thumb over her shoulder. “Now go. Get out of my sight before I change my mind.”

Still sore from his fall, Spike took Matilda’s hand, limping a little as he led her down the alleyway in the direction of her district.

CHAPTER 10

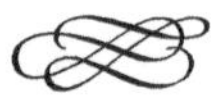

About thirty seconds passed before Spike looked back the way they'd come from. The guards were gone. "What the *hell,* Matilda?"

She shrugged. "I said I'm sorry."

A smaller version of the main street, the alley had cobblestone ground, and the backs of grey single-storey buildings lined either side of it. "I nearly got my skull caved in for that."

"*Sorry.* If I'd have known that would happen, I would have worn my scarf."

"Why didn't you wear it? It's not like you to ignore the rules."

"Like I said to the guards, I *hate* wearing it. I hate the way people treat us when we have them on."

"But it gives us a free pass because we have national service coming up."

She nodded and spoke with a sigh. "I know."

The sound of their steps against the cobblestones filled the space left by the absence of their voices.

Matilda finally said, "I'm sorry I ruined your day."

After rolling his shoulders to relieve some of the tension in his back, Spike shook his head. "You haven't."

"Come on, I nearly got you beaten up by guards, and all I've done is worry about Artan. I really wanted you to enjoy the main event …"

"You don't need to say sorry; I get it. You came today because I wanted you with me. We both knew you wouldn't have chosen it yourself, but I saw you were happy for me. It means a lot. Besides, it would be hard to dampen the experience I've had today. I've seen my favourite protector slay a diseased. I've managed to push a guard over and get away with it. I'm …" He looked at Matilda before he said it, her deep brown eyes fixed on him. Even after all this time, her beauty had the power to disarm him. He gulped and looked at the ground because he wouldn't get the words out otherwise. "I'm here with my favourite person in the world. Nothing can bring me down from that."

"Thank you." She reached across and held his hand.

They clung onto one another for a few seconds before letting go. At present, they were alone in the street, but that could change at any time, and people would have opinions to share with them if they saw them like that. Kids from different districts, did they know what the city said about protectors, politicians, and fools?

"I suppose, not only have I been thinking about Artan," Matilda said, "but I find the way the city handles the main events a bit over the top, you know?"

"It's fine, Tilly. I suppose I like the idea of the main event because they're diseased. It's not like they're people anymore."

"But they were once. People like you and me."

"You tell me I need to be ready for national service, but thinking like that could get you killed. It's the moment of hesitation that gives the creature the advantage."

"How would you like to see someone you cared for turned and then tortured for the amusement of others?"

Puffing his cheeks out as he exhaled, Spike scratched his head. "Well, firstly I haven't ever cared for any of the diseased we've seen so far, but hypothetically, if someone I care for were to be bitten, they're not the person I knew anymore. The second the disease kicks in is the second you need to mourn their passing. Anything beyond that isn't them. I wouldn't personally want to see them killed in the main event, but I think it's necessary for Edin."

A gust of wind flicked Matilda's hair across her face. After pulling it away, she said, "How's that?"

"The people in Edin live oppressed lives. It's out of necessity, right? We all need to do our bit to help the city grow so we can give more freedom to future generations."

Matilda shrugged.

"With over ten thousand people in such a small space, we all need to have roles, and we need to not deviate from them."

"Like bees in a hive," Matilda said.

"The infrastructure can't support freedom of choice. They have to run the place how they do. That being said, it's enough to drive anyone insane. Edin isn't an easy place to live in."

"You're telling me."

"The population grows quicker than the city can." They turned off the street they were currently on and headed down a similar one.

"So?" Matilda shrugged. "What's that got to do with the main event?"

"Catharsis."

"Huh?"

"The citizens can't be mad at how Edin's run."

"But I'd imagine they are, even if they've been conditioned not to say it."

"Fair enough, but I'd guess most of them see the necessity of it."

"So you agree with the restrictions placed on the citizens?"

"It is what it is."

"But you want to be a protector so you're not subjected to them?"

"We all have that option. I'm not saying the way the city's run is perfect, but it works."

"Just about," Matilda said. "And being a protector won't be easy."

"But I'll do it." Before she could say anything else, Spike continued. "So although the citizens can't be openly mad about it, what they can be mad about is the diseased."

"Isn't that like being angry with an inanimate object?"

"No, because ultimately the diseased are the ones oppressing all of us. Were it not for them outside the walls, we'd be free. We'd have more space to live in; we'd be able to choose the jobs we want to do." His cheeks burned when he said, "To be with the people we want to be with."

Only a slight glance from Matilda, but Spike noticed it all the same.

A shake took a hold of Spike, his face hot and no doubt glowing red. He pointed at the part of the perimeter wall closest to them. A constant, it stood as a looming reminder of their limitations. "If it weren't for those diseased freaks out there, we wouldn't all have to live like prisoners. I think sometimes just knowing about the main event makes us feel better. At least they're being made to pay for it. And the protectors give us hope. One day we'll win and life *will* change for the better."

"I'd not thought of it like that. Although I'm not sure I'd agree with people for thinking that way. I mean, the diseased are prisoners too. They're trapped in their own bodies because of their affliction. But I can see the logic in what you're saying." Matilda pulled on her black scarf as if to loosen the knot around her neck.

Before Spike could say anything else, an old woman appeared from around the corner. She had long blonde, almost white, hair and blue eyes that stood so brilliant in her wrinkled face, they damn near glowed. Her hands were red raw. She must have been from the laundry district.

Dipping his head in a nod, Spike said, "Afternoon. And how are you on this very fine day?"

For a moment, she didn't reply, she simply stood in front of them, her eyes glazed as a shake ran through her.

Just as Spike drew a breath to say something else, she burst to life. "I had to stop and talk to you. You remind me of my son—tall, strong, and handsome. You're clearly a fit boy."

Nudging Matilda, Spike flashed her a smile.

"My son didn't come back."

Spike physically sank where he stood.

"It was thirty years ago now. He had aspirations of being a protector like the greats in the arena. They went out after their first month's training to extend the wall for the city." Looking over at the section of wall closer to the national service area, she nodded in the general direction. "He helped build that one over there."

Neither Spike nor Matilda filled the silence as they looked at a section of the wall in the vague direction she'd indicated.

"They got him on his first day after training. His strength meant he was teamed with a weaker group to try to lift them up." A glaze covered her eyes and her shake grew more violent. "He paid the price for being more capable because his team let him down when it really mattered. Apparently he killed seven diseased before he fell. But there were too many. They were overrun."

Looking back at Spike while chewing the inside of her cheek, the old woman leaned forward and took one of his hands in both of hers. Despite her withered appearance, she had a strong and cold grip. As she got closer, the musty smell of damp moved with her. "I don't know what I'm trying to say. I know you have to do national service, and I'm sure you'll be amazing, but please, *please* be careful. *Please.*"

The woman's naked grief—after so many years since her son had passed—lifted a lump in Spike's throat. His attempt at clearing it proved ineffective, so he nodded instead.

The woman wrapped them both in a hug before pulling back again. "Bless you, children. Now I'd best go before the city guards arrest me for being outside my district. I was given twenty minutes to deliver clothes to the mayor." Looking at each of them again, her bottom lip quivered with the rest of her. "God be with you."

Watching the woman walk away, her burdened frame hunched at the shoulders, Spike then looked at Matilda. Wet tracks ran down her cheeks. "Please don't underestimate how hard it's going to be in national service," she said.

Without a word, the two of them walked on.

CHAPTER 11

Although Spike kept telling Matilda everything would be okay in national service, the old woman hadn't helped his cause. That and the fifty percent survival rate, long and brutal days, and young people used as cannon fodder to build a wall that took years to finish … Maybe he needed to accept it wouldn't be easy, but the fact remained: they had to do it, so they might as well go into it with a positive attitude.

They were still within the administration zone and the streets were quiet. Now the arena had emptied, very few people would pass through the place. The many citizens who worked there were either inside busy with the running of the city, or they were the guards on patrol in all the districts.

When they turned down another street in the direction of the ceramics sector, Spike looked across at Matilda—her face pale—and said, "I know it might seem like I'm not taking national service seriously, but I want you to know I'll do everything in my power to make sure we get through it. I'm going into it with my eyes open."

Although Matilda nodded, she didn't look like she'd

composed herself since the old woman's impassioned plea. Her chin raised, she stared straight ahead.

The grey cobblestone ground and walls always made Edin feel a few degrees colder than it was. A slight shiver snapped through Spike. The atmosphere made the chill feel worse, but there seemed little point in going over it again. No one had yet found a way out of national service. And why should they? It was a rite of passage, and one of the most important things anyone could do for Edin.

Spike needed to change the subject. "Do you remember your eighteenth, Tilly?"

She looked at him, one eyebrow raised.

"When you said you were ill, what you actually meant was that you didn't want to go to the arena, right?"

Keeping her chin held high, Matilda returned her attention to where they were headed.

"Why didn't you tell me?"

She kept her focus in front of her. "Because I knew you'd act like this."

"Like what?"

"The way you're acting now. I can *feel* your judgement."

Spike bit back his initial response. She had a point. In a softer tone than before, he said, "Yeah, I suppose you're right. I would have killed for a chance to go to the arena a few months back. For the chance to get two trips in the space of four months."

"And it's not like I could have just given the tickets away. I had to go if I was to take a guest, and I really didn't want to. It was my birthday; the last thing I wanted was to go and watch *that*. I struggle with some of the protectors and their egos. The way they peacock around the ring's a bit gross. The way they peacock around the city like they own it is even worse. I think some of them remind the citizens about how trapped they are rather than how they're fighting daily to look after them."

Yet she'd still gone with him for his birthday. "But surely some of the reason for their behaviour has to be because they know people are jealous of them."

"So they act like arseholes?"

"No, what I mean is they must feel the resentment and react to it before the people have even delivered it. They must always be on the defensive, you know? It's a shame we don't celebrate them more."

"You don't think Magma's celebrated?"

"Oh sure, but he's a superstar. I'm talking about the rest of them. Without them, this city would have fallen decades ago."

"Still," Matilda said, "they could try smiling once in a while. They can go anywhere in the city. They eat free in every restaurant—"

"They can marry whomever they want." Heat flushed Spike's cheeks and he quickly added, "Although, I'd imagine some days they don't have much to smile about. I wonder what it's like outside these walls."

"We'll find out soon enough."

"No, I mean *outside* outside. You know, like far away from here. I wonder where they get the wood from for the fires. What some of the wild forests look like. How many diseased they fight that we never hear about. I wonder how many diseased have been in the largest horde they've come across. Do they ever have to run away from them, or do they always stand and fight?"

When Matilda didn't reply, Spike said, "Don't worry; when I make it, I'll smile every day. They'll call me the happy warrior."

For the first time since leaving the arena, the scowl lifted from Matilda's face. "I like that name."

The conversation died naturally as they approached the ceramics district. The buildings were poorer quality than in the administration zone. Many of them were canted because of the weaker materials they'd been given to build with. The best quality always went to those in power. But what they lacked in solid structures, they made up for in colour. Almost every house had a ceramic wind chime, colourful flower pots, mosaic jugs outside to catch rainwater … One of the most vibrant places in the entire city, it always lifted Spike's spirits to be there. It helped that Matilda lived there too.

A guard stood on either side of the road; they wore their usual scowl. When Spike looked at the one on his right, the guard stared back. Then he dropped his eyes to the scarf around his neck and lingered there. The facade of officialdom gave way to the slightest wince as if he felt pain for what Spike and Matilda were about to embark on. Everyone had lost someone in national service. The guard dipped the briefest of nods at him. "Bless you both. Be safe."

It rarely paid to speak to the guards, so Spike nodded back as both he and Matilda kept walking.

A second later, the rumbling clatter of cartwheels called through the tight cobblestone street. Spike spun around to see the horses were close. He grabbed Matilda and pulled her into a nearby alleyway. The heavy cart flashed past, the ground shaking from both the pounding of the horses' hooves and the turning of the large wooden wheels.

While Spike peered out of the alleyway to watch Magma come to a halt in an opening up ahead, Matilda said, "See what I mean? You can't tell me that's the behaviour of someone who's living a happy and fulfilled existence. And if it is, he's certainly not showing us that."

With Magma so close to him, Matilda's words faded for Spike. He stepped from the alley and walked towards the man, a crowd already gathering around his cart.

As Spike joined the others—many of them shoving and pushing to get close—he felt the gentle press of a palm against the centre of his back. Matilda had caught up with him. Despite her feelings about the protectors, she looked to have shelved it and smiled at him like she had in the arena. A display of genuine joy for the experiences he was having. It was enough to lift the earlier mood and let him appreciate the moment.

Just before Spike turned back to the protector, he saw him. Over Matilda's shoulder, shoved to the side against one of the walls on the road they'd just walked from, sat a boy in a wooden wheelchair. He couldn't have been any more than eight years old. Spike and the boy shared a lingering look before he returned his attention to Matilda. She hadn't seen the boy yet. He glanced at the crowd as it grew, more people piling in from every direction. If he left the group now, he probably wouldn't get close to Magma.

A few more seconds passed, the people behind Spike shoving him forwards with the press of their eagerness, shoving him closer to a chance to talk with his hero. He shook his head and muttered, "Damn it," before turning his back on the cart and his hero and fighting his way back through the crowd.

Free from the crush of bodies, Matilda a step behind him, Spike walked over to the boy. He had muscular arms, but small and withered legs. He'd obviously been in the chair a long time. Dark skinned, but not as dark as Spike, he had black hair and green eyes. The boy smiled, his teeth a brilliant white against his dark complexion.

Hooking a thumb behind him, Spike said, "Do you want to get closer to Magma?"

The boy's jaw fell loose and his eyes widened.

"Well?"

If the boy nodded with any more enthusiasm, he'd give himself whiplash.

"Will you be okay on my shoulders?"

The boy nodded again, no words in him, but he flexed his biceps as if to show he could hold on.

"Are you mute?" Spike said.

"No, sir. I just don't know what to say."

"Don't worry, you don't need to say anything." Lighter than he'd expected him to be, Spike lifted the boy, sat him on his shoulders, and pressed his palms against the base of the kid's back to support him like his chair had.

The crowd surrounding Magma had doubled in the small time he'd been away from it, and more people joined the dense press with every passing second. When he reached the edge of the crowd, Spike bobbed and weaved to see a path to the protector. With the boy on his shoulders, he wouldn't have to get directly next to the cart, just close enough for Magma to see the kid.

Spike looked over both shoulders, making brief eye contact with Matilda. He then cleared his throat and called in his deepest boom, "City guards coming through. Move aside." Like birds scattering, the crowd dispersed. No one argued with the guards. Many had at least witnessed what one of their clubs could do.

By the time the crowd caught on to the hoax, Spike had forced his way close to Magma. Despite the dark glares, many of them looked from Spike to the boy and back to Spike again. Not a single person challenged him.

Magma turned around, his usual frown on his large features, and Spike winced in anticipation of his wrath. No one liked a cheater. But then the protector looked at the boy on his shoulders. For that moment, Magma stared at the kid like he was the only one there. A soft glow of compassion momentarily shone through his deep glare and he smiled. When he reached across and stroked the kid's dark hair, Spike felt the boy quiver with excitement.

The moment passed and Magma's scowl returned. He turned back around and snapped his horses' reins, the people in front of him parting before he shouted, "Go." The thunderous boom of his voice cleared those who hadn't already moved out of the way.

After watching the cart out of sight, Spike returned the boy to his chair. He stepped back, moving aside as the kid's friends rushed over and surrounded him. The boy in the chair beamed while facing an onslaught of giddy questions.

"What did he feel like?"

"Is he hotter than normal people?"

"Did he say anything to you?"

It took for Matilda to come to Spike's side and hold his hand for him to turn away from the kid. It had been a day for her smiling at him, but the one she gave him now shone as bright as the sun. She nodded in the direction of the boy. "That was a nice thing to do. You were close enough to have been able to say something to Magma."

Batting a hand through the air, Spike snorted a laugh. Any disappointment he felt at the missed opportunity vanished when he looked at the boy. "Bloody kids, eh?"

Without saying anything else, Matilda continued smiling and rubbed his back.

Spike returned his attention to the kid and leaned into her warm touch.

CHAPTER 12

When Spike and Matilda stopped outside her house, Spike's throat tightened. Too many unspoken words for far too long. If he didn't say them, he'd drown in regret. She already knew, of course she did, but he needed to tell her how he felt. Their lives would change forever tomorrow. A gentle breeze moved through the tight streets, tickling the wind chimes. Nature often gave song to the ceramic district. A dirge of lost love and missed opportunity. He had to say something. "Matilda?"

"I think we should go for lunch," she said.

"You do?" He cleared his throat and lowered his voice slightly. "You do?"

"You don't want to go?"

"Of course I do. But only if you're happy to leave Artan?"

"Happy isn't a word I'd use, but I won't have a choice tomorrow. He's fourteen; he needs to learn to grow up and look after himself. It's not like we didn't know this day would come. I just want to check on him first. Do you want to come inside with me?"

Again, Spike nodded. She didn't invite him in often.

The second Matilda opened her front door, she gasped.

Spike rushed in after her and clapped his hand over his mouth as he took in the front room. "My god, what happened?"

While Matilda rushed over to Artan, Spike looked at the state of the place. Their sofa had been turned over, plates were smashed on the floor, and many ceramic ornaments had been shattered. The colourful shards covered the room like confetti. Then he looked at Artan. The boy took after Matilda and his mother. They all had dark features, high cheekbones, and brown eyes. A tanned brooding that made all of them beautiful beyond many in the city. As Matilda had gotten closer to eighteen, Spike noticed how she turned the heads of men. It drove him insane, but he never commented. What right did he have?

Despite sharing his sister's looks, Artan's usually boyish beauty was absent today. As Spike took him in, he winced. His dark features were darker with bruising and dried blood. His right eye had swollen closed and he had a deep gash torn open on his left cheek.

"What happened?" Matilda said.

Despite the bruising, Artan smiled. "I figured with you going for national service tomorrow, I needed to show that arsehole he couldn't get away with pushing me around."

"He's already started?" Matilda said.

"He tried."

"Are you okay?"

Artan nodded. "I'm fine. You should see *him*."

Back on her feet, Matilda held her hand down for Artan. "Come on, let's get you cleaned up." Then to Spike, "Are you okay waiting here while I sort him out?"

Despite Spike's concern for Artan, he could see their lunch date slipping away from him. He should have told her how he felt when he had a chance. He'd sound like an arsehole if he said it now. With a tight-lipped smile, he nodded. "Sure, take your time. I'll be waiting here."

"Hi, Spike," Artan said while his sister led him away.

While dipping him a nod, Spike said, "Artan, I hope you're okay?"

Artan smiled.

After watching Matilda and Artan head out of the front room, Spike looked at the carnage again. Like most houses in Edin, the ceiling in Matilda's front room stood about a foot taller than him at just over seven feet. A single-storey building, if they built it much higher, it would have a far greater risk of collapsing on them. Too many families had been lost to failing structures in the past. The house had two bedrooms, a bathroom, a kitchen, and a living room. Just about enough space for four people. One doorway—the one Matilda had just gone through—led to the bedrooms and bathroom, while the other doorway led to the kitchen.

There seemed little chance of them going for lunch now, and Spike couldn't blame her for that. But he'd wait just to make sure she and Artan were okay, and see if they needed anything from him. While he stood there, he filled his lungs with a deep inhale before slowly letting it out, his cheeks bulging. Nothing could change the situation, so he needed to make peace with it. There would be plenty more lunches when he became the next protectors' apprentice.

Matilda didn't let Spike in her house often because of her dad. She could never predict what the atmosphere would be like. When he did visit, if the mood started to turn, she'd give him the nod for him to make his excuses and leave. She'd often come to school the next day with bruises, and he'd hate himself for not sticking around. In his head, he'd beaten her dad down a thousand times, but she'd always told him she needed to handle it herself. And she did. The bruises stopped as she got older and stronger. She learned to fight back.

Spike listened to Matilda's and Artan's steps as they made

their way to their shared room. At least they'd had a trip to the arena for his birthday.

Because he'd been lost in his thoughts, Spike hadn't heard him coming. When he turned around and saw the man in the kitchen doorway, he jumped back. "Um … hi, Mr. Sykes. How are you? How's the ceramic industry?" If he hadn't forced himself to stop there, the questions would have kept coming, his nervous tongue threatening to run away with him.

A short man, Mr. Sykes had thick black hair that grew in every direction. Stubble and eyebrows to match, he looked like he'd been sleeping in bushes for most of his adult life. Always scruffy, he wore clothes that could have been tailored had he cared enough to send them to the tailoring district. Although short, he stretched almost as wide as he did tall and wore his stocky frame with a hunch. Apparently, as a young man, he'd been fierce and had the power to damn near crush rocks with his bare hands. Now he walked with a limp on a right knee that could barely support him. A less stubborn man would have enlisted the aid of a cane.

From the look of Matilda's dad, Artan's assessment of the fight had been accurate. Mr. Sykes had clearly come off much worse than his boy. Both of the man's eyes were swollen and puckered slits. Dried blood clung to his nasal hairs and beard.

About thirty seconds passed where Mr. Sykes did nothing but stare at Spike. Despite the swelling, the man's eyes remained sharp. Penetrative.

Fighting the urge to ball his fists—for Matilda's sake, not her dad's—Spike kept his calm and tried again, "Um …" He shifted his weight from one foot to the other. "It's a beautiful day, wouldn't you say?" He hated how his voice shook, adrenaline flooding his system.

Mr. Sykes continued to watch him, the slightest twist to his features as if regret turned through his wild and hairy face. Almost as if he felt sad for the things he was yet to do to Spike.

The thud of footsteps then sounded out from Matilda and Artan's room. Spike looked in the direction of it as if he could see through the walls. When he looked back at the doorway to the kitchen, Matilda's dad had gone.

Several more thuds as she made her way to him, Matilda appeared a second later. "Artan's telling me he's fine. We can go to lunch if you're ready?"

Spike looked at the doorway leading into the kitchen.

"What is it?" Matilda said.

"Um … nothing." He shook his head. "Nothing."

She cocked her head to one side. "Are you sure? You look pale."

"Yeah, it's nothing." If he told her, they wouldn't have their last meal together before national service. She wouldn't want to leave Artan with her dad coming back so soon, especially with him as wild as he looked. Spike opened the door and stood aside to let her out into the street first. "Come on, let's go."

A twist of guilt tugged on Spike's heart as he watched her step out of the house. But she was right, Artan needed to work it out for himself. She'd be gone tomorrow, so he needed to find his own way.

CHAPTER 13

They'd walked no more than ten metres from Matilda's front door before Spike broke. It didn't matter how much he wanted to have lunch with her, it wasn't up to him to decide if Artan would be okay. "Um, Tilly?"

Matilda stopped in the middle of the street and turned to look at him.

"Your dad came into the front room when you were with Artan."

The colour drained from her face and her mouth fell slightly open. "Oh god. Artan said he hadn't gone to work, but I didn't realise he was still at home. What happened?"

"Nothing. He just stared at me."

"He does that. A lot."

"I think Artan was right though; it looks like he got the better of him. Look, I'll understand if you want to cancel lunch."

After she'd drawn a deep breath, Matilda looked back at her house and squared her shoulders.

Spike took her hand as if to lead her back to her front door. "Come on, be with your brother on your final day."

But Matilda shook her head. "No."

"*No?*"

"I spoke to Artan and he said I should go out with you. That, from tomorrow, he has to deal with Dad on his own. Besides, we can use today as a test run. Dad's always his worst around this time of the year, so if I can leave Artan and come back to see he's coped, I can focus on national service knowing he'll be okay." A heavy sigh, she shrugged as she looked at Spike, tears in her eyes. "He's going to have to be, right?"

Spike nodded. "But only if you're sure?"

"I'm sure."

"Okay. Lunch at Mr. P's?"

She smiled. "Naturally."

CHAPTER 14

When Spike pulled the door open for Matilda, the bell above it rang, announcing their arrival to Mr. P. Before Spike had even entered the restaurant, the heady mix of spices he associated with the place rushed out to meet him, his mouth watering instantly at the infusion of basil, mint, pepper, and god knew what else. Mr. P kept his recipes very close to his chest.

Stepping into the restaurant so he stood next to Matilda, Spike looked around the dark room, squinting to see as best he could. "As ready as I am for tomorrow and beyond, I'm sure as hell going to miss Mr. P's cooking."

As if savouring the moment, Matilda pulled in a deep sniff and nodded. "Me too."

Were his food not as good, Mr. P would have had to close his place down years ago. In the city, you needed to justify your business and prove it mattered to the community. The turnover in restaurants happened quicker than most services. There were many chefs waiting in the wings should people grow tired of their selection of eateries. And because they all had to cook with the same limited ingredients, many establishments failed because of what they had supplied to them on a daily basis more than their culinary skills. Mr. P also had the added incentive of keeping the place open because it allowed him to remain inside during the day. He'd be screwed if they expected him to work in the sun.

Mr. P came as if from nowhere, a wide smile on his pale face. "Here they are," he said, his voice so loud many of the diners turned around to look. "And how are the two lovebirds?"

Matilda stared at the ground. "We've already told you, Mr. P, we'd be mad to fall in love with one another. We might only live in neighbouring districts, but they're as good as worlds apart in this city."

"Ah, come on, don't be coy."

When Spike saw Matilda's cheeks flush red, he said, "It's a hot one today, Mr. P."

Still a few metres away from them, Mr. P halted, gasped, and pulled his hands into his chest as if the sun could find a way into his restaurant. A glance at the door behind Spike, he wiped his white hair back and shook his head. "It's all right for you two. Especially you, Spike."

Spike looked down at the backs of his own hands as if seeing his ebony skin for the first time.

"But that weather out there cooks an albino like me." He shook his head. "What kind of temperature is this for March? Anyway, how can I help you both?"

"We'd like a table for two," Matilda said.

His apparent fear of the weather gone, Mr. P drew a deep breath as if about to deliver bad news, but then he stopped and clapped a hand to his mouth. A camp man, everything came with an eccentric flourish. His eyes flitted from one of their necks to the other's. "It's tomorrow, isn't it?"

Until that moment, Spike had forgotten about his scarf. With a self-conscious tug on the black fabric, Matilda spoke before he could. "Yes, it is, Mr. P."

Tears filled his eyes and he looked between the pair several times before he found his words. "It seems like it was only yesterday when you two lovebirds were starting school. And there's me about to tell you I don't have space today." Long fingers on delicate hands, he pointed at them both before he said, "Wait here. I'll go and find you a table."

Spike dipped a nod of thanks at the restaurateur.

In the minute or two he'd left them for, Mr. P had clearly had a chance to compose himself. His eyes were now dry and his smile wide again. He ran a look up and down Spike. "You're a fit lad. What are you, six feet tall?"

"Six two."

"Do you plan on doing the apprentice trials?"

"I sure do."

"And you, Matilda?"

The twist of Matilda's face forced Mr. P back a step. "No," she said. "I don't even want to go for national service."

"I'm not sure many do, sweetheart."

Before Matilda could respond, Spike said, "What's it like? No one ever talks about it."

The skin at the corners of Mr. P's eyes wrinkled from where he winced. "Just you two look after one another, okay?"

"Of course," Spike said.

"Of course you will. Lovebirds mate for life, don't you know?" As if to spare them their blushes, Mr. P said, "Well, for today, the food's free. Leave the ration stamp with your family so they can get extra another time. I want to make sure we send two of Edin's newest heroes into national service with their bellies full. Today, you can have whatever you like."

A rumble ran through Spike's stomach. "Even rabbit stew?"

"Even rabbit stew, William."

Where Matilda would normally smirk at someone calling him that, her expression remained unchanged. Spike said, "Thank you."

They followed Mr. P through the dark restaurant. The tables were packed so closely together they had to weave between them, their hips snaking as if they moved to a Latin rhythm. When they reached the small stage at the back of the room, Spike and Matilda stopped. Mr. P stepped up onto the slightly elevated area and showed them the best table in the house. It was the only one unoccupied. He often ate there himself at the end of a shift.

Removing the reserved sign, Mr. P wiped the tablecloth—not that Spike saw any need for him to—and then held his hand out to help Matilda up.

Spike jumped onto the stage and pulled a chair away for her to sit on.

After lighting the candle in the middle of the table, Mr. P bowed at the pair. "Have a wonderful meal, you two, and know you go into your national service with my love and prayers."

"You don't have to worry about us, you know that, Mr. P?"

The apparent grief Mr. P had managed to swallow rose in him again, tears filling his eyes for a second time. Words seemed beyond him, so he left them on the stage without speaking again.

When Spike looked across at Matilda, he saw she'd turned paler than before. Maybe the poor light played tricks on him; although, from the way she wrung her hands, maybe it didn't.

Reaching over, he leaned across the table and stroked the back of her forearm. "Don't worry about what Mr. P said. We'll be fine, I promise."

Matilda pulled away from him and steel settled in her eyes. "I'm not sure we will. So much can go wrong between now and you becoming the next protector."

"I'll get through national service."

"You don't know that. Besides, *I* might not. And then after that, there's still too much that can go wrong."

"I don't believe that. I think—"

"Can we just order, please?" Matilda said.

The snap of her reply made Spike pull back. Before he could respond, she picked up the menu and looked at it instead of him.

CHAPTER 15

For the next few minutes, Spike and Matilda ate in silence. The attention of the restaurant remained on them from how Mr. P had announced their arrival. Many of the diners watched on with blank expressions at best, but many more stared pity at them. Spike mirrored Matilda by directing his focus to his plate while he ate the complimentary rough bread and butter. Although, Mr. P had made everything complimentary today.

Matilda spoke first. "I'm sorry, Spike. I've been really negative towards you about being a protector."

"I understand. National service is a big deal. I know I'm unusual in how much I'm looking forward to it."

"It's not about national service. Well, it is, but only kinda."

Although Spike opened his mouth to respond, Matilda cut him off. "I'm ready to tell you about my dad if you'll listen?"

The second she said it, Spike gulped, and the bread he'd been chewing wedged in his throat. His shoulders and neck tightened and his heart quickened as he thought he might choke. It took him several gulps and a sip of water to regain his composure. "I only want you to tell me if you feel ready. I'd like to know, but I don't *need* to."

"And I appreciate you never asking. And for you putting up with me having wicked trust issues. But you must have been curious?"

"Sure."

"I don't know why I haven't spoken to you about it before. Shame, I suppose."

A flutter of anxiety unsettled the rhythm of Spike's breath. "What do *you* have to be ashamed about?"

"I dunno. You saw him earlier."

He thought about the wild man, incommunicado and covered in bruises. "Has he always been like that?"

When Matilda blinked, a tear ran down her cheek. While pressing the back of her shaking hand to her nose, she nodded. "All I can remember of him is the violence, the aggression, the self-loathing. And then the tears that *always* came afterwards. He'd beat the crap out of us, all *three* of us, and then we'd be the ones making sure he was okay once he'd finished." She spoke through gritted teeth. "He's such a pathetic snivelling wretch of a human."

Spike had always known what he did to them, but he was just a kid. What could he have done about it? Fighting to keep his tone even because Matilda didn't need him getting angry, he said, "How did you change it?"

Fire burned through her sadness and her features steeled. "I hit him back. When I got to thirteen, I decided I didn't want to be my mum. I don't want to be that person that lets someone walk all over her." As she looked away, Spike watched her eyes fill with tears again. "She pretends she stays with him for us. That keeping the family together is better than living in a broken home. But she stays with him because she's a coward and would much rather sacrifice her children's happiness than make a change in her wretched life."

"And that's why you have to look after Artan?"

"Someone has to. But I think that's changed. I think Artan has put him in his place." She then said, "It's why I'm so down on the apprenticeship trials."

Spike didn't reply, but his expression must have said everything it needed to because she went on to explain.

"Dad won the protectors' apprenticeship when he was our age."

Spike gasped.

"He breezed past national service and went all the way through the trials. He smashed it. He knew from the start that he'd be the next apprentice because he'd spent his entire life focused on it. Nothing would get in his way."

"So why isn't he a protector now?"

"Injury."

"Damn. Hence his limp?"

Matilda nodded. "In his first week of being an apprentice, he was in the arena and the chain lowering the box with the diseased in it snapped."

"The crate fell on him?"

"Well, he saw it coming, but as he dived out of the way, he tripped and smashed down on his knee."

"So what happened next?"

"Magma took his place."

"Magma was the runner-up that year?"

"Yep. I think that's what made it so hard for Dad. Any other protector and he probably would have been able to get on with his life, but as Magma's reputation rose, he had to watch what he could have been from afar."

"So how did he end up in ceramics?"

"He chose it. They let him live wherever he wanted to. He had to pick something that didn't put many physical demands on him because of his injury. It's where he and Mum met. I think he thought he could live a normal life."

"I don't understand," Spike said. "You said you feel ashamed."

"Wouldn't you?"

"I can't say, I'm not in your situation, but the story you just told me has nothing for *you* to feel ashamed about. If anything, you should be proud how you've come through it and helped Artan. I'd imagine Artan has been grateful to have you around."

Matilda had stopped trying to hold her tears back, wiping her eyes as she said, "But I have to leave him alone now."

"What did he say to you when you took him to his room?"

"That he'd be fine. That he can get himself to school and care for himself. He'll keep his head down and work hard and see me when I get back."

"I'm going to stop offering guarantees," Spike said, "but I think Artan will be fine. The best we can do is focus on what's ahead and make sure we're ready for everything coming our way. I'll be by your side for every step of it and we'll make sure you never have to leave Artan again. Okay?"

While nodding, Matilda drew another deep breath and looked out across the restaurant. Many of the diners were still watching them. The way she glared back—the candlelight reflecting off her glazed eyes—made Spike smile. The strongest person he knew, defiant in her grief, she silently dealt with every one of them. Her stare told them if they had a problem, they'd best say it now. On the rare times when he'd seen her in this frame of mind, he'd never seen anyone accept the invite by voicing their problems. "If you take that fire inside you in national service," he said, "I think you'll tear through it. You'll be back to Artan in no time."

CHAPTER 16

"The one major problem with Mr. P's," Spike said while shielding his eyes against the daylight, "is how damn dark he has it. I get why he needs it that way, but it's always hard to step back outside again." As his eyes adjusted to the light, he noticed the day had dulled a little. There were many more clouds in the sky, the hairs lifting on his exposed arms because of the nip in the air. A stomach full of food, he covered his mouth and burped.

Matilda laughed and shook her head at him. "You animal!" Her mirth left her features as quickly as it had lifted them. The weight of what she'd said to him in the restaurant still clearly dragged her down.

Spike reached across and touched the top of her arm. "Everything will work out."

While nodding, Matilda straightened her back. "You know what? I feel it. Seeing how Artan has dealt with Dad, and now telling you the truth about it all … it's helped a lot. I feel ready to focus on what's ahead. I'm not looking forward to tomorrow, but at least I feel like I can face it now. Thanks for listening."

"Thanks for trusting me."

Matilda winced.

Okay, so maybe she hadn't trusted him yet. Spike surveyed the ceramics district. Some of the more recently built houses stood out because they had bricks from the new kiln in their walls. Most of them went to the national service area to help with the expansion of Edin's footprint, but a small quota went to Edin's citizens. Given time and more bricks in circulation, collapsing houses would be a thing of the past.

With the day growing long, Spike knew Matilda would want to go back to Artan soon. "These next six months will fly by, you know? And then after that—"

"It's off to work. Ceramics for the rest of my life. I'll be building Edin's pots for their shit and piss until my hands don't work anymore. But at least I'll be able to keep an eye on Artan."

"Will you come and watch me when I'm in the trials?"

A slight pause, she looked ready to warn him against being overconfident again. Instead, she smiled. "I wouldn't miss it for the world. But just so you know, I won't be one of those women who visit the square every night."

"I know."

Spike saw Matilda look over in the direction of her house. "Do you want to get back?"

"I do, but I also need to let go at some point, right?"

As much as Spike wanted to say something, he didn't. She had to make the decision about whether to go home or not.

"I can't see me getting much rest, and Artan told me to stay out as long as I like. He insisted he was okay. I think it's about time I let go and stopped trying to mother him. I need to get my mind focused on national service. Whatever I do, I can't avoid the next six months. Would you mind if we went for a walk?"

"I'd love that," Spike said.

"The square?"

"I thought you hated the square?"

"Tomorrow will come. It's time I faced it. I need to go there and I'd like you to be with me."

Spike nodded. "I'd like that too. Let's go."

CHAPTER 17

They arrived at the entrance to the square and Spike looked out over the crowd. The place had started to fill up, as it often did at this time of day. Many of the lovers' benches were unoccupied. They'd come later when the crowds had left. Standing on his tiptoes, he saw some space down by the cage. "The protectors haven't been yet. It will get much busier when they do. Are you sure you still want to do this?"

Matilda nodded.

"In that case, I think we should make the most of the opportunity to get close now. Come on." He reached back and grabbed her hand. "Follow me. I know the best spot."

Although Matilda didn't reply, she let him lead her past the several empty benches close to them and into the heart of the crowd.

Spike moved at a quick pace, knocking and shoving people on his way down. Several tuts and angry shakes of heads, but no more than that. They must have seen his and Matilda's scarves. The amount of pity he'd had to face since putting the thing on, he might as well use it to his advantage now.

As they walked alongside the large cage in the middle of the square, Spike looked in at the stakes protruding from the ground. Twelve in total, they were wedged in the gaps between the cobblestones. They all pointed straight up. Each one no thicker than a spear, they had bloodstained shafts and dried pools around their bases. The stakes were kept locked in a cage because of the risk of infection. There had only ever been records of the virus spreading through saliva, but the city wouldn't risk it. If even one person picked up the disease and someone wasn't there to take them down instantly, it could bring Edin to its knees.

One of the few communal areas in the city, the square was always busy. Especially between the hours of six and eight in the evening. Some nights, Spike had come down here and could barely move for the crowd. His eyes on the space he wanted, he shoved through the next gap, sending a man stumbling a few steps away from him. He and the man stared at one another before the man looked at the black scarves around Spike's and Matilda's necks, shook his head, and turned his back on them.

The daily displays from the protectors brought in the crowds. At other times, those visiting the square were there to meet people from different districts. Lovers before they were separated by finishing national service and being forced to remain in their sector. They would sit on the benches around the place and spend their evenings talking, but definitely not touching. Spike looked at several more benches dotted around the outside of the main area. Of course he'd gone there and watched them at night. The act of a curious kid, even then he saw the sadness hanging over the place. One of the most heavily guarded areas, day and night, those who chose to go there to meet with forbidden romances weren't allowed any physical contact with one another. It seemed that for some, just being able to talk to their love at the end of a day made their life easier. He couldn't imagine never talking to Matilda again.

Spike looked back at Matilda to find her staring straight at him. He couldn't blame her for not wanting that life for herself. It looked like torture. Better to forget about what you'd lost than live the sterile existence of those who sat on the benches.

The super lonely also hung out in the square. They would meet with others in need of company. They clearly preferred to have a conversation with someone they could never be with than stay at home alone every night. Whatever way you sliced it, the square reeked of desperation, death, and despair.

But they weren't here to think about the lonely people. Spike would be the next protector, so he didn't need to worry about it. The temperature might have dropped with the evening getting closer, but the crowd held onto a lot of the day's heat. The funk of sweating bodies hung like an invisible mist. Doing his best to breathe through his mouth, Spike said, "They should be back soon." Matilda had turned pale. "Are you sure you want to watch this?"

"I can't stop the sun setting and rising, Spike. Whatever happens, this is my life for the next six months. I need to let a little bit of that reality in."

Spike dipped a nod at her and then gently rubbed her back to show his support.

Seconds later, the horn announcing the protectors' return sounded. The deep resonance of it swelled through the square, a surge of bodies pushing into Spike and Matilda and forcing them several steps closer to the caged area. They were now close enough to the stakes for the smell of rancid blood—curdled by the sun—to hit them. Spike ruffled his nose. No matter how many times he smelled the vinegar tang of the diseased's spilled essence, he'd never get used to it. A glance at Matilda and he saw that she too scrunched up her face against the stench, sweat now glistening on her brow. "Are you okay?"

With a tight clench to her jaw, Matilda nodded. She had to be.

The horn sounded again—this time much louder—accompanied by the thud of boot heels. Close to fifty guards ran into the square. Those first in moved to either side to make a tunnel all the way to the cage. They shoved many people aside to make room, their billy clubs raised should they get the chance to use them. The citizens knew the drill and rarely obliged their violent urges.

Too many bodies between Spike and the protectors for him to see them. But they had a good spot, so he just needed to wait. The protectors would come to them.

What must have been one of the more senior guards, from the way he held himself, walked slowly down the pathway made by his comrades. The click of his boot heels snapped through the now quiet crowd. "Good evening, ladies and gentlemen. Whether you're here for the first time, or this is a regular event for you, I wanted to take a moment to mention the protectors and the hard work they do keeping Edin safe. Were it not for their tireless efforts outside the city walls, we'd run out of wood, we'd not get any new scavenged materials, and most importantly, the diseased would overrun this city. The thinning of those vile creatures on a daily basis keeps them away from our walls. Edin's walls are strong, but if we let the numbers of diseased grow uncontrollably, they'd push them over in no time. So, without further ado, I want you all to welcome today's protectors."

A cheer lifted the crowd, loud enough to make Spike flinch. Then he joined in. Although he smiled at Matilda, she didn't smile back, her skin several shades paler than before. He hooked a thumb to motion them leaving, but she shook her head.

A few seconds later, the first of the protectors came into view. Tall and broad shouldered, Crush had her hair shaved clean off, her dark scalp shining in the sun. She wore blood-matted furs over her shoulders and scowled at those around her like she'd run them through with her broadsword just to increase her kill tally for the day. She had a brown woven sack tightly gripped in her left hand, which squirmed and writhed with the activity inside it. When she emptied it on the ground, several heads rolled out, their skulls playing a hollow percussion against the hard stone.

One of the heads went farther than the others, the spectators near to Spike all moving a step back from it. Although Matilda went with them, Spike didn't. Instead, he watched it roll to within six inches of his feet and stop. He stared down at its pallid and wrinkled face. He watched its ineffective snapping jaws as it stared through blackened eyes, the blood flow to them cut off where the connection to its body had been severed. The muscles in his legs tensed and he balled his fists. It took all he had to refrain from stamping on it like he would a troublesome bug.

Crush stepped towards Spike. Nearly as tall as him and easily twice his width, she was one of the largest women he'd ever seen. At first she stared straight into his eyes, the crowd silent around them. A few seconds later, her gaze settled on the scarf around his neck. "A brave boy," she said, her voice as deep as Magma's had been. "You'd do well to rein that in over the next six months. In my experience, brave teenage boys are only brave because they're dumb." Her stare moved to Matilda. "A brave girl … now that's a force of nature."

When Crush returned her attention to Spike, he felt the crowd stare at him with her. It sent his pulse into overdrive and his throat dried. He tried to hide his nerves with a shrug, his eyes dropping to her bloodstained broadsword.

Crush must have seen him struggling because her hard scowl softened slightly, moving aside with a twist of sympathy. She patted Spike on the shoulder, hitting him so hard he struggled to hold his balance. "Good luck, boy. Make us proud, and try to come back alive."

Many of those in the crowd were old enough to have already done national service. Crush's words sent a graveyard silence through the place. Spike and Matilda shared a look with one another.

Spike leaned close enough so only Matilda heard him. "Do you want to go?"

She shook her head.

Before Spike could respond, Crush bent down and grabbed the runaway head by both of its rotting ears. She laughed while holding it up in front of her. It bit at the air between them, its teeth sending out a castanet click as they snapped just centimetres from her face. The creature's black tongue wormed from its mouth, a necrotised snake poking its head from a hole. So desperate to taste pure flesh, but it had no way of making it a reality.

Crush then walked into the cage and over to one of the twelve display spikes. The guards each had their own stakes and kept them for as long as they lived. She raised the snapping head in the air and paused for a moment as if to milk the crowd's reaction.

The onlookers fell silent. Spike's stomach tensed.

Lifting the head even higher, Crush roared as she brought it down hard.

A wet squelch as the wooden spike burst through the top of the thing's skull, blood and bone exploding away from it. The crowd cheered as both its eyes and mouth fell open and the head slid down the pole, greasing it with blood and brain matter on its way to the ground. By the time the skull had reached the bottom, the wooden shaft now glistened with the putrid disease.

The cheers and applause grew louder. Despite having seen the show thousands of times, Spike bounced where he stood and grinned as if he'd never witnessed it before. He celebrated. They all celebrated. All of them save Matilda.

When Spike looked at her again, he saw how she'd pulled back mentally, her eyes distant. He mouthed, *Are you okay?*

Matilda shook her head, turned around, and walked away,

shoving some of the people close to her aside in her haste to get out of there.

Spike followed her, listening to the cheers as more of the protectors entered the cage. More cracks of skulls and screams of celebration lit the place up. Good for Matilda for facing it, but maybe it was too much. Especially after Crush's pessimistic well wishes.

CHAPTER 18

When they got to the edge of the square away from the main press of the crowd, Matilda stopped, chewing on the inside of her mouth as she looked back in the direction of the cage. “I’m sorry. I know you wanted to stay longer.”

Spike shook his head. “Don’t worry, I’ve seen it hundreds of times already. And it’s a lot to face at the moment.”

“It just seems so unnecessary. A brutal display just to remind us how great the protectors are. How lucky we are to be a citizen of Edin. Sometimes I question that. So much is forbidden, I wonder if these walls keep them out or us in.”

“I think they bring the heads back each day for the same reason they have the main event in the arena. This is the easiest way to reach all the people who want to see it. To show them the protectors are doing something for them.”

“Catharsis.”

“Exactly.”

“I’d worry about you, you know?”

“Huh?”

“If you became a protector.”

“*If?*”

Matilda didn't respond. Instead, she turned and headed away from the square.

Jogging a step to catch up with her, Spike walked at her side for a second before he noticed one of the benches and stopped. He reached out and grabbed Matilda's arm.

When she saw why he'd pulled her up, she stepped towards the bench he'd been looking at. "Mr. P?"

The albino man turned from pink to crimson and he dropped his eyes to the ground. He sat next to a well-dressed chap who looked like he'd come from the tailors' district. Although clearly from different worlds, they both had the same deep pools of despair in their tired eyes.

Where Mr. P would usually talk to them, he kept his focus on his feet.

Spike moved forward another step and Mr. P raised his hand at him. "Stop!" After a glance around, he said, "Don't talk to me. Not here."

The ultimate forbidden love in Edin, Mr. P did it for Spike and Matilda's protection not his own. There were strong opinions in the city about his type.

"But we don't care," Matilda said and moved towards him.

"I do," Mr. P said. "If you won't look out for your own well-being, then I'll have to. Now go." A wince as if it caused him pain, his voice broke as he growled, "Leave me alone."

They looked from Mr. P to his forbidden love. "Come on," Spike said. "We need to respect Mr. P's wishes. He knows we're not passing judgement." As he moved off, he tugged Matilda's arm to bring her with him. She resisted for a second before letting him lead her away.

CHAPTER 19

As Spike and Matilda left the square, Spike noticed she had more purpose to her stride. Her jaw set, her shoulders back, her pace quick. Not quite evening yet, but with it closing in, many of the fires in the street had already been lit. A line of metal baskets filled with burning wood, she walked over to the nearest one while untying her scarf.

Before Spike could say anything, she'd tossed it into the flames. While watching it burn, his jaw fell. "What are you doing?"

"I'm fed up with this city and its damn rules." She rolled the neck of her shirt up to cover the bottom half of her face. The fabric muffled her voice. "I'm fed up with people being told where they can and can't go, who they can and can't love, where they can and can't work." While bouncing on the spot, she raised her voice, her eyes narrowing. "I'm fed up of kids being sent to slaughter to make this prison we live in bigger and harder to escape from. I can't change any of that, but I can choose if I wear that damn thing around my neck. I refuse to be a slave to this city. If only for tonight."

"But if the guards see you—"

"I'll run. Let's see if those power-hungry arseholes are quick enough to catch me."

"You're not thinking straight, Tilly."

The fire she'd thrown her scarf in reflected in her eyes. Her nostrils flared. "Oh, I'm thinking straighter than I have all day. I've accepted Artan's ready to be left alone, so this moment's for me. I want to have some fun; the question is, are you with me or not?"

The intensity of her glare made Spike squirm, but the question didn't. He'd follow her to hell and back. He removed his scarf too, copying Matilda by covering the bottom half of his face with the collar of his shirt as he tossed the black fabric into the same fire on the side of the street. Adrenaline lifted his pulse and lit up his senses. He half-smiled at her, not that she'd be able to see it. "If we run, you'd best be able to keep up."

Matilda shot air through her upturned shirt. "It's about time you stopped worrying about me. I'm fit enough, Spike. I think you're the one who should concern yourself with catching up."

Instead of replying, Spike followed Matilda's lead as she set off, the same quick march as before. They walked in the direction of the ceramics district and the closest set of guards.

As they drew close to them, Matilda spoke quietly. "Watch me and be ready."

His confidence draining from him, Spike looked at the four guards. He nearly pulled his shirt down to show his face. "What are you going to do?"

But she didn't reply. Instead, she marched like she owned the streets.

"State your business," one of the guards said, the other three leaning against the walls on either side. Despite their casual stance, they were all focused on the pair.

Matilda said nothing.

"I said *state your business.*"

No more than ten feet between them, another one of the guards pushed off from the wall and helped her colleague block the way.

His billy club in his hand, the first guard's voice dropped in tone. "I *said state your business!*"

Five feet away, the need to run coursed through Spike. But Matilda had told him to follow her lead. Even if she'd never trusted him, he needed to trust her.

"My business is my own," Matilda finally said. "You may not enquire about it. Now stand aside, you peasants."

In any other situation, her faked posh accent would have made Spike laugh.

The other two guards stiffened a little at her words, but only the guard who'd originally spoken continued to talk to her. "I beg your pardon? Now unless you want your skull cracked, I suggest you wind your neck in and answer my question."

When Matilda released a banshee cry, even Spike jumped. The guards' eyes spread wide and all four of them flinched when she charged, her arms windmilling like she'd lost her mind.

Spike followed on Matilda's heels as she ran straight for the guard who'd spoken to them, and knocked him backwards with a hard shove, jumping through the gap she'd made as he fell. One of his colleagues swung for Spike, who ducked the swinging club, stumbled from where he'd dropped so low, and ran several clumsy steps before he regained his balance, keeping Matilda in his sight.

As they ran down the street and into the main square in the ceramics district, the guards gave chase and shouted behind them, "Criminals! Stop them now!"

Maybe the residents of the ceramics district didn't hear the guards, but they certainly looked. If questioned as to why they didn't stop the pair, no doubt that was what they'd say.

The thunder of the guards' steps behind them, Spike looked over his shoulder. All four had given chase. When he turned back around, he saw Matilda duck down a tight alley on her right.

Entering the alley a second later, Spike watched his love move like lightning. It had been years since he'd seen her run, but he knew she trained. They all did.

No wider than four feet at the most, the alleyway turned a sharp left. As Matilda vanished around it, she'd already pulled farther away from Spike. When he rounded the corner a few seconds later, he saw the dead end. The guards' footsteps entered the alley behind them. "What the—?" But before he could say anything else, he watched Matilda jump from one wall to the other. Kicking off each one as she ran, she got progressively higher.

The wall on their right stood about ten feet tall. When Matilda caught the top of it, Spike shook his head. But what else could he do? The guards on their heels, he felt the strength leave his legs.

Up on the wall now, Matilda shouted down at him, "You can do it."

Spike leapt at the wall on his left and kicked off it, hitting the right a second later before going back to the left. Each kick felt like it would be the one where his foot slipped, but he found a protruding piece of rock or brickwork every time, lifting as he ran.

On his final leap, Spike reached for the top, his hands burning from where the rough brickwork tore cuts into his palms. Gassed, he fought against his heaving diaphragm and scrabbled to get to the top before he flopped over the wall, gasping as he looked down on the textiles district on the other side.

It took a few seconds, but when Spike looked at Matilda, her eyes showed him she was smiling. "You've done that before, haven't you?"

Before Matilda responded, the guards charged around the corner. Spike wiped his brow to keep the sweat from his eyes.

The one whom Matilda had shoved over led the team again. While pointing an angry finger up at them, he spoke through gritted teeth. "Get down now."

"Or what?" Matilda said.

"Or I'll climb up there and drag you down."

"Go on, then."

An already red face turned redder and the guard stamped his foot. "Someone get me a ladder!"

The fourth and final guard had only just rounded the corner. Not as in shape as the others, she looked at the three staring at her, rolled her eyes, and ran back in the direction she'd come from.

"So you want us to wait here while you go and get a ladder?" Matilda said.

The guard didn't reply to her, pacing back and forth like an angry dog.

"Do you want us to lock ourselves up when you catch us too? Maybe we can chase ourselves for you as well and give ourselves a beating?" She reached down. "Throw your sticks up and I'll make a start."

It happened so quickly Spike missed it. Fortunately Matilda didn't. The guard launched his billy club straight at her, the baton spinning as it flew through the air.

Matilda ducked, the club sailing over her head into the textiles district behind them. "How am I supposed to catch that?" She then threw one of her legs over the side of the wall, turned so she hung down into the textiles district, and dropped to the ground.

The guards looked at Spike, who shrugged before following her over.

When he landed, Spike shook his head at her. "You're nuts."

She smiled, but just before she could pull her shirt down to expose her face again, the sound of more guards called through the streets. “It ain’t over yet,” she said while tugging on his sleeve. “Come on.”

As much as Spike needed to rest, when she took off, he ran after her.

CHAPTER 20

Although they were yet to see them, it sounded like more guards chased them than before. The tighter streets in the textiles district amplified the stampede on their tail. Matilda opened up a lead on Spike again. Like in the ceramics district, his lungs felt like they'd burst just from trying to keep up. It was on her to decide where they were heading.

Not only were the streets tighter, but they zigzagged, making Matilda vanish from his sight and then reappear every few seconds. For now, he could follow her sound, but the guards were getting closer and it wouldn't be long before they drowned her out.

When Spike ran around the next corner, he saw Matilda waiting for him. Not that he would have ever asked her to, but thank god she had. He didn't fancy finding his own way out of there. Although nowhere near as breathless as him, she stood panting. The steps continued closing down on them. Then he saw why she'd stopped. Guards blocked the way ahead.

The alley they were in stretched wider than the one they'd escaped from earlier. Too wide to kick off against the walls to get out of there.

Before Spike could react, Matilda leaned her back against one of the walls and linked her hands together to give him a foot up.

"What about you?"

The guards in front of them screamed and charged. The ones behind would be on them soon. "Just do it," Matilda yelled.

They'd done it before. Spike ran at Matilda, stepped onto her hand and jumped when she lifted. It gave him the extra foot he needed and he stretched up to catch the top of the wall like he'd done to get out of the ceramics district. None of the walls in Edin had smooth tops to them, this one tearing at his palms much like the previous wall had. But Spike moved quickly, pulling himself up and then throwing his legs over the other side before leaning down for Matilda.

While looking from one side to the other, both sets of guards closing in, Spike felt Matilda's hands in his and slipped off the wall backwards, using his weight to drag her up.

Just before Spike dropped over the other side, he saw Matilda lift her right leg and catch the top of the wall with it. He let go, landing on the other side. She nodded down at him. She'd made it, but they needed to get out of there before the guards found another way around.

When Matilda landed next to him, Spike—still fighting for breath—said, "Which way?"

"The plaza."

Spike frowned at her. "We'll be sitting ducks in there."

Matilda turned her head as if listening for something. It helped him hear it too. The running footsteps of guards came at them from every direction. "It sounds like half the city are chasing us," he said. "They're going to beat the crap out of us when they catch us."

"We'll need to make sure they don't catch us, then. We're going to the plaza. You need to trust me. Come on."

Not the time to raise the issue of trust, Spike dragged air into his tight lungs as they set off again.

When they got to the plaza, it suddenly made sense. The textiles district made sheets and fabrics for all of Edin. On sunny days like the one drawing to a close, they hung the fabrics out to dry. It turned the plaza into a giant multicoloured maze.

Matilda dodged and batted the fabric away. Spike followed her as she led him into the centre. They stopped again and Matilda said, "I can hear them coming. They'll know we're in here. We're going to have to use the sheets to our advantage."

"But where shall we go?"

The shout and heavy boots of the approaching guards closed in from every side. It looked like Matilda had most of her attention fixed on that. Surrounded by the shimmering sheets, they had to rely on their ears. "You need to work that out for yourself, Spike."

"Huh?"

"We're going to have to split up."

The first guards entered the plaza. "Where are they?" one of them shouted.

A female voice answered back, "They have to be in here somewhere."

The sounds of more guards came in from other sides.

"We need to close in on them," one shouted.

"We're screwed," Spike said.

Using her right hand, Matilda silently counted down. *Five, four, three, two, one.* On one she ran at a light blue sheet close to them, letting out a shrill and undulating scream as she went.

Spike watched the sheet settle, covering her path, and for a moment he remained frozen. But he had to move. He had to get out of there and hope Matilda would do the same. A red sheet next to him, he sprinted through it and headed in what he hoped to be the least guarded section of the square.

As he ran, Spike listened to Matilda. She continued to scream, drawing the sounds of the guards with her.

The damp fabric felt cold to the touch as it dragged along Spike on his way to the edge. He'd gone through five or six on his way in. After smashing through a fourth one, he saw an exit.

Just before Spike made a break for it, one of the sheets on his right burst to life, wrapped him in a tight grip, lifted him from his feet, and slammed him down against the cobblestone ground.

CHAPTER 21

Before Spike could scream for Matilda, the damp sheet smothered him, two hard fingers shoving it into his mouth. He fought against his need to heave and bit down, but the fingers were out before he'd clamped onto them.

A balled fist, his teeth still gritted, Spike swung for the guard on top of him. Again he missed, and before he could throw another punch, the sheet smothering him got ripped away, giving him sight of her. "Tilly?"

Matilda reached down and put her hand over his mouth. With her other hand, she pressed a finger to her lips to motion for him to be quiet. She then reached down to help him up.

It took a few seconds for Spike to untangle himself from the damp wrap of the sheet.

After pointing in the direction she intended them to go, Matilda nodded at Spike, looking for his acknowledgement. He nodded back and they set off again.

No sign of the guards, they left their shouting and screaming behind in the square, hopeful they'd be long gone by the time the guards realised it. Matilda moved at an easier pace, Spike able to catch his breath and keep up with her.

Matilda turned right down the next street. Like many in Edin, it had cobblestones and was penned in by the walls of one-storey, canted buildings. No bricks from the kiln here, this street looked as old as Edin itself.

When they turned into another alley, Matilda stopped again, the sky growing darker with the onset of night. The cooler temperature came as a relief against Spike's sweating skin, but no doubt he'd feel the bite of the evening if they stopped for longer. To look at Matilda made him shake his head. After he'd pulled the front of his shirt down to uncover his face, he said, "You're insane, you know that?"

She shrugged.

"I didn't think you had that in you. You've always toed the line."

"Maybe I'm fed up with toeing the line."

"Clearly."

The two of them were smiling as they stood in the alley, and before Spike could say anything else, Matilda pointed at the large building close to them: the main factory in the textiles district. "Do you remember when we used to climb on the roof of that thing?"

It made Spike smile to think about it. "And how many times we were chased away because of it."

"And the time we didn't make it home for dinner."

Spike laughed. "Our parents went apeshit, eh?"

A moment of sobriety, Matilda looked at the ground. He'd forgotten about the bruises she came to school with the next day. But she looked up again with steel in her eyes. "That was the last time he beat me. The next time he tried, I fought back. I think it was important for that reason."

"My mum thought I'd been eaten by a diseased," Spike said. "Not that I could have gotten out of the city."

"I dunno." Matilda took several settling breaths. "There's always a way out if you really want to find it."

"And you want to find it?"

"Maybe."

"You know what? The wall at the edge of our largest field looks like it could be climbed. Every time I see it, I plot a route to the top."

Despite the size of the large square building—the second largest structure in Edin after the arena—it looked much smaller than Spike remembered. It had been a few years since he'd walked down this street. With what they had coming tomorrow, everything looked smaller, almost as if the approaching national service forced Spike to view the world through the eyes of a man for the first time in his life. Tomorrow would change everything.

When Matilda walked away from him, Spike said, "Where are you going?"

Another tight alleyway ran along the side of the factory. It probably only existed so the large structure could collapse without taking down the neighbouring buildings. It served no other purpose because it led to a dead end. Even a small gap could mean the difference between just one building falling instead of an entire street going down like dominoes.

Matilda stopped to look up and down the road—the sounds of the guards still in the air. They were far away for now, but they'd get closer. She moved towards the alleyway again.

A similar check to be sure they weren't being watched, Spike followed her.

By the time Spike entered the alley, Matilda's feet were as high as his head. She'd made a star with her body, her left foot and hand against the left wall, her right foot and hand against the right. Alternating between using the press of her feet against the walls on either side of her while she moved her hands higher, and then her hands while she lifted her feet, she moved up.

Only about fifteen feet high, Matilda reached the top, grabbed onto the ledge, and pulled herself up onto the roof. She then disappeared from sight as she walked away from Spike.

One final check, Spike followed her up, bracing against the close walls as he too shuffled to the top and onto the roof in the same way she had, though much slower than she had.

The slightest slope to the wooden roof allowed for drainage. Spike walked up it over to where Matilda now sat. He plunked down next to her, let his feet hang over the edge, and looked at the fenced-in courtyard below. On days when they had fine weather, many of the workers preferred to be in the sunshine. The mess of tools still scattered around showed today had been one of those days. Several large sheets flapped in the gentle breeze like they had in the square.

For a few seconds, neither of them spoke, both taking in the city around them. Most buildings were so small, they could see over the tops of them all the way to the walls on every side. They could even see the large wooden gates that led to the national service area. Yesterday, it wouldn't have bothered Spike to look at them. But now, with national service so close and Matilda's insistence he take it seriously, his heart fluttered at the sight of them.

"Edin seemed a whole lot bigger the last time we were on this roof," Matilda said.

"A lot's happened since then."

"How old were we when we last climbed up here?"

Spike shrugged. "Thirteen."

"Thirteen? You seem pretty certain of that. How do you remember it so clearly?"

A flush of heat smothered Spike's face and he turned away. Because they were slightly higher up, the breeze lifted his hair. "I remember every day we've spent together."

"*Every* day?"

It was too much to look at her, so Spike continued to stare out over the city. His gaze settled on the agricultural section, the place he'd called home for his entire life. He nodded. "Yeah."

"Okay, what was I wearing on my thirteenth birthday?"

Even as the wind picked up, the heat in Spike's cheeks grew hotter. "Don't do this, Tilly."

Jabbing his arm with a playful punch, she laughed. "I knew you couldn't remember."

"In the same way I used to think this factory was huge, I used to think the fields in the agricultural district stretched for miles. But they look so small from up here. The walls look so close. We're one bad harvest away from starvation."

"Like the famine just before we were born," Matilda said. "I pray we never have to see that in our lifetime."

Although Matilda drew a breath to say something else, Spike cut her off. "You were wearing a blue polka-dot dress. You seemed really awkward in it because you were turning into a young woman and trying to deal with your changing body. But you had nothing to feel self-conscious about. We ate at Mr. P's. He even found you a chocolate cake for dessert. Then we climbed up here."

Slack-jawed, Matilda continued to stare at him. "You remember all that?"

Spike nodded. "You got upset with me because I didn't compliment you on how beautiful you looked."

"God, I was a bossy cow."

"But you did look beautiful. You looked amazing." Turning away, Spike faced the arena. "You always look amazing." He kept his focus directed out over the rooftops. "You mentioned you wanted to run away. If you decide to, please tell me."

"Why?"

"I'll come with you. I'll come with you and Artan if that's what you really want."

"What about your dream to become a protector?"

"I do want to be one, but my dream's ultimately about freedom. Freedom to go where I please and not live the life of a slave. I could have that outside these walls."

"But at what cost?"

"I'm not sure. We don't know what's out there. But I'll risk it if it means spending the rest of my life with you." Spike sighed. "It's not my first choice, but I just wanted to say if it's something you need to do, then come and get me, okay? The carriage is picking us up in the morning for national service. If you come to me before then and say you want to go, I'll come with you. I'll take you to the wall I think we can climb." Spike stood up before Matilda could say anything else. "I need to go and spend a bit of time with my parents before tomorrow. Whatever happens, I'll see you soon, okay?"

Matilda nodded.

"Just promise me you'll come and get me if you decide to leave?"

She nodded again. "You're one of the kindest people I know, Spike."

After leaning down and stroking her long brown hair from her face, Spike looked into the dark eyes he knew so well and said, "If I don't see you tonight, I'll see you in the morning."

Again, Matilda nodded. Before Spike could turn and leave, she stood up and grabbed both of his hands in hers. She looked into his eyes. "I promised myself I'd never do this." She leaned towards him.

Despite all the exercise they'd done that evening, Spike's heart beat harder than ever when they kissed. After they'd pulled away, he said, "What was that for? I thought we needed to hold back and not fall in love."

A slight wince, Matilda said, "Have you not fallen in love?"

"I fell in love years ago. You know that."

"Well, I suppose tonight's a night for breaking rules."

"Have you broken your rule to not trust anyone other than Artan?"

The slightest smile lit Matilda's face and she gently shook her head before leaning in and kissing him again.

When she'd pulled away for a second time, Matilda said, "I've wanted to do that for ages. I don't know what's going to happen in national service, but I don't want to regret never kissing you."

Spike squeezed her hands. "Just wake me up if you want to get out of the city. I'd follow you to the end of the world and back."

Again, Matilda smiled.

After letting go of her, Spike stepped backwards before turning around and running to the edge of the roof. While slipping off the side, Matilda called after him, "Be careful on your way home."

CHAPTER 22

She'd kissed him! Spike had been friends with Matilda for years, and for a lot of that time, he'd liked her in a way he shouldn't. In a way reserved for protectors, politicians, and fools. But he hadn't chosen those feelings, and once they'd risen up in him, he most certainly couldn't deny them. Besides, *she'd* kissed *him*, not the other way around.

The sky had the slightest blue tinge where the sun still cast a subtle influence over the day. Most of the light in the city now came from the fires lining the streets. A bounce in his step, Spike strolled through the agricultural district. Plain compared to textiles and ceramics, the place smelled of mud, the streets dirty from where many boots had dragged some of the field home with them.

When Spike rounded the corner to see his house and his dad sitting outside it, he slowed his pace. The closer he got, the more his legs resisted his forward momentum, especially when he saw the chamber pots by his dad's feet. He'd told Matilda he'd be waiting for her should she come. "Um … hi, Dad."

It looked like it caused his dad pain to smile, but he did it anyway. "Thought I'd wait for you. I wasn't the best company last night, so I was wondering if you'd like to take one last walk to the wall before …" He cleared his throat. "Where's your scarf?"

Spike shrugged while tugging at his collar. "I didn't want to wear it anymore. It's tiring getting treated like a victim by everyone."

From the frown on his dad's face, Spike guessed he wanted to say something about the dangers of walking the streets without a black scarf on. A paternal need to protect, even when the protection came across as pessimism. Instead, he nodded, his shoulders relaxing as he clearly let it go. "Fair enough. You won't need it tonight anyway."

A large man, when Spike's dad got to his feet, he stood slightly taller than Spike. A thick frame from working the fields in the agricultural district, it would take Spike years to develop the same level of strength his old man had. Spike might have had a six-pack and pecs, but his dad could drag a cart filled with hay if one of their horses let them down. His dad would wrestle Magma to the ground if he needed to.

It had been a long time since Spike had seen hair on the top of his dad's head. Grey around the sides and back, his dark bald scalp looked like a slab of leather from where it had been exposed to the sun for years, very little escaping it in the fields. Spike's skin was a few shades lighter than his dad's on account of his pale mother, but not so light that he burned from spending too long in the sun. His mum had to wear hats and layers in the fields; otherwise she turned into a blister and couldn't move for a week. Even after all these years of being out in the elements, her skin hadn't ever adjusted to it. "Where's Mum?"

"You know what your mother's like. She's in bits already. It wouldn't do to have her sobbing as we walked through the city. You can't remove that kind of attention like you can a black scarf."

Spike's dad first handed him a coat, which he slipped on. As the day had come to a close, he'd regretted leaving the house in only a T-shirt. Although, he'd take hypothermia for another kiss from Matilda. After doing the buttons up, his dad gave him the smaller of the two chamber pots before picking up the other one himself.

A bittersweet job because it gave them the chance to walk through the city whenever they pleased, but they had to have a sloshing bucket filled with piss and shit for the excuse to do it. At least they'd emptied them the previous night. The pots still stank, but didn't weigh as much as they could have.

As they set off, Spike looked back at his house. If Matilda did come for him, surely it would be much later in the night. With so many people still awake, it would be madness to try to escape now. Spike said, "So how was your day?"

"Fine, the usual. Ploughing fields, sowing seeds, praying for rain …"

"Were you and Mum in the same field today?"

"No."

Conversation normally flowed easily between them, but it felt like conversing with a stranger tonight. As much as Spike wanted to suggest they go home, he knew it would break his dad's heart. While staring in front of him, the flickering torches in their metal baskets animating the shadows in his peripheral vision, he looked in the direction of the small communal plaza close to them. "Do you think there will be anyone at the dentist today?"

It broke through his dad's scowl, the slightest twist of a smile lifting his face. When he looked at Spike, his eyes were alive. "Is it mean to say I hope so?"

"No. We all have to do it eventually."

As if confirming Spike's statement, his dad's top lip bulged where he played with the gap from his most recent removal. "Besides," his dad said, "as entertaining as it is to watch, I feel like the support afterwards is genuine and important for the patient. You get a lot of love from the crowd after sitting in the chair. Believe me, you need it!"

When they rounded the next corner, the small square opened up in front of them. They'd entered at the highest point, the plaza sloping down to the other side, giving them a clear view of the chair in the middle. It had a shelter over it, the top covered in fabrics from the textiles district. Not waterproof, but it helped when it rained. All four sides were open for the spectators to see the patient, flaming baskets providing the light. Both Spike and his dad stopped to look.

"Why do they make a public show of this?" Spike said.

"I think it makes it easier for others to go through with the procedure when they need to. We all know it's a horrific thing to have to do, but to see others cope with it at least normalises it."

"Did it make it easier for you to have it done?"

"I'm not sure. I don't know what it would have been like to have it done any other way."

The man in the chair glistened with sweat. Pale, he looked ready to vomit. Wide eyes fixed on the dentist as if he wanted to shut out everyone else there, the man visibly shook.

Dentists in Edin weren't employed for their finesse. The woman looked as much an executioner as she did a medic. A bloodstained, off-white bandana across the lower half of her face, she said nothing, raising her spike and mallet while the man reclined in the seat.

A knot tied in Spike's stomach as the crowd around him fell silent. Thankfully, he hadn't yet had a toothache. But it would come. It came for everyone sooner or later.

Spike shifted from one foot to the other as if he could evade his discomfort.

Because Spike had seen many dentists before, he recognised the competence of the one in front of him. With total confidence, she pressed the spike against the man's tooth, the chink of metal meeting enamel. She then raised her hammer. Although the man shifted where he sat, the dentist kept the spike pinned to the tooth. When she moved, she moved fast, sending one sharp whack against the flattened head of the spike.

The man's scream took flight, bouncing off the closed walls around them. While he yelled, the dentist grabbed him, shoved him forward, and slammed a hard slap against his back. Blood exploded from his mouth. Hopefully the tooth came out with it.

Despite the applause, Spike stood frozen to the spot. It took for his dad to nudge him before he started clapping too.

"You need to do the supporting bit," his dad said. "That man needs celebrating for what he's just been through."

It took a few minutes of cheering and clapping before the colour returned to the man's face, blood and spit dribbling from his chin. When he stood up and offered the crowd a smile, they cheered louder at being given a glimpse of the gap in his bottom row of teeth. The man then pressed his hands together in thanks to the dentist and his audience, bowing at them both before he stumbled away on wobbly legs.

Spike's dad put his arm around Spike and pulled him in close, squeezing him tightly. "Come on," he said, nodding in the direction of Edin's towering back wall. "Let's get going."

Maybe he stayed in his dad's embrace for a few seconds longer than he needed to, but his dad didn't seem to mind, so Spike made the most of it. At the end of national service he'd get into the protector trials. After he'd won the apprenticeship, he'd be on the path to becoming a protector. Protectors didn't stand in public squares hugging their dads, so he needed to wring every last drop out of it now.

CHAPTER 23

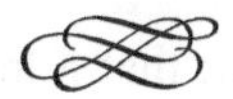

The large wall cast a long shadow. The only natural light came from the crescent moon, which shone down on the street behind them. Every other glow came from the flaming baskets lining either side of their path. "The wall looks different," Spike said, his arms aching from carrying the heavy chamber pot. It had already been a long day. When he finally got his head down, he'd sleep like the dead. "It's like I'm seeing it for the first and the last time. The next time we come back here, so much will have changed."

After he'd heaved a sigh, his dad nodded. "Six months, maybe more."

"Definitely more. I'll be the next protectors' apprentice."

"Have you had a good birthday?"

Spike could still taste Matilda's kisses and he grinned to think about it. "I have."

Spike led the way up the first wooden ramp, his steps in stereo as he walked in time with both his dad behind him and those around him. No matter how many trips he'd made up the wooden structure, the ascent always had a sobriety to it. He'd witnessed so much death from looking out over the wall.

The long walkway stretched at least fifty feet before the ramp to the next level. Spike craned his neck to see to the top. "They've moved the spot we need to dump the waste from."

"The ground must have been getting too boggy outside."

Just to get him talking if nothing else, Spike said, "What do you think created the disease?"

"I gave up thinking about that a long time ago. I realised I'd never know the truth of it, so why worry? As long as we have these walls protecting us, we'll be safe." Before Spike could respond, his dad said, "Look, you've probably guessed I was waiting for you tonight so we could talk. There was no need for us to dump the waste, but your mum wanted to make sure I said a few things to you."

"Man to man?"

"If you like."

Spike watched several people climb the slope to the next platform before he followed them.

"She … *We* wanted to say to you that you shouldn't … um, you shouldn't fall in love too soon."

"Hmm," Spike said.

"What?"

"I wasn't expecting you to say that. I thought this would be another chat about how horrific national service is."

"I've already said my bit about that."

"Well, I haven't. Fallen in love, I mean."

"I saw how you were walking when you came home tonight."

"*Walking?*"

"Look." His dad pinched the top of his nose as if trying to ward off a headache. "We just wanted to say it. Just in case you do."

Would Matilda come for Spike in the night? Would she bring Artan and decide they needed to get out of there? Would they take their fate into their own hands rather than jumping through Edin's hoops to get the city's blessing to honour their hearts?

"Love's a hard thing to walk away from, and even harder to accept when neither of the people in love have chosen the separation."

The slight wobble in his dad's voice spoke of a past Spike didn't want to know about. His parents might not have been madly in love with one another, but it worked. They made it work.

"I've learned," his dad went on, "that happiness in this city comes from acceptance. Acceptance of the work you have to do, the rules you have to obey, the people you have to choose from. Acceptance that only one person can become the protectors' apprentice each year."

A flare of adrenaline drove Spike's words. "You don't think I'm good enough?"

While casting a glance at the people around them, his dad spoke in a quiet voice as if to counter Spike's outburst. "I didn't say that. We just want to make sure we protect you against heartache."

Spike stopped and turned to look at his dad. The line of people behind them walked around, many of them carrying their chamber pots by their rope handles. "*If* I don't make it as a protector, I'll be sad. I won't be any less sad for not trying as hard now though. Why set myself up for failure before I've failed?"

"I'm not saying you shouldn't try so hard."

"I have to believe this can happen, Dad. If I don't, it won't. It's so hard that if I go in defeated, then I've already lost. I know what you're trying to do, but your thinking's flawed. It makes more sense to put everything I have into going for it now and then deal with whatever comes in the future. I can work hard. All I need to do is make sure I work harder than anyone else. That'll get me through." When another person tutted at Spike for blocking the way, he clenched his jaw to contain his reaction before shaking his head at his dad and moving on.

"Besides," Spike said, "I want freedom. I love and respect you and Mum, but I don't want your life. I want to be able to move through the city whenever I choose and live in any district I fancy. I want to be with who I want to be with."

A shake ran through his dad's words. "You think the life of a protector is freedom?"

Despite the darkening sky, Spike could still see into the distance, the wind blowing his hair back as he looked at the moon reflecting off the vast lake. Several diseased ran through the long grass. He might have shared the same form and genetics as the things outside the walls, but he felt no connection to them. Their arms flailed and snapped as if electric currents burst through them. They bit at the air, their heads turning in sharp and jagged movements like dogs catching flies. They screamed at nothing other than maybe the torment inside their own bodies.

"You serve the people," Spike's dad went on, resting his chamber pot on the top of the rough wall. "Fame is anything but freedom. Being a member of a society is anything but freedom. There are rules, codes of conduct that living within these walls requires of you, no matter who you are. You want freedom?"

When Spike looked at his dad, he nodded out to the horizon. "Then go out there."

And maybe he would. If Matilda came for him, he'd go. He loved his mum and dad, but he didn't want their life. Maybe running away would be easier than fighting against the system to be the next protector. As Spike drew a breath to respond, the sound of the loud horn below cut him off. It stopped him emptying his pot over the side. His dad waited too.

"Two days in a row," Spike's dad said.

A second later, the crack of the lock being freed on the door below rippled out across the long grass. The diseased, alerted by the horn, were already running at the gate, their screams lighting up the night, the long grass swishing against their forward momentum. Spike watched them close down on the wall, the same anxious shot of adrenaline running through him that he always felt. He'd seen so many people leave the city. Would that be him, Matilda, and Artan tonight? Maybe the latest evicted could teach him a thing or two. Mostly they showed them what not to do. Also, Spike, Matilda, and Artan wouldn't have the horn announcing their exit.

One final and long note sounded from the horn. "They're letting out two people?" Spike said. A look along the wall to either side of him, he saw everyone waiting, their pots still not emptied.

It took for several people over to his left to jeer and boo before Spike saw the two men below. No two evictions were the same. The two men were running with what looked like everything they had. One of them wore the smart dress of someone from the tailors' district, while the other one had the shock white hair of an albino. They were far away and it was dark, but not so far he didn't recognise them. "Mr. P!"

"Who?" Spike's dad said.

"That man with white hair has a restaurant in the ceramics district. His name's Mr. P."

"What do you think he's done wrong?"

"I have no idea. He seemed like a nice man."

A woman on Spike's right leaned close to him. "They often do, love. It's the nice ones you should be wary of."

It didn't make any sense, but Spike let it go.

As the two men ran, those on the wall closest to them toppled their pots over the side. Downwind from them, Spike fought against his heave when the smell hit him. He even felt the pinpricks from some of the moisture riding on the wind. Unlike

Spike, the men below were too far away for the waste to hit them.

Where there had been four or five diseased only moments before, that number had now trebled. The horn had called to them, and they were ready for whatever the city had to offer.

Like Spike had seen with the young man yesterday, Mr. P and his lover ran for a gap in the diseased's lines. Spike shook his head. "They've got no chance of getting through."

His dad sighed next to him.

The diseased had closed the distance on the two men to just a few feet. The hellish screams of torment lit up the evening. Then the first creature tackled the smartly dressed man to the ground. Even with the distance between them, Spike heard him let out an *oomph.*

Mr. P made it through and Spike's heart lifted. "He might be okay." But before he'd gotten to the end of his sentence, a second creature took the man down.

The boos and hisses stopped, giving way to the screams and yells of the enraged creatures below. Many sounded frustrated at not being the ones to catch one of the two men.

A matter of seconds later and the two diseased who'd tackled the men were on their feet again and wandering aimlessly. They had fresh blood around their mouths.

The well-dressed man then twitched. Spasms snapped through his arms as he writhed and rolled on the ground. He moved as if his blood boiled. Mr. P then came to life too. The pair of them jumped to their feet in a snarling and hissing rage. Lines of claret already streaked down their faces and they bared their teeth, snapping at the air around them. What had once been Mr. P and his forbidden love had now been turned into another two wretched diseased to add to the countless army outside the city's walls.

When Spike's dad nudged him, Spike blinked away the start of his tears and wiped his eyes.

"You okay?"

Spike nodded. "It's all a bit overwhelming."

"I know. Tomorrow's a big day."

"And I liked Mr. P." Maybe the restaurateur had done something wrong; maybe he hadn't. Either way, if Matilda came for him in the night, he'd now have no hesitation about leaving.

CHAPTER 24

Spike woke with a start, his head spinning as he sat up in bed. His heart pounded, pumping what felt like thick blood through his fatigued body. Still dark in his room, he looked around and couldn't see any reason why he'd woken up.

A heaviness in his eyelids pulled them closed and Spike gave in to it, falling back against his pillow. Once he'd lain down again, he heard it, the noise that must have awakened him in the first place. It drove any tiredness from his system.

Then a third gentle tap at his window.

Dressed in just his boxer shorts, the chill of the night clinging to his skin, Spike got out of his bed, pulled the curtain back, and smiled at the two faces staring in at him.

Both Matilda and Artan waved. Their familial resemblance almost made him laugh. Their mouths were pulled tight and they had an identical furrow to their brows. After opening the window, he looked from one to the other. "So we're really going to do this, then?"

"Have you changed your mind?" Matilda said.

A shake of his head, Spike then pointed at his packed bag in the corner of the room. After throwing his clothes on, he retrieved it, passed it out through the window, and stood up on his chair before climbing out after it. Just before he closed the window behind himself, he looked in the direction of his parents' room. Hopefully they'd understand. They'd want him to be happy.

SPIKE AND MATILDA WALKED HAND IN HAND, BUT HE WAITED until they were away from the houses and crossing one of the largest fields in the agricultural district before he spoke. He pointed over to a corner in Edin's perimeter wall, their path lit by the moon. "That's our way out of here."

Both Matilda and Artan looked where he pointed. Matilda's grip tightened, but neither of them replied.

The moist and uneven ground of the ploughed field made it tricky to cross. Spike's feet twisted and turned, the cloying mud making his shoes heavier with every step. The field seemed to be questioning their decision to leave. When he looked at Artan and Matilda again, he said, "What's going on with you two?"

After a moment of silence, Matilda said, "I wasn't going to come tonight, but before Dad went to bed, he told me he was going to kill Artan while I was away."

What looked like a continuation of a previous argument, Artan shook his head. "He can try. In fact, I'd like him to. I want another excuse to put him in his place."

Matilda turned her head away from him, her jaw set.

"The man's all hot air, Tilly. He only beat us when we didn't fight back. He wouldn't dare try it now."

They were about halfway across the field, the reek of damp mud in the air. Spike looked around to make sure they weren't being watched. The shadows made it hard to tell, but it looked clear.

"All I know," Matilda said, "is I'm not spending the rest of my life working in ceramics. I managed to get out of the district tonight with Artan because I used this."

So dark, Spike hadn't noticed she had another black scarf around her neck.

"I made it out of an old dress. I got away with it because it's night-time; otherwise they would have seen it for the fake it is. I told them I wanted to go for a walk with my brother before tomorrow. This is the last time I'll be able to move through Edin so easily, so it's our last chance to get out of here. I just can't handle this place anymore. With the way they treat their citizens, it's no wonder Dad's lost his head. It's enough to drive anyone mad."

To listen to her talk about how Edin treated its citizens took Spike back to earlier that evening. What would she say if she found out about Mr. P? Maybe she didn't need to know about it just yet. "So you didn't think you were going to leave before that?" They were close to the wall now.

"No. But I can't stay after what Dad said to him. If anything happens to Artan, I won't forgive myself."

"How many times do I have to tell you?" Artan said. "I'll be fine."

When they reached the edge of the field, Spike showed them where the two walls met. Stones poked out all the way up it like steps. "I reckon we can climb out here."

"And you think the other side's okay?" Matilda said.

Spike shrugged. "I dunno."

"Only one way to find out." Matilda walked over to the wall and started to climb.

When Matilda had held Spike's hand, he felt like he could go anywhere and do anything. But now she'd let go, he saw the wall from a different perspective. She'd already climbed several feet up it. What if they didn't have a way down on the other side?

What if the diseased were waiting for them like they waited for the evicted? In Artan's face, he saw his own worries staring back at him. "Tilly?" he said. "Are you sure you've thought this through?"

Matilda stopped. "Are you changing your mind?"

"I've told you countless times that I'll be okay," Artan said. "It seems a bit rash to run away."

"Saving your life seems rash?"

Spike spoke before Artan could reply. "I'll be the next protector."

"You *might* be. And if you are, it's a year away."

"A year isn't long to have freedom for the rest of our lives."

"And what if you don't make it, Spike? What then? If you're not the next protector, and you don't become a politician, what does that make you?" She pointed up the wall. "We have an opportunity to get out of here tonight."

"But we don't know what's out there," Artan said.

"Exactly," Spike said. "We know the rules in here. We know what I need to do." He reached up to her. "You need to trust me, Tilly."

For a few seconds, she stared at his outstretched hand and shook her head. "You're right, we don't know what's out there, but I know what life in here looks like if you don't make it. I'd risk only lasting five minutes outside the walls over spending the rest of my life in ceramics. This is our best chance to get out of here."

Spike kept his hand reached out to her. "I'll be the next protector. Trust me."

The pause seemed to last an age, and Spike listened to Artan inhale and then let his breath go as if he'd thought about speaking and then changed his mind.

Matilda tutted and shook her head before she finally climbed down the wall, ignoring Spike's hand as she jumped off. She landed in the mud with a squelch.

Although Spike stepped towards her, she focused on the ground and walked past him. "I hope I don't live to regret this choice. Come on, Artan, let's go home."

CHAPTER 25

"*William!*"

Spike opened his eyes and gasped, his world spinning from the abrupt awakening. Not only had his mother's shriek cut straight to his core, but the heat in his room pressed in on him like the ceiling had collapsed. An awful taste in his mouth, he ran his tongue across his teeth to try to get rid of the morning funk.

"*William!*" Louder this time and more shrill. Even from the other room its bone-saw ring cut through him. He'd not had enough sleep because of their late night trip to the wall.

Fully intending to get up, Spike lifted his head and dropped it again a second later. It felt too heavy for his neck. He clamped his hands over his eyes with a slap and let his exhaustion leak from him in what felt like the most appropriate sound for that moment. "Urghhhhhh."

The thud of angry steps made their way towards his room, culminating in his door flying open, his mum filling the doorway. A hand on one of her wide hips, the other leaning against the door frame, she glared at him, her face a taut mess of anxiety and stress. A usually kind-looking woman, her strained and crimson features banished any hint of the calm and compassionate mum he knew. “How many times do I have to call you, William?”

“I don’t answer to that. It’s *not* my name.”

“It’s the one I gave you, so it’s the one I’ll call you. You’re not a damn dog. Do you know what time it is?”

Covering his face with his hands again, Spike groaned. “Too early.”

When he heard his mum step aside, Spike pulled his hands away to see Matilda standing in his doorway. He double-checked to see the light of a new day on the other side of his curtains. “Are you okay now?”

Matilda shrugged.

“*William*,” his mum said, “the coach is *outside!*”

The words lit Spike’s fuse and he jumped from his bed. “Why didn’t you wake me up earlier?”

“You’re in national service now, boy. Do you expect me to travel to the other side of the city to wake you up every morning there too?”

Fire surged through Spike, but before he released it on her, he looked into her eyes. A glaze of tears covered them.

His legs shaking from getting up too quickly, Spike rubbed his face hard. Instead of waking him up more, it just hurt. Dressed only in a pair of boxer shorts, he looked around the room for where he’d discarded his clothes when he came back from the wall. He’d rested his packed bag by the door.

Before their kiss and their abandoned escape, Spike wouldn’t have thought twice about standing in front of Matilda dressed only in his boxer shorts. “Um …” He cleared his throat. “I’ll be ready in one minute.”

They stared at one another for a few seconds, neither of them moving. Her face expressionless, he couldn’t get a read on her. It took for his mum to slap him on the arm and shout, “Hurry up!” to get him going again.

While hopping on one leg and slipping the other one into his trousers, he glared at his mum. "It would have helped if you'd woken me up earlier."

Clearly too much for her, her eyes filled, her bottom lip bent out of shape, and she burst into tears. She pressed the back of her hand to her nose as if it would stop them. When it didn't, she took a deep breath. "I was hoping they'd forget you, all right?"

Spike pulled his other leg into his trousers. Just about to shout at her again, he looked at Matilda. She didn't have a mum as kind as his. He shouldn't be so ungrateful. He walked over and hugged his mum. "You don't need to worry about me. I'm going to be fine." He looked at Matilda. "*We're* going to be fine, and I'm going to be the next protectors' apprentice. Just you wait and see."

Instead of replying to him, Spike's mum leaned into his chest, her shoulders bobbing as her small body shook.

Although Spike spoke to his mum, he stared at Matilda, whose face remained fixed. "I promise you. I *will* be the next apprentice."

Shaking her head, her tears flowing freely, Spike's mum pulled away from him and left the room.

Matilda had a distant look in her eyes, and her usually dark skin had turned pale.

"Look, I'm sorry last night didn't go how we planned, but I think you made the right choice. Everything's going to work out."

The light caught the slight sheen of sweat on Matilda's brow.

"Are you okay?" Spike said.

Matilda's eyes widened, and before she could say anything, she heaved, her cheeks blowing out. A hand clamped to her mouth, she stared at Spike for a second before running in the direction of the bathroom. Although she locked herself in, the echo of her vomiting called through the house.

Spike knew her well enough to leave her alone at that moment. While pulling his shirt from the back of his chair, shaking with his haste, he heard his mum knock on the bathroom door. "I've left a glass of water outside for you, dear. Just let me know if you need anything else."

The only response she offered came in the form of another booming heave followed by a wet splash as she filled one of the chamber pots. Good job Spike and his dad had emptied them the previous evening. Splash back from a full chamber pot could be brutal. The thought of his visit to the wall with his dad the previous evening came back to him. The thought of Mr. P and his lover. But he pushed it down. Whatever the reason for Mr. P's eviction, he didn't need to talk to Matilda about it. Not with the stress of national service ahead of them. Not with her worry about Artan.

When Spike's mum walked back into his room, her eyes were red and swollen, but she'd stopped crying. The warmth he associated with her had returned and her features had softened.

"Everything will be okay, Mum."

Pursing her buckling lips, she replied with several jerking nods, a fresh glaze of tears covering her eyes. Although she straightened her posture, it did nothing to suppress her clear sadness. "I'm sorry. I've always hoped that national service would have been abandoned by the time you turned eighteen. I was even praying for it up until last night. You're my baby boy. My only child. They shouldn't be taking you from me."

"Don't worry. I've trained long and hard for this. I'm going in prepared. Not only am I going in prepared, but I'm going to smash through it. I'm going to be a protector."

She smiled through her sadness.

Looking past her, Spike turned his palms to the ceiling. "Where's Dad?"

She shook her head and Spike's stomach sank. She then pulled something from her pocket, her closed fist concealing it while she held it out to him.

Spike opened his palm and she dropped a cold lump of metal onto it. It looked like a ring. Silver and chunky, it had a large skull on the front of it.

"Your dad couldn't be here. It was tearing him up too much. He really loves you. It's just … well, you know how Dad gets. He didn't want to make you feel any worse about today by breaking down in front of you."

Clearing the lump from his throat, Spike drew a deep breath. "If he didn't want to make me feel any worse about it, why isn't he here? I wanted to say goodbye to my dad." Before his mum answered, he held a halting palm in her direction. "Don't answer that. You don't need to take responsibility for his actions. And thank you."

"Thank you?"

"Thank you for being here for me. For always being here for me. Even when it's hard for you."

Wringing her hands, Spike's mum nodded while she looked at the floor. "Before he left for work, he asked me to explain why he's given you his ring. It's a silly thing, really, but he wore it all the way through his national service and he feels like it brought him luck."

Holding it up to the light, Spike then slipped it over his middle finger. Making a fist, he smiled. "I suppose this will be great for cracking the diseased's skulls. I'll think about you both every day."

Matilda reappeared in the doorway. Not quite as pale as before, she cradled the glass of water and offered Spike's mum a weak smile as she took another sip. "Thanks for the drink, Jules."

"Are you feeling better now, dear?"

Pushing her eyes closed, Matilda kept them shut for a few seconds. When she opened them again, steel had settled across her brown stare. She dipped one slow composed nod. "Yes. I am now. I just needed to get rid of my last-minute nerves."

"And Artan's okay?" Spike said.

Ice clung to her words. "He's fine. Me being sick just then was about me and nothing else. It's all out now. I'm ready."

Spike said, "Me too."

Spike's mum then removed something else from her pocket as she stepped forward and tied Matilda's hair in a topknot.

Matilda lifted her hand to the metal clip and ran her fingers over the intricate design.

Any trace of sadness left Spike's mum as she clasped her hands together in front of her chest and beamed at Matilda. "Ah, it's perfect. It suits you."

"What is it, Jules?"

"It's a hummingbird. I just gave William a ring from his father."

Spike lifted his hand to show her. "Cool, huh?"

Matilda nodded and turned back to his mum.

"Like Spike's father wore the ring through his national service, I wore the hummingbird through mine. Call us silly, but we're both quite superstitious. We think they helped us survive. I don't have any other children, so I want you to have it. You're like a daughter to—" Tears stopped her finishing her sentence.

How could Spike be expected not to fall in love with her when his mother clearly already had? After shaking his head at his mum, he hugged her once more.

Spike's mum pushed him away after a few seconds, her cheeks sodden again. "Go, the coach is waiting."

After tucking his shirt in, Spike kissed his mum's forehead, lifted his bag, and said, "Right, Tilly, let's do this."

CHAPTER 26

When they stepped outside, Spike squinted against the bright sun and locked eyes with the coach driver, a thick, squat man with yellow teeth and sideburns that ran all the way along his jawline. He had red skin, although not naturally red. Hard to tell if a rash or frustration caused it.

The coach driver tugged on his horses' reins, their agitation clear in their twitching movements. Although he maintained eye contact with Spike, he leaned towards the skittish animals and spoke in a soft voice. "Calm down, girls. We're nearly ready to go." He then spat on the ground in front of Spike, the phlegmy ejection wobbling but holding its form. "Finally ready, are ya? You'll get your arse kicked during national service if you make people wait like this."

To look at the driver's spit turned Spike's stomach, so he looked back at the man and ground his jaw.

The coach driver returned the glare with interest as if he'd be glad of an excuse to swing for him.

Spike jumped when someone grabbed him from behind and spun him around. His mum hugged him one last time and whispered in his ear, "Make sure you come back, son."

Stepping away from their embrace, he held the tops of her arms and looked into her blue eyes. "I will, Mum, I prom—"

She cut him off by holding a halting finger between them. "*Don't* say that. You can't promise. Just try as hard as you can."

"Of course, Mum."

When Matilda hugged Spike's mum, the coach driver tutted. "Take your time. It's not like we're already late or anything."

"Allow a mother a moment to say goodbye to her son," Spike said.

"You've got a lot to learn about respect, boy. And you'd best learn it quick; otherwise this will be the last time she sees you. Now shut up, and get in the back."

Were it not for Matilda tugging on his arm, Spike wouldn't have gotten into the coach. He bent down to pick his bag up and followed her as she climbed into the small carriage.

The confined space smelled of wood and had just about enough room inside for them and their bags. "Hopefully we're not stopping for anyone else," Spike said, his right shoulder pressed against Matilda's left.

They closed the door, his mum appearing at the window. She blew a kiss at both of them. "I love you."

Nodding, Spike squirmed on the hard wooden bench and said, "I love you too, Mum. Although, you'll feel silly about this goodbye when I come home ready to start the apprenticeship trials."

"I hope so, Spike. I really hope so."

Before he could say anything else, the coach driver called out, "Yeargh!"

The lurch of the horses setting off threw Spike back, his head cracking against the hard wooden wall behind him as his mother's anxious face disappeared from sight.

As they trotted down the street—every bump in the road sending a jolt through the hard carriage—Spike poked his head out of the window and looked back towards his house. His mum stood in the same spot, waving him off while crying freely. "She's such an embarrassment."

Although Matilda didn't look back, she shoved her arm out of the window and waved so his mum could see. "You shouldn't take it for granted. I didn't say goodbye to my family this morning. Artan and I said our goodbyes last night."

"And your mum?"

Matilda shrugged, and before Spike could say anything else, she said, "What about your dad? Where was he?"

As much as he'd tried to be reasonable about it in front of his mum, Spike drew a deep breath to compose himself before he said, "He couldn't face it."

"But what about you? Didn't he think *you'd* want to say goodbye?"

The thought of it made Spike's eyes itch, so he turned to look out of the window. "I'm not sure he thought about me."

THE CARRIAGE PASSED THE TOWN SQUARE ON THEIR LEFT, THE scenery flashing past so quickly it made Spike feel nauseated to watch it. Despite their speed, he still caught a glimpse of the caged stakes in the middle. Each one had a stack of heads skewered on it from the night before. They were piled one on top of the other from the ground up like hellish totem poles.

By the time they'd passed the square, Spike had regained his composure. Their pace made his bottom sore on the hard bench and whipped up a breeze in the small carriage. He looked across Matilda out of her window. Heat lifted on his face to see the textile factory, the tallest building of any around it. The kiss already felt like a lifetime ago, back in a time when they were still children, when they were innocent. They shouldn't have, but they could kiss one another then. They could fall in love, consequences be damned. To look at Matilda's long brown hair tossed by the wind—most of it tied on the top of her head with his mum's hummingbird clip—her perfect tanned skin, her soft lips … "Nothing's going to stand in my way, Tilly. I *will* be the next apprentice. I'll do whatever it takes." He reached across and held her hand.

Matilda pulled away. "You can't promise anything. We're both ready for this. That's the best we can do."

The coach suddenly jolted as it abruptly slowed its pace. The driver's loud growl called through the street. "Coming through! National service passengers! Stand aside."

Spike shifted on the bench to get more comfortable. They kept moving forward, but at a much slower pace than before. People appeared on either side of the carriage from where it cut a path through them. Many of those they passed looked in, their faces ashen. Some of them made crosses over their chests as if the carriage were a hearse. A glance back at Matilda and Spike saw the tension had returned to her features. He said it as much for himself as he did for her. "We're going to get through this."

"I hope so," she said. "I really don't want to regret not getting out when we had a chance."

IT TOOK SEVERAL MINUTES FOR THEM TO PASS THROUGH THE BUSY crowd, and for the entire time Spike and Matilda stared straight ahead. Better to ignore them. They didn't need anyone else telling them how screwed they were.

They got clear of the busy streets and reentered the agricultural district. A much less densely populated area, it too sat on their left like the square had. The fields stretched away from them, although not for the miles and miles Spike once thought they did as a child. Their space was most definitely finite. National service had to happen for that reason if no other.

Although they'd been picked up from the agricultural district, it was the largest of all of the city's sectors because of the fields. It meant the coach driver had to take them out of it and back in again on his way to the gates leading to the national service area.

Spike rested back in his seat as they picked up speed again. He saw Matilda staring across the field they'd walked over the previous night. "I think we're away from the worst of it now," he said. "No more people to look at us or treat us like we're already dead."

But the coach slowed down again. Not quite as abruptly as before. "Bloody cows!" the driver yelled. "Get out of the way, you damn oafs."

Spike looked out of the window and froze. The ring on his finger seemed to treble in weight.

Standing with his fork pressed into the ground, Spike's dad rested on the handle and stared straight at him.

The coach then came to a standstill, mere metres separating Spike and his dad. The slightest pinch of crow's feet crimped the skin at either side of his dad's eyes before he abandoned his fork and walked over to the carriage.

Even watching his dad walk towards him took Spike's breath. Matilda reached across and squeezed his hand.

The cows continued to hold the carriage up, his dad showing little interest in clearing them. He reached the carriage and sighed, scratching his weathered scalp. "Good luck, son. I'm sorry …" He paused, his eyes filling with tears. A wet clearing of his throat, he said, "I'm sorry I didn't wait for you this morning. It was cowardly of me."

Spike laughed through his grief. "You created the roadblock?"

The coach driver took his shouting to another level. He might have even been aiming it at Spike's dad, but if he did, Spike's dad ignored him. "Get these cows out of the way. *Now!*"

"I've said everything I needed to say over the past two nights," Spike's dad said. "Now go and smash through national service, become the next apprentice, and make it work for you and Matilda. You deserve it." He dipped his head to peer in at Matilda. "You both do."

Although the coach driver continued to scream and shout, Spike didn't hear what he said. Instead, he watched his dad back away. He'd never seen him cry before. His dad pressed two fingers to his lips and kissed them.

Spike's world blurred and his eyes burned. A wet sniff to stop his nose from running, he then dipped a nod at his dad and returned the gesture. His tears soaked the tips of his fingers. Before he could see clearly again, the carriage jerked forward and they moved off again. His dad out of sight, he faced Matilda to see she had tears in her eyes too. Resting her hand on his shoulder as she looked into his eyes, the wet glaze in her stare swelled until the dam broke and tears ran down her cheeks.

"We'll be okay, Tilly."

While chewing her bottom lip, she held his gaze before saying, "I hope so. I really do."

CHAPTER 27

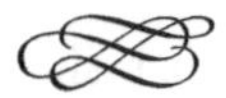

They passed the hand-painted signs at such a pace it took for three of them to fly by before Spike had put the gist of the message together. Although they weren't identical, they all delivered the same order: *No civvies beyond this point.*

The scenery grew ever more sparse, the walls closing in to funnel the coach towards the gates leading to the national service area. Spike only knew the gates by reputation and from seeing them from the back wall. Unless you were in national service, you had no business here.

Once Spike had drawn a deep breath and let it out again, he turned to see Matilda watching him. Her anxious expression had eased a little. "How are you feeling?" she said.

"Ready. I've trained for this. I'm going to go all the way. You?"

A tilt of her head to the side as if conceding the point. "It has to happen. My mind's here now and not with Artan. I need to let him grow up. One step at a time, eh?"

"One step at a time."

The coach driver then brought them to another hard stop. The varnished wooden seat offered little resistance as it threw them both against the opposite wall and then to the floor. "Hey!" Spike shouted. "What the hell are you playing at, you maniac?"

"Shut up," the driver shouted back, "and get out!"

After he'd dragged himself back onto the seat, Spike waited for Matilda to do the same. No reason to rush now. The driver could wait. "Are you okay?"

"Yeah." Matilda rubbed her shin. "A little whack, nothing more." They both picked up their bags before Spike opened the door and led them from the carriage.

Aware of the hard stare from the driver, Spike ignored him, stretched his arms to the sky, and filled his lungs with a deep inhale. "The air seems fresher here."

"No smells of industry," Matilda said. "No kilns, no dye, no glaze for the pots."

"No manure."

The large gates stood as tall as the wall they were built into. At least twenty feet from the ground, both them and the walls on either side had barbed wire running along the top. The only way through would be with consent.

With everything else going on, Spike had almost forgotten about the coach driver until the man cleared his throat. "Oh," Spike said, "you want some attention, do you?"

The coach driver stared at Spike while dragging in a heavy snort. He then spat at Matilda.

Fire rushed through Spike and he looked down at the phlegmy lump. Green and wobbly like before. "What's wrong with you, you fool?"

"How dare you talk to me like that, boy."

"That nearly hit her!"

"That was my intention."

"You're an animal, you know that?"

"And what are you going to do about it, child?"

The gentle touch of Matilda at his back helped Spike relax

and he looked at the man's spit again. "You need to get yourself checked out. That shouldn't come from a normal body."

"Driving self-entitled brats like you two around is what's doing it. It's bad for my health."

Spike smiled and shook his head. "You're not worth it."

A redder face than before, the coach driver worked his mouth as if he might spit again. If he did, Spike wouldn't hold back a second time.

"You know," the coach driver said, "going into national service in love isn't a wise move."

As much as Spike wanted to deny it, he didn't, grinding his jaw while waiting for the man to continue.

The lack of reply appeared to wind the coach driver tighter than before. A sneer lifted his top lip. "I hope I don't see you two again. I'm sure there are kids more deserving of coming home alive than you."

Matilda gasped at the man's venom. As Spike drew a breath to reply, the coach driver snapped his horses' reins, ran them in a wide circle, and galloped away, leaving Spike and Matilda on their own in front of the large wooden gates.

"What a spiteful man," Matilda said. "You did well not getting too dragged into it." She nodded at the gates. "You ready for this?" She led the way.

Two steps later, Spike caught up to her and they walked in the long shadow cast by the huge gates. Spike shuddered. Maybe the temperature hadn't dropped too much lower, but it sure as hell felt like it.

The height of the gates made Spike dizzy. Sure, he'd climbed the wall to empty the chamber pots plenty of times before, and although the gates weren't as tall, everyone climbed the wooden structure. Only a select few went through the gates each year and even fewer passed back the other way.

Continuing up the dusty cobblestone road—the saliva in his

mouth turning into a thick paste—Spike studied the wall on either side. It had been built by the cadets before them. Some parts were constructed from new bricks straight from the kiln, while other parts were made from all kinds of rocks and stones. The high demands on the kiln meant it would be a long time before it met the city's needs. A large portion of its output headed through the gates in front of them to help build the external wall. Yet, despite the ramshackle mess of materials used to construct it, the wall on either side of them still looked impregnable. At some point, they'd tear it down when they were ready to extend the city.

Spike watched the gates as they drew closer, expecting something to happen. Nothing did. He raised his hand to knock, but before he could rap his knuckles against the wood, a deep *clunk* sounded on the other side. A second later, the gates shook as someone opened them, the colossal hinges groaning in protest.

A sound of chains being dragged along the ground came at them, the gates obscuring their view. They grew louder as they ran across the cobblestones with increasing velocity. It sounded like a tethered dog charging, eager to see off trespassers. An inclination to run balling in his calves, Spike opened his mouth to ask Matilda if she knew where the noise was coming from. But before he could say anything, a diseased's scream accompanied the creature bursting through the gap. Wild limbs, blood-red eyes, a snapping mouth. It leapt straight at Spike, driving the wind from him as it connected, taking both of them to the ground.

CHAPTER 28

Smothered by the writhing weight and the foetid stink of the thing, Spike shook and twisted to get the creature off him, but it was too heavy. It snarled, its hot breath pushing against his face. The thing had his arms pinned, restraining him. He pulled back from it so hard, he hurt his head against the cobblestones. With its mouth spread wide enough for Spike to see down its throat, the thing lunged at him.

Unable to do anything but turn his face, Spike waited for the searing pain of its bite to tear into his flesh.

But the pressure of the thing suddenly lifted, the creature flying away to the side and hitting the ground next to him.

Gasping, Spike watched Matilda jump over him and lay into the monster with a flurry of kicks, each one hard enough to send out a deep thud. The beast curled into a protective ball against her attack.

The sound of chains then snapped taut, and before Matilda could kick the thing to death, it shot away from her. Where it had been driven to take Spike down, its mouth now stretched wide from where the chains throttled it.

A moment to compose himself, Spike looked up to see a

woman just outside the gates. No taller than five feet five inches, she reeled in the disgusting beast. She belittled his frantic pulse and quickened breaths by making it look easy. To her, the creature was no more than a lively pet.

Despite her size, the woman had arms as thick as Spike's thighs. They bulged as she dragged the thing. When she had it close to her, it spun around and reached its skinny arms in her direction. A swift kick to its face gave off a loud *crack!*

The woman then pressed her boot against the creature's neck, pinning it to the ground. It tried to squirm free, but from the twist of her face it looked like she had the strength to pin a horse there if she needed to. Were Spike not so consumed with his own shame, he might have been impressed by her.

As Spike got to his feet, the woman pulled her long blonde dreadlocks from her face and said, "You didn't deal with that one very well, did you?"

"Obviously!" Spike said. He threw his arms in the air. "What's wrong with you anyway? That thing could have turned me into one of *them*, and for what? Your entertainment?"

"Relax, will you?"

"*Relax?* Did you see what just happened?"

The woman leaned down and put her hand close to the diseased's face. Its legs kicked and writhed, scraping over the ground as it remained beneath her pressure, unable to get to her. When she took her foot away, the beast snarled and sprang from the ground. It clamped onto her bare hand.

Both Spike and Matilda jumped back and gasped, but before either of them could say anything, the creature slipped off the woman with a wet clop before landing on the ground again. No teeth marks where it had latched on, just a patch of glistening saliva.

After kicking the creature again, her face twisted with hatred for the thing, the woman watched it for a few seconds. She'd kicked it so hard it lay dazed on the ground. She then drove a hard bang against the door with her fist. Someone from inside pulled the chain, the barely conscious diseased scraping over the rough cobblestones as it got dragged back into the complex. "As you can see, it has no teeth. It can't bite you."

"But what if I'd swallowed some of its saliva?"

"Then you're useless and we don't want you out in national service in the first place. You'll have other people relying on you, so you need to be worth something out in the field. Like your friend here."

"He'd have done the same for me," Matilda said, although Spike could have sworn he heard shame in her words.

But the woman ignored her and kept her attention on Spike. "Think of what we just did as the idiot test."

"The idiot test?"

"An idiot swallows the diseased's saliva, so you passed … just." With a dull tone, she added, "Congratulations."

"You mean some people don't pass?"

"We don't want to take idiots outside the walls with us."

In all the commotion, Spike hadn't noticed the broadsword and crossbow on the woman's back. A large two-handed weapon, the sword stretched nearly as long as she stood tall. Not that she'd struggle to use it. With biceps like hers, she could pop the head off a bull if she got it in a headlock.

Because the woman continued to stare at them without speaking and Spike's heart rate had settled a little, he held his hand in her direction. "I think we got off on the wrong foot."

"*You* did." The woman nodded in Matilda's direction. "She didn't. I didn't."

The need to argue rose in him, but Spike swallowed it down again. "I'm Spike and this is Matilda."

"Did I ask for your names?"

He flinched at the abrupt retort.

"Let me guess," the woman said. "Like every boy that comes through these gates, you have designs of being the next protector?"

Although Spike opened his mouth, she spoke again before he could respond. "We don't get nearly as many girls thinking they can do it. Many of them don't think they have it in them, but they do. They're often *more* capable. They just have a touch of self-awareness that helps them see their own weaknesses. The ability to acknowledge them means they can improve and grow stronger. And from looking at how the idiot test just played out, I'd suggest you start learning from your friend here."

Spike looked at Matilda, but she didn't look back, her flushed cheeks a clear sign of her discomfort.

"But before you think about any of that, you two morons need to learn a few things about national service. First and foremost, this isn't working in the factories or in the fields. This is *proper* work. *Dangerous* work. You don't shake my hand like we're equals. You call me *boss*. You got that?"

The pair replied in unison, "Yes, boss."

The woman nodded, turned around, and walked back through the gate while shouting over her shoulder, "Now follow me."

Seeing Matilda's cheeks push out as she exhaled hard, Spike held back and let her lead the way.

As he stepped through the gates, Spike looked around for the diseased and the person who'd reined it in.

The woman with the dreadlocks snorted a laugh at him. "It's no good being alert now. When you're out in the field, you'll already be dead by this point."

Spike clenched his jaw and looked at Matilda again. She'd turned pale. As much as he wanted to promise her everything would be okay, he didn't. Instead, he took in the national service area. A large open patch of grass in front of him, it stretched all the way to another set of gates like the ones they'd just walked through. A crowd had gathered in front of them, and he nearly asked the woman who they were. But he'd already had more than he could take of her.

The stocky woman moved at quite a pace for her short legs. Spike jogged a couple of steps to keep up before looking around again. A large wall on his left cut off a section of the national service area. It had a gate in it that led through to the space beyond. Over his right shoulder and behind him, he saw a wooden fence. It too had a gate in it. They'd surely find out soon enough what lay on the other side of each one.

As fascinating as Spike found his surroundings, he kept glancing at the crowd down by the gates. What were they doing there? Again, the question rose and died in him.

Between them and the gates at the end stood several huts. Many of them were about the size of an average house and must have been where the cadets slept. There were a couple of larger buildings that must have been used for the more communal activities. Made from wood, they looked like they could be taken down and reassembled in the new national service area whenever they were ready to move on.

The short and stocky woman stopped by a pile of bags and pointed down at them. "Leave your things here. You need to go and meet Sarge by the main gates. And you need to be quick about it, the last class of cadets are coming home now. It's their final day today."

"You could have told us that sooner."

"*What?*" the woman said.

"Well …" Spike threw a hand in the direction of the gathered crowd. "They look like they're waiting and we're holding them up."

"They're not waiting for you. The other cadets will be coming home whether you're in the crowd or not. Jeez, you think the world revolves around you, don't you? Let me guess, you're an only child?"

Although Spike didn't say anything else to the woman, Matilda dipped her a nod on her way past and said, "Thank you." She didn't look at Spike.

The woman spoke in a loud voice, clearly for Spike's benefit. "You'll go far, sweetheart. Good luck."

Spike watched Matilda break into a jog towards the crowd before he set off after her.

CHAPTER 29

A thickset man with tightly cropped grey hair stood at the front of the crowd and glared at Spike and Matilda as they approached. In his sixties, he'd clearly had an active life and wore his strength like an old bull. He might not have the pace he once did, but he undoubtedly more than made up for it with guile and brute strength. Not the kind of man to get on the wrong side of.

The kids in front of him must have all been about the same age as Spike and Matilda. All in national service for the first time, Spike saw many of them had the pale complexion appropriate for the journey they were about to embark on.

As subtle as they'd tried to be in joining the back of the group, the man raised his eyebrows at them. "How good of you to join us."

Even Spike knew when to keep his mouth shut. He moved closer to the back of the group to make it harder for the man to see him. He stared at the grass at his feet.

"Today is the final day for those who were in national service before you. There were thirty-two of them six months ago. You'll see how many are left shortly. We're here to congratulate them on their hard work. The wall's close to being finished. They've done a great job and need to be celebrated for it."

Before the man could say anything else, a horn sounded on the other side of the gates, lifting the hairs on the back of Spike's neck. The horn to say they were outside, he'd heard it on occasion as far away as the agricultural district. It had taken a lifetime to get here, and now he'd arrived, he'd make sure he came home as the next apprentice.

A guard on either side of the gates, they had two wheels each. They each turned one, the rush of chains running over wood as they dragged the slack in. Both chains snapped taut and the gates wobbled before a gap opened down the centre of them. It split wider apart as the large wooden doors slowly moved inwards.

Within seconds, the cadets in front of Spike gasped and muttered. He bobbed his head to get a better view, seeing through the crowd to catch sight of the dirty faces of those returning. Boys and girls not much older than him and those around him, although their eyes told a different story. They wore the look Spike had seen so many times when he'd asked about national service in the past. A look that said once they returned to society, they'd never talk about it again.

The guards on either side of the gates bobbed up and down while they spun the wheels with increasing velocity, the whooshing of the metal chains singing against the wood as the cadets entered.

Several guards amongst the experienced cadets, they all filed into the place. When the flow stopped, Spike stood on his tiptoes to see behind them and the long grass of the world outside. There were no more cadets. Only about twelve had entered. He heard one of the boys close to him whisper, "Is that it?"

One of the guards on the gate looked at the older man at the front. The older man nodded.

The same energy they'd opened the gates with, the two men went to the wheels next to the ones they'd been turning and spun them, closing the gates again. It prevented Spike from getting a clear view of what lay beyond the city.

A sombre air had settled and no one spoke. Then one of the cadets who'd returned from building the walls screamed. Her shriek rang out and seemed to stop time momentarily, turning Spike's blood cold and lifting gooseflesh on his arms. The girl panted, the whites of her eyes stark on her face as she pointed at the boy beside her. "He's been bitten!"

Those close to her jumped backwards, the guards in the group raising their weapons and turning on the boy. While the cadets scattered, the boy held his hands up. "It's just a cut, honestly."

Spike saw the new recruits around him throw glances at one another and then at the guards in front of them. Several stepped away, moving from the gates and past Spike and Matilda, back in the direction they'd just come from. But he wouldn't be fooled again. He could see right through it. Another trick to test the mettle of the new recruits. He wouldn't fail this test.

The more experienced cadets and the new recruits picked up their pace, Matilda joining those in getting away from the boy. As much as Spike thought about running, he kept his feet rooted to the spot. Fool him once, shame on them …

Not enough guards near the injured boy to surround him, they raised their weapons and formed a semicircle between him and the closing gates. Three of them had broadswords, one gripped two handheld axes, and two more had smaller blades.

The boy pulled his shirt up to show the guards his wound. Just above his hip, the dark red gash belched blood. It looked authentic. They'd clearly picked the best actor there. He cried and shook his head. "Honestly, I hurt myself building the wall."

None of the guards responded. Instead, they stepped closer to the boy, their weapons still raised. More of the newer cadets moved back, Spike now the closest of the lot.

The boy shook his head again. "Screw this," he said and took off, running away from them and straight at Spike. The truth of his infection sat in his eyes. No blood, not even any signs of it, his blue gaze was spread wide with well-acted fear. Spike would be the only one who hadn't fallen for it.

Ten feet and no more between Spike and the boy. Then everything changed. Even with the distance separating them, he saw the blue of the boy's eyes give way to red as the veins swelled and burst, filling in the sclera at first and then covering his irises. His features switched to snarling fury. The coordination of his run twisted and twitched from where his legs betrayed his intention. His lips pulled back in a snarl. He reached out at Spike—his attention fully fixed on him—and he roared.

No time to move, Spike held his arms up in front of him as if the action would somehow protect him from the monster.

A snap sounded to Spike's left, but he didn't look. The first he knew of the crossbow's bolt came from when it entered the right side of the infected boy's head and exploded out of the left, dragging a cloud of blood with it.

At the last moment, Spike jumped aside, the diseased boy running several wobbly steps before he landed face down on the grass.

Panting as he rode out his adrenaline rush, Spike looked to his left to see the short and stocky woman who'd let him in through the gate. She still had her crossbow raised to her shoulder and looked down the barrel of it at him. As she lowered it, she shook her head. She then turned to the grizzled man who'd been at the front of the group of rookies. "You want to keep an eye on this fool; he's a liability."

When Spike shouted back at her, he did it loud enough so

everyone heard him. "I thought it was another test like the one coming into the gates."

The grizzled man this time: "And if it was? What were you hoping to achieve by not running? You could have tried to take it down at the very least. That would have been arrogant, but arrogant's better than stupid."

If Spike had had a good answer, he would have given it.

CHAPTER 30

"April the first!" Despite all the new recruits being there, Sarge stared straight at Spike as if addressing him personally. "I dunno what I've done to deserve this, but when I look at this line of losers and halfwits standing before me, I feel like I'm being taken for a fool."

Behind Sarge stood seven guards. Not protectors, but they had the grizzled look of men and women who'd seen action. The woman who'd both opened the gate to Spike and Matilda and then killed the diseased with her crossbow stood among them. They lined up shoulder to shoulder in front of the gates leading outside.

About twenty minutes had passed since the cadets in the class before them had returned from their final national service. Spike looked at his feet, at the patch of blood where the boy had been taken down. They'd removed his corpse so they could burn it—as they did with all the infected—but they'd not tried to clean up the mess made by his demise. When he made him stand in that spot, Sarge had called it a good reminder of Spike's incompetence.

"Look at you," Sarge said, dragging Spike's attention up so they made eye contact again. "I've got a month to turn you idiots into soldiers." Pinching the top of his nose as if fighting off a headache, Sarge looked at the ground and muttered to himself, "I swear the recruits get softer every year."

Still stinging from the humiliation on the way in and then when the boy turned, Spike leaned close to Matilda. "He's a fine one to talk; look at the old codger."

Sarge snapped his head up and jabbed a finger in Spike's direction. "You, boy! Step forwards."

Spike felt every pair of eyes on him as he took a step away from the line. He'd clearly not spoken as quietly as he'd intended to. Definitely not the smartest move with the amount of attention he'd already received from Sarge.

As Sarge marched towards him, a limp in his walk, the ground seemed to shake beneath his heavy gait. Stopping just inches from Spike, his light blue eyes bored into him after he'd looked him down and then up again.

Listening to Sarge's heavy breaths, Spike's heart damn near beat its way free from his chest as he waited for the man to speak.

"So you think I can't cut it anymore, boy?" He laughed. "And I'm guessing you think you can? Did you see what happened to you earlier?"

His stomach tense, Spike fought against the adrenaline rushing through him. He stared straight at Sarge so he didn't have to see the faces of his fellow cadets.

"I'll tell you what, if you can do more press-ups than me, I'll let you go back into line without punishment. I'll even forget how much you've already screwed up. Wipe the slate clean. How's that sound?"

Although Spike opened his mouth to reply, Sarge cut him off by raising a halting finger. "*But,* if you can't, I expect you to wear your trousers around your ankles for the entire time we're out here. I might even dig out a fool's hat for you to wear. What do you say?"

Some of the cadets giggled until Sarge shot them a hard glare. "To give you a chance, I'll do my press-ups one-handed."

Was he insane? Spike had been doing press-ups for years now. All he'd done since he was fourteen was train. If he didn't do it, Sarge wouldn't ever lay off him. But if he did it and failed … He wouldn't fail. Dipping a sharp nod, he dropped to the floor. "On your count."

Going down on his knees, groaning as he bent his old body, Sarge put one hand behind his back and the other one out in front of him, splaying his thick fingers as he formed a tripod frame. "Ready?"

Spike nodded.

"One." Despite only using one arm, Sarge snapped down and back up again.

AT FIFTY, SPIKE'S ARMS WERE ON FIRE.

At seventy-five, Spike's entire body shook and sweat burned his eyes.

At one hundred, the other cadets were cheering Sarge, who looked as fresh as he had at the beginning. "You ready to drop yet, boy?"

At one hundred and seventeen, Spike's arms gave up and he hit the ground, the dust sticking to his sweating skin, some of it going into his mouth.

Sarge jumped to his feet and looked down on Spike. "Looks to me like you've failed every single test so far. Now get up."

As much as he wanted to, when Spike tried, his fatigued arms trembled and gave way beneath him again. After another failed attempt, two boys stepped out of the line at Sarge's command and helped him stand.

Sarge nodded at Spike's belt. "Now drop 'em, fool."

When Spike went for his buckle, his hands—clumsy with fatigue—weren't up to the task. Heat flushed his face. Bad enough he had to do this in front of strangers, but in front of Matilda …

Sarge shook his head and the other officers laughed. "Bloody hell, fool, I was only joking. Now get back in line and wind your neck in. You've stood out for all the wrong reasons so far. It's going to be an uphill climb for you, son."

Pacing up and down in front of the new recruits, Sarge now stared at each and every one in turn. "Lesson number one: underestimate anyone and you're likely to come unstuck. Underestimate a diseased, and you're dead." Again he paused to look at Spike. "Unless Ore's there to save your life." The short woman with the long blonde dreadlocks and crossbow strapped to her back stared straight ahead.

By the time Sarge got level with Spike again, he leaned so close Spike saw the flecks of orange in his blue eyes and felt the warmth of his breath against his face. "And if you speak out like that again, it'll be more than your pride that's hurt, understand?"

Dropping his head, Spike looked at the ground. "Yes, sir."

Spike stepped back a pace when Sarge yelled, "I didn't hear you!"

Stamping his foot, Spike lifted his head, fixed his gaze on Sarge, and shouted so his voice broke and his throat hurt. "Yes, sir!"

Hard to tell, but it looked like the slightest flicker of a smile tickled the old man's features. "So he has a spine." He nodded his approval at the guards behind him. "Maybe we can do something with that."

Resuming his hobbled walk in front of the recruits, Sarge sneered, snorted as he dragged snot into his mouth, and spat on the ground. "Forty-two of you idiots stand before me. Now there was either something in the air to make your parents procreate at the same time, or we're starting to see a real shift in population growth. I'm going to assume you have horny parents. Shall we take a moment to consider that?" He let the silence hang, many of the cadets twisting their faces from what he'd just said.

Grinning, Sarge said, "That was a lovely moment, wasn't it? Now, out of the forty-two of you useless fools, only twenty will survive. And I'm being generous. Take a look at the person next to you. They won't be here at the end of this."

When Matilda raised her eyebrows at Spike, he gently shook his head. They'd be there, no matter what had happened so far. She'd do better to look to her other side.

"I'd imagine a lot of you are here with aspirations to become the next protectors' apprentice."

Spike stood straighter than before.

Sarge shook his head at him. "I'd give those dreams up now. It's hard, and most of you don't have the minerals for it."

Whenever Spike had told someone about his dreams, he'd always been told how hard it was. Hard work didn't frighten him. Whatever it took, he'd do it. He'd run harder, farther, and push more than any other recruit fighting him for his place. If he had more grit than anyone else, he'd win. He might not be able to change the past, but he could influence the future. He'd make sure they had no other choice but to select him for the trials.

Hawking up some more phlegm, Sarge spat it on the ground again. "Should you survive, then we pick a maximum of seven recruits for the trials. One member from each team.

Stopping by a squat boy, Sarge pointed at him. "You! Step forward."

Without flinching, the boy did as he was ordered. Short, squat, and pure muscle, he snapped his heels together and lifted his broad chest like he'd been in the army for years.

Leaving the boy standing there, Sarge patrolled the line again. "This here, boys and girls, is Ranger Hopkins."

The wind soared across the field.

"I take it from the silence that none of you recognise that surname? That's understandable. After all, Magma's surname isn't that well known."

Gasps ran down the line and the murmurings of hushed conversations started up. Spike noticed Matilda glance at the boy. The son of the man who'd finished second best to her dad.

"Anyone who's aiming for the protectors' apprenticeship will have to outdo this little daddy's boy here. Unless you can walk on water or do something equally miraculous, I'd suggest giving up now, because you ain't gonna beat him."

Despite the sinking feeling in his chest, Spike kept his frame straight. It didn't matter who they put him up against because he wanted it more. And to be the best, he had to beat the best. Magma's son or not, he didn't have Spike's determination. A glance at Matilda beside him. His reason couldn't be as strong as Spike's. Nothing would stop him becoming the next apprentice. Nothing.

"Anyway," Sarge said, "we can think about becoming a protector in six months' time. Who knows? You might get lucky; Ranger might have been killed in the field by then."

Although he must have been aware of everyone looking at him, Ranger's face remained stoic and staring ahead. Spike might have made himself look useless so far, but maybe that would work in his favour. Unlike Ranger, he didn't have a target on his back. Better to be the underdog than the one to beat.

Sarge turned away from the recruits and faced the gates that opened into the wild lands. He spread his arms wide. "The wall extension is close to being finished. If enough of you can stay alive, this might be the national service where it gets completed. I'm not holding my breath. After just one month's training, you band of halfwits will be sent outside the city to die. The last lot became tediously slow after half of them were slaughtered in one day. The population in this city's growing all the time, so extending the wall is crucial if we're all to survive. We need more fields to grow food and more space for houses. God help us, but the future of this city hangs from you lot of frayed ropes."

Sarge turned back around again, wearing a wide grin. "Cheery prospect, ain't it? Now, do I need to tell you that the diseased on the other side of this wall won't give you a break? They'll do everything in their power to sink their teeth into you, and there won't always be a team leader to bail you out. When you step outside those gates, you're at war with an enemy that has no heart. You stop to think and you're dead. In the next four weeks, we're going to throw everything we can at you. See that over there." He pointed into the distance at the gates they'd entered the national service area through. "That's your childhood leaving. Wave goodbye to it."

One of the recruits waved. Sarge stared at the girl for several seconds. "As you can see, we have a walled-off section on one side of this area and a fenced-off section on the other. You're probably wondering what's behind them."

Spike took in the two sections he'd looked at when he entered the place.

"We have the training area on one side," Sarge said, "and the hole on the other. You'll become acquainted with the training area soon. Let's hope you never get to find out about the hole."

Another pause, Sarge cut through the silence by unsheathing the broadsword on his back. Not quite Jezebel, but it still rang and held the note for a few seconds. "This is your weapon. This will save the lives of you and your teammates. You'd best learn how to use it. You'd best love it because it'll be your only friend when you're in danger. When you're outside, it's every person for themselves. Each dorm has a line of broadswords on the wall by the doors. You'll use them for training with your team leaders, and when you can be trusted, you'll be allowed to carry them."

While throwing practice swings, Sarge said, "You lot will be divided into teams of six. In each team, three of you will defend and three will build the wall." While pointing at the men and women lined up in front of the gate, he said, "Seven teams with seven team leaders. Your team leader will do what they can to keep you safe, but working with rookies is like herding cats, so make sure you keep your wits about you and make decisions when they need to be made. Hesitancy is your enemy out there. Above all, save yourself first. There ain't any heroes here, only the diseased and those waiting to become one."

Spike looked at the seven officers stood behind Sarge. Like Ore, they all had their shoulders pulled back and their chins raised.

"And before we pick the teams," Sarge said, forcing a smile, "I wanted to talk about relationships."

Maybe Spike imagined it, but he could have sworn he saw Ranger look over at Matilda.

"They don't happen. *Ever!* You don't fall in love here, especially with someone from another district."

As Magma's son, Ranger could fall in love with whomever he pleased. Spike clenched his jaw to watch the boy look at Matilda again.

"Oh," Sarge said, "the teams will be rewarded and docked points depending on how well they perform. You can earn points by killing the diseased, and you can lose points when someone dies. The team leaders and I can also deduct points for things like lateness, untidiness—" pausing, he looked at Spike "—insolence, ineptitude, idiocy."

Although Spike felt the attention of the others on him, he held his chin high. Better to be the underdog than a target. While everyone focused on Ranger, he'd show them all exactly what he could do.

Turning around, Sarge pointed at the smaller of the two large buildings. "That's the dining hall. I want you all over there now. It's time to pick teams."

Another surge of adrenaline tightened Spike's stomach. But not the adrenaline from having a diseased charge at him; this shot of adrenaline rode in on the wings of giddy butterflies in his chest. It had taken him a lifetime to get here. It didn't matter what had gone on before that moment, he now had a chance to prove himself. He'd show them exactly why he should be picked as Edin's next apprentice. He'd make all of them eat their words.

CHAPTER 31

The dining hall looked like many of the other buildings in the national service area, except larger—much larger. The second largest structure Spike had seen since walking through the gates. Nine long dining tables sat in the open space. Two neat rows of four in the main area and a top table, which had been positioned on an elevated platform and ran perpendicular to the others. Each table would seat twelve comfortably. From what Sarge had said to them outside, they'd never all been filled. Not even close. It would probably take a few more years of population growth before they had enough cadets for that.

The wooden floor had a dark tinge to it from where it had been mopped, the damp pulling the smell of wood from the floor-boards. Those in the national service area interacted so frequently with the diseased, sanitation had to be of the utmost importance.

The warmth of the day had entered the room and turned the air thick. Sweat itched Spike's collar and he squirmed on the hard wooden bench he'd chosen to sit on.

The cadets had gathered in smaller groups around the room. The largest collection of them sat at Ranger's table. The only full table in the place. He might have a target on his back, but among the worthless rookies, he was as good as royalty. The chatter of multiple conversations rose to the pitched ceiling and swirled as an indecipherable white noise above them.

Sarge and the seven guards were currently sitting at the top table, also talking amongst themselves. The wall behind them had many names etched on it. At first Spike wondered if it might have been to commemorate the fallen, but when he read it, he saw names he recognised: Magma, Chucker Smith, Woody Carlson, Jake Biggs. The fallen clearly didn't deserve commemorating. Edin celebrated winners. For a second, he closed his eyes, etching his own name on the hall of fame he held in his mind. When he opened them again, he glanced over at Ranger, who smiled and laughed with his new friends. That would be his own child in years to come, celebrated because of the greatness of his old man. A hero through legacy. Except Spike would train him well enough so he could follow in his footsteps. Ranger didn't stand a chance against him.

Ranger looked over and Spike quickly turned away. Nudging Matilda, he covered his mouth and said, "I can't believe Magma's son is in this year's qualifiers." He glanced over at him again. He'd already gone back to talking to his new friends.

Matilda placed her hand on Spike's back, but when she spoke, her voice was distant. "They're not allowed to give him preferential treatment." Maybe, like everyone else, she thought he didn't stand a chance.

"Yeah, right." Another look at the boy, Spike caught him throw a glance at Matilda. Fire rose in him, but he drew a deep breath to pull it down.

Keeping his attention on Ranger, Spike watched him look at Matilda again. He couldn't take his eyes off her. He then fixed on Spike, smiled, winked, looked back at Matilda and licked his lips.

Holding eye contact with the boy, Spike said, "But you know what? It doesn't matter. To be the best, you have to beat the best.

I'm going to make Ranger wish he hadn't come to do national service at the same time as me."

When a boy—short, squat, and with closely cropped brown hair—sat down opposite them, both Spike and Matilda fell silent and stared at him. Solid and round like a mole, he had a slight squint to his brown eyes as if the daylight bothered him. He smiled a wonky grin and offered them his hand. "Hugh Rodgers."

Hugh's hand swamped Spike's, and when he squeezed his sweaty grip, Spike laughed to stop himself from wincing at the strength of it. "Easy there, fella. Can I have my hand back now, please?"

Flushed cheeks, Hugh dropped his attention to the table. "Sorry, I didn't mean to hurt you. My dad says I'm too clumsy." His words fell from his mouth, each one running into the next. "I pulled a door off the hinges at home before leaving to come here. I break everything." He looked up at them again, turned even redder, and dropped his focus once more. "Sorry."

The kid had something endearing about him. Spike shook his head and laughed. "Don't worry about it. I'm Spike and this is Matilda."

The boy's grin widened and his face relaxed. Although, his words still came out quickly. "I'm not supposed to be here, you know? I've been working in the labs for the past few years. We've been developing an antidote for the disease. We normally take an exam to prove our value to the lab so we don't have to do national service. It's not a hard exam if you revise. The man who ran the lab, Richard Stein, said I wouldn't have to take it. It was a given that I was staying. At least, that's what he told me. He said my work on the antidote was too important, that he'd teach me everything he knew, and that I should focus on learning from him rather than studying."

Leaning towards the boy, Matilda turned her palms to the ceiling. "So what happened?"

"Richard was fired just before the exams, and his replacement, Mike Canner, came in on a power trip. He started throwing his weight around like he was trying to manage a group of protectors rather than scientists. We really didn't need someone to assert their authority over us like he did. None of us are type A personalities."

Spike's jaw dropped. "He made you do the exam?"

"Yep. I wasn't prepared *at all.* The annoying thing is, straight after that, he was fired for incompetence. He got the job on a blag and was exposed for being a fraud. His aggression stemmed from his inability to do the role. But it was too late for me by then." When Hugh glanced up at the head table, Spike did the same. Sarge shifted in his seat as if in preparation to address the group.

Shrugging, Hugh sighed. "So I'm here now."

Before Spike could reply, Sarge's chair screeched as he stood up, his heavy steps beating against the wooden stage as he walked around the front of his table. "Right, thickos, I want you all standing against the far wall now. Do it quickly and quietly."

It took about a minute for everyone to go where they'd been told to, many of them weaving through the tables to get to the other side of the room.

"It's time to draw the teams. There are seven teams, and they all have stupid names, but it's not the names that count, it's how you perform. You need to learn to work well with whatever team you end up in. Your life counts on you working as a unit. For the next six months, your team should be everything to you. You should train together, sleep in the same dorm together, work together, and if you fail miserably"—he lowered his voice—"*die* together."

Hugh stood on Spike's right and whimpered at the last comment.

Holding up two small black cloth bags, Sarge kept them elevated long enough for the entire room to see. "I'll draw boys' names from this bag"—he shook the one in his right hand—"and girls' names from this one." Pausing, he looked at all the new recruits. "Does everyone understand, or do you need diagrams to make it easier?"

Silence met his question and he smiled. "Good, let's start."

When Sarge plunged his hand into one of the sacks, Spike's stomach sank with it. Why hadn't he thought about it sooner? He and Matilda might not end up on the same team. The words rushed to the end of his tongue, but he kept them in. Sarge wouldn't do him any favours. He wouldn't change how the teams were drawn so one recruit could be with their girlfriend. In fact, if anything, he'd split them up. A glance at Matilda and he saw the crease to her brow as she watched the man on the stage. If they were in separate teams, he wouldn't see much of her for the next six months. What if she got in trouble beyond the wall? What if she ended up in the same team as Ranger?

His heart racing and his stomach turning backflips, Spike watched Sarge struggle with the small slip of paper, his large hands lacking the finesse required for the task.

When he finally unfolded it, he held it in a pinch and frowned at it for a few seconds. He read the name as a question. "Drew Peacock?" Although a boy put his hand in the air, Sarge hadn't yet looked up, his dark frown still fixed on the slip. "Is this a windup? Droopy cock?"

Looking up, Sarge's blue eyes fixed on the boy. "Is that *really* your name?"

Swiping his side-parted hair over, the boy blushed and nodded.

"Do your parents hate you? It's a good job your surname's not Hunt. They would have probably called you Michael."

Most of the cadets sniggered.

Sarge watched the crimson-faced boy move his side-parting over again. "You look like you're about to enter a bloody ball-room-dancing competition, not go to war. Are you here to dance, boy?"

The boy's hair wobbled when he shook his head and his side-parting failed him yet again. He swiped it back across. "No, sir."

"You're in team Yeti." Pointing to a table in the corner, Sarge said, "Over there."

The boy scuttled over to the table indicated to him as Sarge pulled out another name. "Flight Stingray." A heavy sigh, he shook his head. "Someone's having a laugh with me, right?"

Flight stepped forward and Sarge already looked exhausted by the process. He spoke in monotone. "You're in team Phoenix."

As the names were drawn, the cadets moved to their team tables. Minotaur, Dragon, Bigfoot, Chupacabra, Yeti, Cyclops, and Phoenix. One table remained empty. If the intake continued to increase, no doubt they'd find another stupid name to give to a new team.

After well over three-quarters of the names had been drawn from the bags, Spike finally heard his. "William Johnson." He stepped forward and glanced over at Hugh, who sat at team Minotaur's table. The boy's mouth had fallen slightly open. Maybe he should start introducing himself as William to save the confusion.

Sarge pointed at a table. "Team Minotaur."

Spike walked over and sat down next to Hugh, who beamed a smile at him. Matilda remained standing against the wall.

Pulling the next name out, Sarge sighed and rolled his eyes. "The golden boy, Ranger Hopkins. Team Bigfoot."

Thank God he wasn't in Spike's team. Just one recruit from each team made it through to the trials. It would be better to compete against him then.

After a few more rounds, they'd gotten down to just two cadets, and team Minotaur still had a space. Thankfully, team Bigfoot didn't. Spike's pulse quickened to look over at Matilda. Please let it be her.

Sarge fumbled with a piece of paper. "And the final member of team Minotaur."

His throat dry, a nauseating rock in his stomach, Spike drew short and rapid breaths. While spinning his dad's skull ring on his finger, he stared at his love. She didn't look back.

Sarge cleared his throat and paused for what felt like a lifetime before he said, "Olga Vasquez."

CHAPTER 32

The city hadn't been extended for years, which meant the dorms would have remained in the same spot for that time too. A steady stream of hard-worked teenagers living there should have made the place stink, but when Spike entered the building, the fresh lavender scent caught him off guard.

Lined up in the small corridor in front of the three bedrooms, Spike had the other two boys from team Minotaur on his left and the three girls on his right. They all stared at their leader in front of them, a line of broadswords on the wall behind him. He hadn't told them his name yet. In fact, he hadn't told them anything.

When Spike looked at the girls again, his stomach tightened. None of them were to blame for not being Matilda, but that didn't make him hate the fact any less. It would take a great effort not to resent them for it.

The man in front of them appeared to be about the same age as Sarge, but unlike Sarge, he wore his years well. Clean shaven, he had a thick head of brown hair. Dressed in an immaculate combat uniform, Spike could see this man knew how to iron a crease down the front of his trousers. Despite the attention of all the recruits already on him, he still felt the need to drive his hands together in a loud clap to get their attention. This man did things by the book.

"Right, boys and girls, you can call me Bleach. I'm your team leader. As you can see, my barracks are spotless, and I expect them to stay that way. You make your bed every day, you sweep and mop the floors every day, and you clean the bathrooms every day. I don't want to have to live in your stink and mess. If you follow my rules, I'll have much less of a reason to be pissed off with you.

"First, I want you all to introduce yourselves. Hopefully we'll all be here for the next month at least, so you need to get to know one another." Pointing at Hugh, Bleach said, "You."

Stepping forwards, his face glowing red, Hugh cleared his throat. When he scratched his cheek, Spike saw his hand shake. The mole of a boy introduced himself to the wooden floor. "My name's Hugh Rodgers. I've been working in the science lab for the past several years, helping research towards an antidote for the disease." After stepping back into line, he kept his attention down and wrung his large hands.

The next boy stepped forwards. A slim lad, he stood about five feet ten inches and had slicked-back hair, high cheekbones and bright blue eyes. Spike noticed all the girls look at him. "I'm Max Slink. I've been in school until now. My parents are in construction. We're hoping we can start building two-storey houses and taller once the kiln's output increases. It'll really help with the space issues in the city. If I'm not the next protector, I plan to return to my district to help with that work."

The next protector! Spike stared at Max. If he wanted to get the apprenticeship, he'd have to want it more than Spike. It took for Bleach to clear his throat for Spike to realise he should be stepping forward. While looking into his leader's eyes, a grey tint dulling the green of them, he said, "I'm Spike."

Bleach raised his large right hand to halt Spike and leaned in as if trying to hear him better. "You're *who?*"

"Spike."

"*Spike?*"

The silence hung in the air and everyone stared at Spike. His throat tightened and he felt Max watching him more than the others. He drew a deep breath before speaking in a low murmur, "I'm William. William Johnson."

Disgust twisted Bleach's features and he shook his head. "You ain't a protector yet, *boy.* Spike's a name you've got to earn."

As Spike stepped back into line, he looked across at Max. They stared at one another. He had no beef with him, but the boy had better believe he'd earn his moniker.

The shortest girl of the three stepped forward next. She stood just over five feet tall. Despite her size, she didn't seem intimidated by the occasion. What Spike had initially seen as fear in her pale skin appeared to simply be a part of her complexion. A wide smile, she dipped the slightest bow at Bleach. "I'm Olga Vasquez." When she stepped back into the line, she looked at Spike and smiled. Her curves and confidence made him look back.

The next girl: "I'm Elizabeth Troy." Her voice shook as she spoke. "If I get through this, I'm going to work in research in the labs."

And finally: "I'm Heidi Sparx and I'm going to work in textiles."

Clapping his hands again, Bleach grinned. "Okay, so now the introductions are over, I'm going to explain what these next six months are all about. As you know, you'll be helping extend the city walls. We've all seen the diseased." He paused to look at Spike. "Some of us much closer up than others."

They all nodded.

"Well, it's different when you're outside those walls. There isn't anyone to look after you out there, especially when they come at you in a swarm. The diseased might look weak and frail, but they're savages. They're stronger than you, faster than you, and what we find out too many times when we run national service is they're smarter than a lot of you too. Their teeth are their weapons and they're masters of them. They'll have your throat out before you can blink. The only thing I can promise is that at the end of these six months, there will be less of you here than there is now."

When Spike heard Hugh gulp, he looked over to see his lips moving as if he were silently praying.

"The first month is full-on training. This is where we're the strictest. As of now, you're on a curfew. You have to be in bed by twenty-one hundred hours, and lights go out at twenty-one thirty. Once you get through training, you'll be given more freedom. Until then, you need to keep your head down and work hard. What you learn in this next month has the potential to keep you alive and, more importantly, to help you keep the team alive, so pay attention."

Maybe being away from Matilda wasn't such a bad thing. If Spike had to make it through these next six months and then into the trials, he had to stay focused. Besides, Matilda had it in her to get through on her own. Were it not for Artan, he'd have put his money on her being the next protector.

Looking along the line of cadets, Bleach raised his eyebrows. "Any questions?"

Before Spike realised no one else had, he'd raised his hand. As much as he wanted to put it down, Bleach had already focused on him. "Yes?"

Spike tugged at his collar as if it would help him lower his rapidly increasing body temperature. "Um …" Why did he raise his hand?

"'Um' isn't a question, *William*."

Spike dragged some of the lavender fresh air into his lungs and swallowed a hot gulp. "What do we have to do to qualify for the apprentice trials?"

Watching his fellow cadets rather than Bleach, Spike saw Max suddenly focus on their leader. None of the others looked interested. Although, he couldn't get a read on Olga.

"What you do, *boy*, is you get your head down and think about it in six months' time. For now, you need to be the best soldier you can be. The protectors' apprenticeship will come around, don't worry. Just make sure you're still alive when it does. By doing that, you'll have a good chance of getting in."

After straightening his uniform, Bleach looked at his group again. "Well, if that's all?"

Silence.

"Okay. You have the next few hours to make yourself comfortable in your new dorms." Bleach pointed at the door on his left—"That's the boys' room"—and then the one on his right—"and that one belongs to the girls. The one in the middle's mine. I don't do well with being woke up, just so we're clear with that now. After dinner, we'll turn in early because tomorrow's going to be a busy day."

When Bleach left the dorm, Spike watched the girls go into their room. By the time he'd looked into the boys' room, Hugh and Max had already moved off. He walked in to see Max throw his bag on one of the top bunks. "This is my bed."

Spike scoffed. "Very democratic."

"What did you say?"

Not that he hadn't already assessed him, but to make a show of it this time, Spike looked the boy up and down. Smaller and slimmer than him, there would only be one winner when it came to the apprenticeship. "It's a bit of a dick move to take the bed you want without any discussion. What if we all want a top bunk?"

When Max stepped forward, it halved the distance between them. "Well, it looks like *you* have a problem then. I called the top bunk first; you and Hugh can fight over the other one."

Grinding his jaw, Spike opened his mouth to speak, but Hugh cut him off.

"I prefer the bottom."

"You sure?"

While nodding, Hugh focused on his toes. "I don't like heights."

Spike looked at Max again and the tension faded between them when Max smirked. A second later, they were both laughing.

With a stamp on the wooden floor, Hugh put his hands on his hips as he looked from one of them to the other. "What's so funny?"

Looking first at the bunk bed and then back to his short friend, Spike shook his head. "Well, it's hardly high off the ground."

"It's high enough. Besides, it's more of a problem when I'm sleeping. I have the worst nightmares if I'm high up."

"Whatever, Hugh. It works out for all of us, so that's all that matters." Dropping his bag on the floor by the second bunk, Spike kicked his shoes off and jumped up. Hugh slipped onto the bed beneath him.

Lying on his back and with his hands behind his head, Spike stared up at the white ceiling and relaxed into the soft sheets. Maybe it would do him good to room with Max. He had to be comfortable competing with his peers.

Just as he was starting to unwind, Hugh said, "So what do you think it will take to get into the apprenticeship trials?"

Neither Spike nor Max replied, the silence hanging heavy between them.

Finally, Max said, "I'm not sure, but I'd say hard work and keeping your head down."

Maybe he meant it as a dig, maybe not. Either way, Spike wouldn't bite. Things could be worse. The next six months would be much harder if all the other cadets saw him as the one to beat. They'd see who remained standing when they got to the end of national service.

CHAPTER 33

Spike rested his weight on his knees and leaned forward as he dragged air into his tight lungs. Sweat burned his eyes. He could have held back in their warm-up and saved some of his energy, but, in light of his introduction to national service, he felt like he couldn't give any less than one hundred percent. And while everyone focused on Ranger, he'd subtly show the leaders what he could do.

The combined funk of many overworked bodies permeated the thick air in the hot gym. Another warm April day. The dining hall had seemed large from the inside, but the gym dwarfed it. At least twice the size, if not more.

A red curtain ran along one of the walls. Only four teams had made it in so far: Minotaur, Dragon, Cyclops, and Yeti. Their leaders—Bleach, Tank, Ore, and Flame—stood in front of the curtain, talking to one another in hushed tones.

Dressed in the red tracksuit of team Minotaur, Spike looked at the other recruits from the other teams. Dragon wore green, Cyclops blue, and Yeti white. It took several attempts, but when he finally caught Matilda's eye, he dipped a nod at her. She returned a tight smile before looking down and straightening her green tracksuit. The teams didn't mix, but he still raised a thumb in her direction. Was she okay? A furtive look at the team leaders by the curtain, she barely returned his gesture before slightly turning her back on him.

Before Spike could get her attention again, a loud bang crashed into the main doors. Half-jumping, he spun around. The double doors had been kicked open and team Bigfoot strode in, Ranger in the lead.

Stunned silence filled the room. Just over twenty recruits already there, they all watched the team's bold entrance. The silence hung for a few seconds before a girl in team Cyclops said, "What the hell?"

Even Ranger, with his straight back, broad chest, and confident swagger, couldn't pull it off. Like all of the other teams, they wore identical tracksuits. How Spike would have loved to be a fly on the wall when they were given their gear.

The stunned silence burst with the room erupting into laughter. A boy from team Yeti called out, "Team Skidmark has entered the building."

Although Ranger scanned the laughing faces for who'd said it, his eyes didn't settle. He flushed red, clearly still trying to find the perpetrator while opening and closing his mouth. But he said nothing. What could he say? Especially as the other team leaders were also laughing at them.

Although the other teams entered, it took for Sarge to walk through the double doors before the laughter died. He took the middle of the room, team Skidmark moving aside. "Right, you little wastes of space, this is day one of training. Today's gonna be damn hard. This entire month is going to be damn hard. So be prepared. However, before we start, I have something to show you." Sarge nodded at Bleach.

Bleach grabbed a handful of the red curtain before pulling it aside to reveal a wall of glass about seven feet tall by about twenty feet wide. It gave them a view into two rooms of equal size, a vertical partition separating them. Both of the rooms were dark. They both appeared to be empty.

Like everyone around him, Spike held his breath, putting pressure on his toes from leaning forward as if it would help him see better into the unknown.

Sarge walked over to the glass, balled his right fist, and drove three heavy blows against it. *Boom, boom, boom.*

The silence in the room damn near choked Spike, his throat turning dry and his pulse quickening.

Next to him, Hugh's voice wavered when he said, "What is this?"

But nothing happened.

The other cadets exchanged glances and shrugs. Had Sarge lost the plot?

Sarge's expression remained stony while he raised his fist again. A clenched jaw, he pounded against the glass a second time. Harder than before.

Still nothing happened.

Time seemed to stand still before Sarge finally turned to face the cadets. When he opened his mouth to speak, a shrill scream cut him off.

The sound snapped Spike's shoulders to his neck. He jumped backwards when he saw a diseased burst from the darkness. It slammed against the window face first. The sound went off like a bomb and the collision drove the creature back several wobbly steps before it fell into the darkness again. It left behind a splatter of blood the size of a fist.

Silence hung in the room, Spike's heart beating so hard he worried the others would hear it. Hugh shifted a step towards him. Any closer and their shoulders would have touched.

Spike's lungs tightened and his breaths quickened as he watched the creature appear again. He heard his own panicked breaths in his head and glanced to see if anyone else noticed. Everyone watched the diseased.

Back on its feet, it stumbled on wobbly legs and shook its head as if it could clear its dizziness. It then roared again and charged. Spike jumped back another pace. The same loud connection of face against glass, it stumbled back. But it didn't fall over this time.

The moment he'd clearly been waiting for, Sarge flashed the cadets a crooked smile before he pushed his face close to the glass. A much gentler knock this time, he said, "This, boys and girls, is a diseased." The diseased's bleeding eyes flitted wildly as it looked at the recruits. The walls of the room felt like they were closing in on Spike and he wanted to turn away. He wanted to get out of there. It didn't look like anyone else felt the same.

A fierce lust for violence burned in the diseased's crimson glare. Much slower this time, it pressed its face to the other side of the transparent wall as if trying to push through it. Its rotten lips splayed, showing its yellow teeth from where it opened and closed its jaw. Similar yellow teeth would have taken a bite from Spike had Ore not saved him. The sound of enamel against glass tormented him. It called to him as if mocking his fear.

Sarge pulled away from the window. "You've all seen a diseased." He looked at Spike. "Some of you from a closer perspective than others."

Spike felt the others looking at him and he physically shrank by an inch or two. But he avoided their attention by watching the creature on the other side of the glass, its pallid skin wrinkled and pitted as if it had had the life sucked from it.

"But you won't have been able to see them this close up. This is the enemy. This is what you'll be facing in a month's time. If this thing running at you makes you piss your pants—" he paused to look at Spike again "—then you need to change that before you step outside the gates. For the sake of both you and your team."

What if Spike couldn't? What would he do then?

The wooden floor amplified Sarge's heavy limp. *Thud, thud, thud.* He stopped in front of the other dark room behind the glass.

An adrenaline-fuelled shake running through him, Spike covered it as best he could by holding his hands behind his back. He looked at the other cadets. None of them had noticed. He returned his attention to the room, squinting to see into it. It looked empty like the first one had.

The ripping sound of a curtain tore across a rail, flooding the rooms with light from a window in the ceiling. The loud sound and sudden illumination sent another nerve-rattling shot of adrenaline into Spike's bloodstream. He looked at the rooms. They were clinical in appearance. Tiled in white. The room with the diseased in it had bloodstains on the floors and walls. It looked like there had been a massacre in there. The other side looked immaculate.

A door then opened into the empty cell, and Fright—team Chupacabra's leader—walked in, pulling a sheep behind her. Although the creature resisted, Fright had no trouble dragging it into the room against its will. Deep black bags beneath her eyes, she looked like something from a horror story as she stared out at the cadets. No expression on her thick features, she left the sheep on its own as she exited the room and closed the door.

The diseased in the other room pulled away from the glass and turned to face the partition wall instead. It lifted its nose as if sniffing the air. Spike assumed the blood covering its eyes rendered it blind. It must be guided by its sense of smell. The wretched thing looked drunk as it stumbled into the dividing wall. Palsied movements, it slowly dragged its hands down it, raking its fingers like it could claw its way through to the beating heart on the other side. Could it hear Spike's beating heart at that moment? Could the rest of the room hear it?

Sarge cleared his throat, the sound going off like a gunshot in the near silence. Spike jumped again, and this time, he looked across to see Ranger had clocked it. A wicked smile lifted his smug face.

"What you've seen of the diseased is them being dominated," Sarge said. Although Spike kept his eyes forward, his cheeks burned to feel Ranger's attention on him. "It's almost comical watching a protector take one down. Or seeing the snapping heads in the square. Some of you might have even seen people evicted from Edin."

Spike thought about Mr. P.

"But this, boys and girls, is what one of these creatures looks like when *they're* in control. When the odds are more in their favour, which they most certainly are on the other side of the main gates."

A cold rush ran through Spike and he pulled at his collar. He looked behind him at the gym's entrance. What would they say if he went out for air?

When someone said, "It's shitting itself," Spike looked at the sheep. But they weren't referring to the docile animal. Watching the diseased lift a leg, he saw the rich brown sludge spill from the bottom of its trousers and spread out on the white floor. It looked like it had more blood than shit in it.

Spike noticed Matilda's face twisting as she watched on, transfixed like everyone else. He ignored Ranger, even though he saw the boy's smile in his peripheral vision.

Walking so he was level with the dividing wall, Sarge pointed at it. "Now, as you can see, this wall is the only thing keeping the sheep alive at the moment. The second we pull it up, the sheep's a goner. If you learn how to fight back, then you might avoid the same fate." Balling his fist, Sarge banged against the window again.

A loud rattling sound of chains called out and the partition wall lifted. The grating clack of the winch rattled Spike's nerves.

He looked at the exit again, his legs twitching with his need to get out of there. He couldn't be the next protector. Who was he kidding? A look at Matilda showed him the sadness in her eyes. She knew it too.

The second a gap lifted beneath the wall, the diseased dropped to its knees and pressed its face to the floor. It poked its nose through the space, its scrabbling feet driving it forward. It looked like it thought it might be able to shove its entire body through the tight gap.

When the space had grown to about ten centimetres, the diseased reached one of its arms through. A long and atrophied limb, its hand spasmed while clawing in the direction of the sheep. Similarly wiry limbs had reached for Spike twice, and he'd failed to protect against them both times.

The sheep remained frozen to the spot, trembling as it looked at the hand. It didn't make a sound. Spike remembered his dad telling him that a sheep's only defence came from being quiet. The loudest sheep showed its predator it was weak. It made it stand out as an injured and easy target. Keeping quiet was the best defence they had. Keeping quiet and standing still. While twirling the heavy ring around his shaking finger, he watched on.

The wall lifted high enough for the diseased to turn its head sideways and shove it under. It stretched its neck forwards, its tongue shooting from its mouth like a snake tasting the room beyond. With better co-ordination, it would have twisted to get its shoulders through. Instead, they caught and prevented it from getting any closer.

Raising his hand, Sarge shouted, "Halt."

The wall stopped.

Dropping down, he pointed at the diseased. "Now, as you can see, this thing's pushing so hard to get through, it's shearing one of its ears off."

Spike drew a deep breath, but he couldn't fill his cramped

lungs. His throat tightened as he stared at the creature's half-attached ear.

"But if you look at its face," Sarge continued, "it doesn't seem to have any awareness of the injury it's causing itself. Driven by a single purpose to attack, they forget everything else. I'm not sure they even feel it. The only things I can tell you these things feel for sure are hate and a desire to destroy."

Spike's entire body shook as he watched black blood belch from the creature's torn ear.

When Sarge whistled, Spike jumped back again. Close enough to the doors, he could sneak out. But could he do it without anyone noticing? He held his chest while watching the wall lift again.

After a few more seconds of the diseased shimmying and twisting—its bare feet clawing against the floor for leverage—it got through. Jumping up, it ran at the sheep full tilt and Spike yelled.

The diseased connected with a loud thud and the sheep bleated. Almost human in its scream, the diseased silenced it by biting into its throat.

Spike watched the sheep kick wildly, his face on fire with shame at his outburst. Blood spread out beneath the sheep. One of its thrashing legs connected with the diseased. The kick sounded with a wet crack, but the creature didn't stop. It didn't seem to notice.

Several convulsions snapped through the sheep before it fell limp.

With its death, Spike felt the slightest release in his chest and pulled a deeper breath into his lungs.

The diseased sat up, blood coating its maw. Its mouth stretched wide and it hissed while looking around the room as if searching for something else to attack.

The monster's rage soon abated. It got to its feet and

wandered off. Sarge stepped in front of the glass again. "As you can see, *these* diseased aren't to be messed with. They're killing machines, hell-bent on your total destruction. Outside those walls isn't a controlled environment. If you survive national service, it's because you've earned it."

After Sarge knocked on the glass again, Spike watched Fright stride into the room for a second time, a broadsword in her two-handed grip.

The diseased flicked its head in Fright's direction. Bloody saliva dripped from its loose maw. Its lips pulled back in a snarl and it hissed like a bag of angry snakes. It exploded towards her, Spike wincing in anticipation of it connecting.

The diseased closed the gap between them in two long strides.

With a swing of her sword, Fright decapitated it and jumped to the side as the headless body crashed into the white, tiled wall. An explosion of blood from where it connected, she stamped on its still-snapping head.

After a moment's silence, the room gasped again to see one of the sheep's legs kick out in a sharp spasm. "As you can see, the diseased didn't eat the sheep, it just killed it. This is what happens when you get bitten. Don't wait for your friend to change; end them before it's too late."

The sheep stood up on bandy legs and released a shrill bleat. A hellish call of torment, it charged at Fright, snapping its teeth as it ran. With another well-timed swing, she took the sheep's head off and watched its body collapse in a heap next to the diseased's.

Wild eyes and bared teeth designed to chew grass not flesh, the sheep's mouth snapped in its decapitated head. Fright drove the tip of her sword into the top of the thing's skull. Its tongue lolled from its mouth as it became suddenly inanimate. Its eyes remained stretched wide on its dead face.

Despite the battle and the carnage in the rooms beyond the

windows, Fright didn't have a single drop of blood on her. Minimum effort, maximum effect.

Sarge broke the silence by clapping his hands and Spike jumped again.

While applauding Fright's display, Sarge said, "This is what you're up against. If one's running at you, you need to act fast and with deadly accuracy. Don't do what William did yesterday."

The attention of the room back on him, Spike's breathing sped up again. He'd chosen not to fight the thing. But he didn't say that. What did it matter? He hadn't acted when he should have. He dropped his focus to the floor. Even if he hadn't panicked by the gates, he'd just panicked now. When faced with a diseased out in the open, he might panic again. He'd persuaded Matilda to stay in Edin on a promise that he'd be the next protector. He'd been lucky to get past day one.

When Sarge delivered his final words in his battle-worn growl, Spike's stomach sank. "You panic, and either you or your teammates are dead."

Spike saw the same sadistic grin on Ranger's face.

CHAPTER 34

Although the curtain had been closed for a few minutes, Spike kept glancing at it, his chest still tight, his legs weak from the spent adrenaline. But at least the need to escape had left him, and at least it didn't feel like his heart wanted to burst free from his chest. An anomaly, hopefully he'd react better the next time he saw one of the things.

Sarge had lined the rookies up against the opposite wall so they faced the now drawn red curtain. He drew a line on the floor at one end of the hall with chalk before moving to the other, his hobbled gait beating a slow metronome against the wooden floor. When he got there, he drew another line and groaned as he straightened his back.

None of the rookies spoke while Sarge walked to the middle of the room. He waited for a few seconds as if milking the tension. "These next few weeks are about training. I'll get all of you fitter by the end of this month, and hopefully some of you will learn how to fight the diseased too." He paused to look at Spike, the attention quickening Spike's pulse.

Sarge held a whistle up. "This here is called the bleep test. I want you all to line up on that line." He pointed to his right.

"When I blow my whistle, you need to run to the other line. When I blow it again, you turn around and run back. The time between each whistle will gradually get shorter as you progress through the levels. The last runner left gets three points for their team, second to last gets two, and third to last gets one."

While drawing a deep breath, his lungs still tight, Spike looked at his competitors. Some in the room—like Hugh—looked like they'd struggle to make it to the line once, but how many others had his level of fitness? Ranger would be in shape. Max looked like it too. But it didn't matter. He'd run every day for the last six years. He was ready for this. Even if it felt like he couldn't breathe at that moment, his conditioning would take over.

"Before you start," Sarge said, raising a finger, "I need to explain what happens to those who drop out." He grinned. "Press-ups. Those who drop out will have to do press-ups until the last runner has finished. So you'd best think long and hard about stopping. If you have more in the tank, use it. You need to learn how to run that extra mile. You need to learn that your head will give up long before your body does. Now line up over there and wait for my whistle."

On their way over to the first line, Spike dropped his attention to the floor as he passed Ranger. The stocky cadet shoulder barged him, sending him a couple of steps to the right. It quickened his pulse again, forcing him to fight against his faster breaths.

"Wow, look at you. We've seen how you deal with the diseased, but you look like you're even struggling to walk to the line."

Team Bigfoot had gathered around Ranger as a wall of brown. As much as Spike wanted to reply, he kept it in. He'd prove what he could do when the test started.

~

Blowing two hard blasts on his whistle, Sarge's gravelly voice filled the gymnasium. "Level three."

Pushing off from the line, Spike turned around and jogged to the next one. He felt behind the pace already, his lungs still tight and his pulse pounding through his skull.

Next to him, Hugh sounded like an old locomotive. Puffing and panting, his flat feet slapped down with every step.

When Hugh missed the line on one of the whistles, Spike got behind him and shoved him in the back. "Come on, Hugh, you're going to be doing press-ups for a long time if you stop now."

His mouth stretched wide and his face contorting, Hugh clearly didn't have a response in him.

Peep!

When they were behind on the second whistle, Spike's breaths came in heavier waves too. Many of the other cadets were coping fine. He sped up and left his friend. "Sorry, dude, I can't go out now."

Catching up, Spike turned on the next shrill peep to see Hugh —hands on his knees—bent over in the middle of the gym. Bleach shook his head as he marched over to him, grabbed him by the top of his arm, and dragged him off to the side like he would a naughty child.

Although Spike didn't watch Hugh, he heard him heave. A second later, the sound of vomit hit the gym's wooden floor. A quick glance showed him Bleach taking the boy outside.

The sharp tang of sick joined the heady funk of sweat and dust in the hot room. It closed in on Spike, and although he tugged at his collar, it did nothing to help him breathe better. Screwing his face up against the reek, he tried breathing through his mouth.

By the end of level six, over half the rookies had already dropped out. Sarge moved into the middle of the room while those remaining ran on either side of him. He blew two hard peeps, the sound rattling through Spike's skull. "Level seven."

When Ranger pulled up, his hands on his hips, Spike nearly stopped too, his legs wobbling as he fought against his balance. Several of those supposed to be doing press-ups gasped as they watched on from the sidelines. What the hell? Admittedly, Ranger didn't have the physique of a runner, but surely he could have gone farther than that? Maybe he wasn't as strong as he pretended to be.

As Ranger walked over to the side—his mouth stretched wide and his face puce—his features contorted like he might vomit too. When he caught Spike looking his way, his already distorted face twisted harder and his dark eyes narrowed.

Although Sarge had made the threat, he didn't enforce press-ups on the dropouts. From what Spike could see, Hugh hadn't even returned to the gym.

At level fourteen, there were just three of them left. The dropouts were now sat at the side watching, cheering the candidates on. At least most of them were cheering. Ranger had a sour twist to his features, which he focused on Spike, and every time Spike passed him, he had another word of abuse.

"Drop.

"Give up.

"You're going to get beaten by a girl.

"You'll lose your nerve when you see a diseased anyway."

With Matilda on one side and Max on the other, Spike lifted his chin and kept filling his tight lungs to the steady rhythm of his feet hitting the wooden floor. If he focused on the feeling in his body, he would have given up ages ago, but he kept his attention on the line and getting to that, his fitness doing the work for him. He didn't care if Matilda beat him, but Max …

MATILDA PULLED UP AT LEVEL SIXTEEN TO A COLLECTIVE GROAN of disappointment. It seemed like the crowd's favourite had just dropped out.

Spike tried to make eye contact with her on his way back down the hall, but she looked away. Stars swam in his vision from where he struggled to breathe and he heard Ranger say, "Well done, sweetheart," as Matilda found her seat.

It broke Spike's focus, and from the look on Ranger's face, it had meant to.

"He looks like he's struggling," Ranger said, cackling a vicious laugh.

There might have been two *hims* in the race still, but everyone knew who Magma's son referred to.

TWO SHRILL PEEPS AND SARGE CALLED OUT, "LEVEL SEVENTEEN."

At a near sprint now, Spike's lungs burned and his feet slammed down with every step. Although Max didn't look to be faring much better. Red-faced, he glistened with sweat and gurned as he fought to breathe. Spike only had to run one extra length than him to win. Max would break before he did.

Peep.

Turn.

Peep.

Turn.

THE STRENGTH NEARLY LEAVING HIM, SPIKE WOBBLED AGAIN.

Ranger got to his feet. "He's gonna go."

A look across at Max, Spike frowned hard and dug deep. He beat the whistle to the next line. As much as he wanted to win and as much as he wanted to beat Max, he now wanted to prove it to Ranger more than anyone. Magma's son or not, he wouldn't stand in the way of Spike becoming the next protector. He'd finish second at best. Like his old man. Whatever it took to overcome him and his fear of the diseased, Spike would do it.

Passing Max on his way back down the hall, Spike glanced at him again. Although he looked awful, Spike probably looked no better. But Max was done. He saw it in his eyes.

When he arrived at the other line before the whistle sounded, Spike turned to see Max had pulled up. He ran one more length because he could. Then he stopped, walked to the side of the hall, winked at the embittered Ranger, and fell to the floor. As he lay on his back, the taste of bile rose in his throat from the effort of the run. Sweat burned his eyes while his breaths ran away with him. But he'd done it.

If he worked hard enough, he could overcome anything. Including his fear.

CHAPTER 35

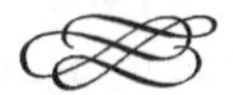

The rain came down so hard it stung the top of Spike's head and his exposed arms. His team around him, he leaned close to them, all of them slightly stooped because of the onslaught. "At least it'll be cooler in the gym. The heat this week's damn near killed me."

Although they were directly competing with one another, Max and Spike had managed to remain civil, and it was Max who replied, "It's been too much, hasn't it? What do you think we're doing today?"

Olga this time: "Whatever it is, I hope it's not as intense as the past few days have been. One more burpee and I might throw up my internal organs."

As the conversation between them died, Spike looked at all the other teams gathered there while he stretched some of the aches and pains from his body. He'd pushed himself to his limit every single day and then every night in weapons training with Bleach, and while the first day of training didn't go as planned, he'd grown as the week went on and given a good account of himself. If Sarge had paid attention, he would have seen a contender emerge. Although, the man never offered praise, so he found it hard to tell whether Sarge paid attention or not.

Team Minotaur stood outside the dining hall like all the other teams. They lined up how they sat at their tables inside. Team Dragon and Bigfoot were neighbours, so Ranger currently stood close to Matilda. From Spike's perspective, Magma's son looked to be spending most of his time trying to get Matilda's attention in one way or another. After saying something else to her, the boy turned around with a smile and winked at Spike. Over the past few days, Ranger had picked up a number one fan, who laughed at his every act. The boy's name was Lance Cull. A tall and broad lad, he had blond hair, teeth nearly as yellow as the diseased, and awful acne.

Not the first time Ranger and Lance had tried to goad him, but Spike's pulse quickened at the affront like it had every other time he'd done it. His stomach tight, he clenched his jaw while staring back at the boy and his pet sycophant. Ranger and Lance's behaviour would have been easier to take though were Matilda not ignoring him. Since they'd been separated into teams, she'd barely looked at him. Maybe his error at the beginning had taken away her confidence that he could get them a better life.

While twirling his dad's skull ring, Spike looked at the hummingbird clip in Matilda's hair.

Before Spike could think on it any further, Sarge's voice called out as he stepped from the dining hall, his usual scowl deepened by the hard onslaught of rain. "Right."

The cadets all faced the man.

"Follow me."

The same process every morning, Sarge walked off in the direction of the gym and they all followed, team Dragon moving off first, all the way back to team Minotaur.

Even as he walked—the ground squelching beneath his feet—Spike saw Ranger talking to Matilda. At least Matilda never reacted, especially on walks like this. No one spoke unless Sarge spoke to them first. Despite the fire in her belly, Matilda needed to have a good reason to go against the rules. What he'd give to be on the roof of the textiles factory with her again.

Instead of stopping at the gym like they had on every other day, Sarge marched straight past it and headed in the direction of the training area. A large walled-off section, Spike had stared at it many times over the past week. He'd stared at both the wall and the fence leading to the hole. He'd learned that the apprentices competed in the training area when the trials started next month. It would be good to see the place so it felt familiar to him in six months' time.

The gates leading through to the training area were much like the ones leading out of the city's back wall—the gates Spike had seen Mr. P ejected from. They were no more than eight feet tall and six feet wide.

The heavy bolt cracked open when Sarge dragged it free. The hinges creaked as he pulled the gates wide and led them through.

As the last team in, Spike had to judge the place based on the reactions of those ahead of him. Every single cadet stared around them after they'd crossed the threshold, their eyes and mouths wide.

Following his team through the now open gates, Spike's jaw fell too. An arena larger than the one they had the main event in, he looked at the banked rows of seats that formed a large circle around a central pit. It was less permanent than the main event arena, however, because it had been constructed from wood to make it more mobile. Like every structure on this side of the gates, it had to be ready to move when they'd finished extending the wall. The main space in the middle, a ring with a diameter of at least fifty feet, stretched much wider than the arena's too. Whatever they did in the trials, they had enough room to make it spectacular.

Several activity stations had been set up in the ring, but before Spike could spend too much time looking at them, Tank—team Dragon's leader—walked across in front of the cadets. A wide man with shock-white skin and black tattoos on his face, he scowled at the rookies, the rain bouncing off him as if he were impervious to it.

A glance at the other cadets showed Spike the same confusion he felt. Why Tank? Sarge took the lead on everything.

"This is the end of your first week. It's been a long week and you've all worked very hard. Today, you'll be competing against one another for team points. The winning team get a lie-in tomorrow."

Just the thought of it made Spike's body ache more than it had a few moments previously. He hated getting up at the crack of dawn.

"The team leaders will take turns setting challenges for you. Mine was supposed to be a gentler introduction, but because of the rain, I'm not sure it will be."

Eight tree stumps, each one about four feet tall, were lined up. The space between them grew larger as they went along. "You need to jump from one of these to the next. You fail to make the jump and you're out." The first gap looked easy enough at about five feet. The final one must have been eight if not more.

A rope hung down from a platform about twenty feet up. "Next, you need to climb the rope. I was going to make you do it using just the strength in your arms, but the fact that it's wet is challenge enough."

When Tank walked over to several axes embedded in lumps of wood, Spike didn't know what to think.

"A big part of being outside the walls for those who want to be the next apprentice is chopping wood. You need to be able to do it well. You have four swings to chop this wood into four pieces of roughly equal size. And then finally …" He walked to the last obstacle. A ring of latticed wood, it had ropes and pulleys attached to it. It looked like an eight-foot-wide dream catcher like the ones he'd seen in the textiles district. "This is a simple case of hanging on. You hold these wooden bars. The last one to fall is the winner. Again, I'm sure the rain will make it infinitely harder. Right, my team first. Dragon"—he pointed at the logs—"get over there."

Ginger Slink went first, slipping slightly as he climbed onto the wet tree stump. Each one had a diameter of about two feet. As much of a fool as Spike had made of himself, at least in this trial he didn't have to be the example of failure for everyone to follow.

"You ready?" Tank said.

Ginger looked at him but didn't reply.

"Go!"

Spike's heart leapt to watch Ginger make the first jump, his feet slipping when he landed on the second log. All the cadets let out sighs and gasps of relief when the boy didn't fall.

Using a two-footed approach, Ginger moved to the edge of the next log, bent his knees, swung his arms, and leapt again. He made it.

Three, four, and five—the same tactic with each one—Ginger crossed the increasingly wider gaps. When he jumped to the sixth stump, he landed with one foot, his other one falling back, but he grabbed on with his hands, crouching down and hugging the stump to remain on it.

The two-footed tactic no good now, Ginger stepped back on the sixth log before running to make the jump. But when he pushed off, his launching foot slipped out behind him, stealing his momentum. He landed face first and nowhere near his intended target.

Tank walked over to the boy—who lay face down in the mud—and offered him his hand. Other than his pride, Ginger didn't appear to have hurt anything. "At least the wet ground has given you a soft landing," Tank said. He then pointed the boy away from him. "You're out."

Matilda next, Spike's heart beat in his throat to watch her climb up onto the first log. No one spoke as she drew a breath and focused on what lay ahead. If anyone could do it, she could. After chasing her through the city on their last night, he'd seen what she had in her. If she couldn't do it, he had no chance.

Suddenly Matilda burst to life, taking two steps across the top of the first stump before launching for the second. Unlike Ginger, she didn't stop, one step across the top of the second stump before she leapt for the third. By the time she'd gotten to the fourth one, some of the crowd were cheering. The same set of concentration on her face, she passed over it onto the fifth, then the sixth, then the seventh. Although Spike had remained quiet until that moment, when he watched her make the final leap, he shouted, "Go on, Tilly."

Matilda nailed the last jump before continuing forward off the final stump to land double footed on the soggy ground.

The cadets all shouted and clapped for her, Spike harder than any others.

Tank's full-bellied laugh sounded like it didn't belong to him, almost mechanical in tone. "Well, that, boys and girls, is how it's done. Nancy, you're up next."

But Nancy Humberto shook her head.

"What do you mean, no?"

"I'm not doing it," she said. "I know I won't make it."

Tank closed his eyes and drew a deep breath. When he opened them again, he looked at Abbie Shrink, who also shook her head.

This time he released a hard shot of air, his cheeks puffing and the whites of his eyes standing out on his face. He looked close to shouting before Jane Strange clambered up onto the first stump. "At last! Someone else with the stones to give it a go."

JANE STRANGE FELL AT THE FIRST JUMP LIKE MANY OF THE following cadets. Many more refused, Hugh being one of them. And Spike couldn't blame them. None of them had designs to be the next protector and they weren't built for the task. Several of the cadets who hadn't made it were still lying down nursing injuries. Elysium Cooch still had blood pouring from her nose. But twelve of them had made it to the other side, including Ranger, Max, and Olga.

Tank slapped Spike so hard on the back, he stumbled forward. "The final cadet. Can you make it thirteen through to round two?"

With all of the other team leaders watching, Spike glanced at Bleach, who, for the first time since he'd met him, almost smiled. Maybe not close to a smile, but the look of utter disdain had certainly left his face.

Being the final one to do the task, Spike had gone through a gamut of emotions. At points he thought he'd smash it, but then he saw someone else slip and fall. His legs shook as he stood up on the first stump, and when he looked along the eight steps, he saw Ranger waiting at the end, staring back at him.

Olga shoved Magma's son aside, moving him out of Spike's line of sight. "You can do it, Spike."

"William," Ranger said.

The rain coming down harder than ever, Spike filled his lungs. He'd do his best to copy Matilda's technique.

Spike reached stump two with ease, then three and four. Like Matilda had, he took a step in between each one and leapt for the next. Stump five, stump six, stump seven. But when he got to the seventh stump, instead of using his momentum to jump for the final one, his courage abandoned him and he stopped, his shoes slipping a little beneath him. Many of the cadets gasped. The longest jump of the lot and he now had no run-up.

"Oh, look," Ranger said. "He's nearly made it, and surprise, surprise, he's bottled it again."

Tank's voice cut through the rain like a thunderclap. "Shut up, Ranger, you jumped-up little moron. Give him the same respect everyone gave you before I disqualify you for putting the other contestants off."

It worked, silencing Ranger and making the boy's pale face redden. But it did nothing to imbue Spike with confidence. As he looked at the gap, he shook his head. No way could he make the last jump.

CHAPTER 36

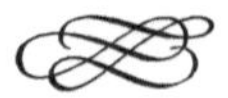

Spike led with his right foot stretched out in front of him. The gap seemed impossibly wide, but he made it … just. However, the second he put pressure down, his foot slipped, fire racing up his right shin as it sheered along the edge of the stump. His knee slammed on the hard surface, rods of electric pain streaking up his thighs, sending nausea into his stomach.

Caught between screaming and vomiting, Spike reached out and hugged the final stump, gripping on with all he had. Although he'd landed it, his head spun from the pain and he could still fall off.

A few seconds later, Spike stood up on wobbly legs to the sound of applause and cheers.

His shin still on fire, Spike tested his kneecap by moving his right leg. It still worked. A small amount of pressure on it to test it would still hold his weight, he jumped off the stump and landed with the rest of the successful cadets. Olga and Max congratulated him while the rest of them, including Matilda, turned their backs on him. Surely he'd just shown her he could do this. While not the best, he had what it took to get through.

~

ALL THIRTEEN OF THEM MANAGED THE ROPE CLIMB, THE NEW rules of being able to use their feet making it easier than intended.

"Spike," Tank said, "you first with splitting the wood. You're from the agricultural district, so this should be a doddle for you, right?"

But Spike didn't reply. Instead, he walked away from the group of thirteen over to one of the axes and logs. On his way past Ranger, he heard the boy hiss, "You're going to fail," but he paid him no mind.

The rest of the cadets watched on, everyone soaked through. The wind whipping up, Spike wiped his hands on his sodden trousers and wriggled an axe free from its stump. While testing the weight of the thing, he tightened his grip on the handle. Lighter than the one they had at home, he still knew how to use it.

Spike rested the head of his axe on his lump of wood to get his range before he wound it back and drove a hard swing at his target. The *shoom* of the cut rang out and a piece of wood about a quarter of the size of the main log fell away.

Two more swings, he cut another quarter and then cut the final piece in half. Not even Ranger could comment when he'd finished and stacked the four almost identical pieces on the stump. The cadets applauded him, and Tank acknowledged his success with a nod. There hadn't been many times in training where Spike had been able to prove his competence. Although Matilda still continued to ignore him.

Spike took his place by the final obstacle and waited while the others tried to join him.

~

Only Ranger made it through to the final task with Spike. All of the others gave it a good go, but they either failed to split the log enough times or their axe glanced off their intended target. When Matilda did it, he wanted to call out her mistakes to her. Hold the axe by the end of the handle and watch the piece of wood she was cutting, not the head of the axe. But in light of the frosty turn their relationship had taken, she'd probably ignore him anyway.

"Two contenders left," Tank said, leading them over to the final challenge. "How perfect." The sound of his steps echoed as he walked up onto the wooden platform beneath the circular latticework of wood. "You've both done well, but there can only be one winner. The boy who holds on longest will get maximum points. You ready?"

"I am," Ranger said, but Spike didn't reply, letting the stocky boy lead the way up to the platform.

Spike had seen the pulleys when Tank first showed them the final task. No doubt they'd lift the latticework high in the air. But how high? It didn't matter. He just needed to hold on.

As much as Spike would have chosen differently, Tank lined him and Ranger up so they faced one another on opposite sides of the wooden frame.

"Ranger," Tank said, "you ready?"

Instead of responding to Tank, Ranger stared at Spike. "Of course."

"William?"

Spike nodded.

Tank stepped off the wooden platform to the sound of a winch turning. Spike looked to see Ore—the woman who'd saved him from being killed on day one—operating it. The wooden lattice lifted above them, dragging Spike's arms up with it. By the time he'd reached full stretch, Ranger's feet had already left the ground.

The cadets cheered, their words mixing together as a swell of excitement. As much as Ranger wanted to look at Spike, Spike turned his face away, the stinging rain slamming against him. He closed his eyes, focusing on his breaths to keep himself calm.

At least a minute passed before Spike opened his eyes again. He looked at Ranger opposite him and saw the twist of his features. He was struggling already. When he looked down, he saw they were at least six feet above the wooden platform. Matilda and the other runners-up stood closer than the rest of the crowd. She still didn't look at him.

It took for Fright to walk over to the wooden platform for Spike to see a section of it could be pulled away. It would make the six-foot drop more like ten as they fell through the middle of the structure.

"Now, boys and girls," Tank said, "when you're outside these walls, you will be challenged. You'll have to do things like jumping, climbing, and chopping, and if you don't, you'll die." He nodded at Fright, who pulled a section of the platform away. It released the shrill cry of the diseased below them.

"So," Tank went on, "we wanted to recreate the consequences in training." He turned to look up at Spike and Ranger. "You boys best hold on, because points are now the least of your worries."

Spike shook to look down. Not only had his drop nearly doubled, but it would land one of them in a well filled with the diseased.

"You have five minutes to hold on," Tank shouted.

"You won't do it," Ranger said.

As much as Spike had tried to ignore Ranger up until that moment, he broke and looked at the boy opposite him.

"You might as well let go now, William. Show everyone what

you're made of. End it here before you get your team killed beyond the wall."

The sound of his own pulse a kick drum through his skull, Spike looked down again. The diseased stretched their atrophied arms up and worked their mouths. Mouths filled with yellow teeth. This wasn't a test. This was life and death.

Spike shook his head and closed his eyes, but it didn't stop the shake running through him. His heart sped up. Impossible to hold onto the wooden bar above, he shook his head again. No, he had to get through this. He had to be stronger than this. He had to prove to them he could be the next apprentice.

Suddenly his grip failed, the lattice of wood rushing away from him as he fell.

CHAPTER 37

The first Spike knew of the net beneath him came when it took his weight, his neck snapping backwards when his fall stopped much sooner than he expected. It sagged, dropping him down close to the diseased, their rotten vinegar stench smothering him as several clawing fingers swiped against his back.

The tension in the net lifted Spike a little, pulling him out of the creatures' range. The same feeling he'd had in the hall, invisible hands reached up and throttled him, tightening around his throat, making it harder to breathe. His heart pounded with such ferocity it felt like it had trebled in size, the kick drum boom consuming him.

The rain lashed against Spike as he lay on his back gasping. It came down so hard he almost couldn't see Ranger hanging on above. Almost. But it would have taken a lot to miss the sadistic grin peering down on him. The clack of the winch sounded outside the well, Ranger lowering with it.

Even with Ranger over him, the sound of the creatures below took most of Spike's attention. Their tormented moans and groans. Their snarling, hissing fury. Paralysed in the net, his body had betrayed him again, and worst of all, he lay there like a fly in a spider's web, waiting for Ranger to get lowered to him so he could witness his weakness up close.

"Stop!"

The sound of the winch halted and Spike looked for the person who'd said it.

When he saw Bleach's face appear over the top of him, he stared into his grey eyes, his breaths still rapid. Although his team leader frowned down at him—another person passing their judgement—Spike watched him wink as he shouted, "I think he's hurt himself. Hold the winch."

"Do you expect me to hang around here all day?" Ranger shouted.

"You're a strong lad. I'm sure you'll last an extra few seconds." Leaning over and reaching down into the well, Bleach spoke so only Spike heard him. "This is your only chance to save face. No one has to see you're panicking if you play along, okay?"

Being called out on his panic somehow made it more real. Spike shook his head and gasped where he lay.

"Come on, boy, I'm just trying to throw you a bone here. We'll deal with this away from prying eyes. I won't offer this again."

A look at the large outstretched hand, Spike glanced up at Ranger's feet dangling above him. Bleach leant over the well in a way that meant Ranger couldn't see him anymore.

Spike reached up and took Bleach's hand.

The strength of his team leader made him gasp as the big man dragged him out of the hole like a mother cat moving her kitten. "You've hurt your right ankle from landing awkwardly."

Affecting a limp, Spike hobbled out of the well, put his arm around his team leader, and bobbed down the stairs with his aid. The rain hammered against the back of his head from where he focused on the wooden steps and then the soggy ground.

Bleach cleared the way. “Stand back, everyone. Give him some room. And while you’re there, give it up for a great competitor.”

Hard to tell where the sound of the rain ended and the applause began, Spike kept his attention on the ground. Stars swam in his vision from where his throat tightened further.

Again speaking so only Spike heard him, Bleach said, “Just focus on putting one step in front of the other. Don’t think about anything else. Just one step at a time. Your breaths will come back to you.”

Before he knew it, Spike could only hear the rain, the sound of the crowd left behind in the training area.

They were walking past the gym when he finally let go of his limp and moved away from Bleach’s paternal half hug. “I don’t understand. I used to go to the square all the time and watch the protectors come back with the heads. It didn’t even bother me when we were in the arena and they had the creature in the box.”

“But it’s different. They were just heads, and the diseased in the main event is contained in a glass prison.”

“The one in the gym was behind glass.”

“But that was after what happened at the gates.” So Bleach had noticed his panic in the gym. “You can’t underestimate the shock of what happened to you with that turned cadet. You nearly died; that’s bound to leave an impression.”

The words lifted Spike’s pulse as if transporting him back to that moment. He managed to settle it with another deep breath. “Thanks for bailing me out.”

“It’s okay.”

He didn’t need to tell Spike that time was running out. In three weeks he needed to make sure he could cope on his own. But at that moment, only his steps mattered. He put one foot in front of the other, his chest loosening with each page.

CHAPTER 38

The rain continued to come down hard, driving against the top of Spike's head as he and Bleach walked to the dining hall to join the rest of the cadets. They hadn't spoken much, taking the time away from everyone to get changed into drier clothes. Not that it made any difference after thirty seconds of being re-exposed to the elements.

Bleach walked ahead of Spike when they got to the dining hall's entrance, and opened the door for him. "Everything's going to be fine. You're not there yet, but we still have about three weeks to make sure you're ready to go outside the gates. I can see you've got it in you. But it's not about what I can see, it's about you seeing it too."

The words gave Spike enough of a lift to help him step into the hall. He pulled his shoulders back and nodded to himself. He could do it.

The aromatic uppercut from the humid room nearly drove Spike backwards. A pungent mix of stew, damp, and sweaty teenage bodies mixed into a near palpable funk. While breathing through his mouth, he looked over at Matilda. Like always, she had Ranger in her ear. He'd never hear what the cretin said to her, and as much as his mind would imagine it if he let it run wild, it wouldn't serve any purpose to go there. It would do nothing to help him become the next apprentice like he'd promised her, and his expectation of what the boy said would probably be far more offensive than the reality. Matilda could look after herself and she'd let Ranger know if he crossed a line.

The cadets closest to Spike fell quiet at his entrance, a ripple effect moving away from them back across the hall. He watched the faces turn his way until the silence hit Ranger. The boy wore his usual smug grin, winking at Spike when they made eye contact.

Bleach broke the quiet. "William's okay. I was being oversensitive. Having broken my ankle myself when I was a kid, I was worried he'd done the same. But he's all okay and ready to continue competing."

"As long as we don't come across any more diseased," Ranger said.

Other than the guffawing Lance at Ranger's side, the comment fell dead. Hopefully that meant no one else knew he'd panicked. Or maybe they just kept their mouths shut to avoid Sarge's wrath.

But where Sarge would normally discipline Ranger, he chose not to. He didn't even look close to it. Maybe he agreed with him.

A shove in the back from Bleach, Spike stumbled forward before he took his encouragement and found his place at team Minotaur's table. As he sat down, the attention of his team on him, Hugh leaned close to him and whispered, "Are you okay?"

Spike nodded and focused on the table, spooning a bland mouthful of stew as a low murmur of conversation started up around them.

A few seconds and mouthfuls later, the screech of Sarge's chair, followed by his heavy gait across the stage, silenced the room again. He held a stick of chalk in his thick pinch as he walked over to a blackboard attached to the wall. It had each of the teams' names on it, points already filled out for all of them save for Minotaur, Dragon, and Bigfoot. The other teams were all within a few digits of one another at around the thirty-point mark.

"Right, you drowned rats, we have three teams this year who are all marking themselves out as the ones to beat. The luck of the draw has put a lot of the fittest cadets in Minotaur, Bigfoot, and Dragon. That's just the way it is. The rest of you need to get better."

In the column that read *Dragon,* Sarge wrote the number sixty-eight. The scratching of his chalk against the board was the only sound in the room. In *Bigfoot,* he wrote seventy-one, and finally in *Minotaur,* he wrote seventy-five.

Hugh made Spike jump by shouting the loudest, leaping up from his seat and punching the air. The attention of the room on him, Hugh cleared his throat, flushed red, and sat back down again.

Olga winked at him. "I appreciate the enthusiasm, Hugh."

The boy turned even redder.

Hugh had already quieted the room, but Sarge let the silence swell before he finally said, "Now, as promised, we're going to let the team with the most points this week have a lie-in tomorrow."

Just the mention of lying in released some of Spike's tension. For the first time since they'd been there, he stooped to Ranger's level, looking over at the boy and grinning at him. This time, Ranger chose to keep his eyes on the board at the front. Although, the flush of his cheeks suggested he knew Spike watched him.

After clearing his throat, Sarge said, "Well done to this week's winners, and enjoy your lie-in. The rest of you can get up an hour earlier to get more training in so you don't lag any further behind team Bigfoot."

"Bigfoot?" Like Hugh, Olga both stood up and silenced the room. "Don't you mean Minotaur?"

"You think I don't know what I mean?"

It took Olga a couple of seconds before she pointed at the blackboard. "We're at the top. Team Minotaur."

Sarge held up the index finger of his right hand, a smile twitching at the edges of his mouth. "Ah, but that's because I haven't made any adjustments yet."

Still on her feet, still the focus of the room's attention, Olga tilted her head to one side. "*Adjustments?*"

"Just one. For putting himself in danger on the first day …"

Spike's stomach sank and he felt the room shift from looking at Olga to looking at him again. Sweat lifted on his palms and the smell of the stew in front of him turned his stomach.

"… and showing he's a first-class liability. I'm docking you ten points. You can all thank William for that."

While Olga sat down, Spike mouthed *sorry* at his team, his cheeks burning as he looked at the table again. The sounds of celebration came from team Bigfoot, swirling in the pitched ceiling above them. He refused to look over as Ranger's voice rang out above all of them. "William's clearly a liability. I wouldn't have him protect my boots, let alone an entire city."

At least half the dining hall laughed.

CHAPTER 39

As Spike entered the arena again, he focused on keeping his frame loose against the tension trying to turn through him. Would the trainers expose them to the diseased for a second week? He shook his head. It didn't matter if they did. His panic had been an anomaly. He'd dealt with it now. If he saw a diseased today, he'd cope. The last time he'd been caught unprepared. He'd felt tired and it had pushed him that little bit too far.

Another week had passed. Another week of training in the gym. Team Dragon, Minotaur, and Bigfoot were still all close at the top of the leaderboard. Bigfoot, after their rest the previous week, had come back to training re-energised and were still at the top because of it.

Spike filled his lungs and looked around. He'd be here in about six months' time, showing the crowd and anyone else who wanted to see just what he could do. He'd show them how the diseased didn't bother him. In a few weeks' time, last season's contenders would be battling it out. If only they were allowed to watch. It would give them a heads-up on what they'd be facing. Although maybe they were better off not knowing.

When Bleach clapped his hands, Spike jumped and looked at

his team leader. They never knew who'd be taking the training, but of all the team leaders, he hadn't expected his own.

"Stressful, isn't it?" Bleach said, pacing up and down in front of the cadets. "Standing here, in this arena, not knowing what's ahead. Now imagine fighting for the apprenticeship. You'll be going through all the anxiety you feel now, but with an audience of over three hundred watching on."

Although Spike cleared his throat and shifted his stance, neither action helped him slip away from his discomfort. But he'd be fine when he got there. He'd have had five months' experience outside the walls, so nothing would faze him.

"You!"

Spike looked down the line to see Bleach had singled out Mercy De'ath from team Yeti. A girl with hair so blond it looked close to white, she had pale skin and brilliant green eyes. Hard to tell where her white tracksuit ended and she began. Long limbed, she looked elvish. She snapped her heels together and stared at Bleach, awaiting something more from him.

A thick rock of chalk in his grip, Bleach held it out to her and said, "Follow me."

Mercy stepped forward and took the chalk.

Bleach pointed down at the flat stone ground. "I want you to walk behind me while drawing a line and only stop when I tell you to."

After she'd dipped a sharp nod at him, Mercy squatted down with the chalk and pressed it against the ground.

No wonder Bleach didn't want to do it. Spike's back ached just from watching her follow him, duckwalking as she kept the chalk pressed against the ground and drew a straight line.

When they'd walked about one hundred feet, Bleach turned a right-angled left and got her following him away from the cadets.

About fifty feet later, Bleach turned another left, dragging Mercy back so the next line matched and ran parallel to the first.

He then turned ninety degrees to the right, got Mercy to draw another straight line of about fifty feet before turning right again and running a third long line along the ground. It ran parallel to the other two.

By the time they'd gotten to the end of the third long line, Max said, "What the hell is he doing?"

The only reply came in the form of a hard glare from Gauze, team Phoenix's leader.

They were now so far away Spike couldn't hear what Bleach said to Mercy, but after a few seconds of talking to one another, he watched the girl in the white tracksuit run around and fill in the lines while Bleach walked back over to them.

By the time Bleach had reached them, Mercy had mapped out a square in chalk and drawn a cross through the middle of it, dividing it up into four smaller squares.

"The corners of the squares," Bleach said, "make up nine points on this pitch. Three along the bottom, three across the middle, and three along the top. I'm going to divide you up into teams of four and five, grouping you with people of a similar athletic ability. You will then race against each other from one point to the next, sprinting as fast as you can. The team on the first point will sprint to the team on the second point, who will then sprint to the team on the third point. It sounds easy, but you'll soon find it's not. This exercise is about your powers of recovery. If I think you're not putting in maximum effort, you're out. If you can't run anymore, you're out. When one complete team drops, you take your cue to run when the team closest behind you gets to the end of their point. Any questions?"

Like all of the other cadets, Spike looked at those around him, flinching when he met Ranger's stare. The boy smiled at him like he always did. The teams were yet to be picked, but he already knew they'd be in the same group.

~

"I'M LOOKING FORWARD TO ANOTHER DAY OFF TOMORROW," Ranger said.

Spike looked at the others. Max, Matilda, and Olga—none of them replied or even looked at Ranger.

When Spike shifted close to Matilda to try to say something, she stepped away from him. Before he could make another move, Bleach shouted, "Go!"

They took off, sprinting from the first to the second point. The moment they reached point number two, Hugh and his team sprinted for point three.

A quickened pulse from the first run, Spike linked his fingers behind his head and tried to make eye contact with Matilda.

Ranger stepped between them. "When do you think the diseased will come?"

The comment sent a surge through Spike, which he did his best to hide. He scanned the arena for signs of diseased. Surely Bleach had a twist planned for this game.

As if he could read his mind, Ranger nudged Spike and said, "I think you might be okay at this one. Your team leader's probably done you a favour."

Katie Rich, Fran Jacobs, Tom French, and Amy Furore came thundering up behind Spike and the others, triggering them to sprint to point three.

Bleach cupped his mouth with his hands and shouted, "Remember to give it all you've got."

His chest slightly tighter than before, Spike watched Hugh give up, his shoulders slumped as he skulked away from his team.

"A dropout already?" Bleach said. "You disappoint me, Hugh."

Matilda, Olga, Max, and Spike didn't speak, all of them breathing more heavily than when they'd started. And why did they need to talk when Ranger did enough for all of them? "That boy's dead weight. He's going to get your team killed when you go outside the walls."

The team behind caught up again in a galloping rush, so Spike and the others burst to life. Only three sprints, but he already felt how the short recovery time would chip away at them.

Two more of Hugh's group gave up. Flight Stingray and Jenny Crumb.

Nice to see one of Ranger's team pull up. Spike watched him wince as he heckled his teammate. "Jenny! Come on, you can do better than that." But she ignored him. Something she'd probably got quite good at doing over the past few weeks.

By the time it came back around to them, four more cadets had dropped. Spike sprinted again, pulling deeper breaths than before to find the speed he needed to keep going.

When they stopped this time, Max bent over and put his hands on his knees. Spike tapped his teammate on the shoulder and said, "You'll recover better like this." He linked his fingers and held them behind his head. After several breaths, sweat running into his eyes, he said, "It opens up the lungs more."

Red-faced and glistening, Max nodded his thanks at Spike and did as he'd just shown him.

Eight more had pulled out by the time the team behind them caught up again.

At the next point, Spike noticed Ranger glance his way before he shifted closer to Matilda. "How are you doing, Tilly? If you get a bit stiff after this and want a massage or something …?"

The offer of a massage didn't bother Spike. It seemed like the kind of thing Ranger would say. But he'd called her *Tilly.* No one else called her that.

Matilda looked from Ranger to Spike and then turned her back on both of them as if they were each as bad as the other.

The thunder of footsteps behind, Spike took off again. The

team on the point before them were now down to two because Katie Rich and Amy Furore had both pulled off to the side. The entire field had halved since he'd last checked. When Spike saw Heidi Sparx from his team vomit clear liquid at the side of the pitch, he focused on his breathing again to try to settle the knot in his own stomach.

Because two entire teams were out, it had shortened their recovery time. Surrounded by the heavy panting of his team, Spike fought his own battle to hold on. There were only nine runners left. Five of them still in his group.

Spike found it impossible to avoid Ranger, who moved closer to him and nudged him hard enough to send him stumbling to one side. "With no diseased, you might stand a chance of winning this one. I mean, it's not like facing those freaks is something we need to get competent at."

They sprinted again. For all Ranger's bravado, Spike saw how hard he now breathed. They were all tiring.

Just three teams left, Spike watched the team closest to them —now four places back—finish their sprint, and he ran again, his legs heavy, his mouth stretched wide as he tried to fill his tight lungs.

"Who needs to deal with the diseased in this world anyway?" Ranger tried again.

It took a great effort to speak, but Spike did it anyway. "Why don't you do one, Ranger?" They sprinted again.

The only team left, all five of them still together, Bleach shouted over to them, "Go on my word."

Even worse because they couldn't see their turn coming around to them, Spike watched Bleach.

"Go!"

Spike saw his own fatigue in those around him, all of them slowing down as they got close to the line.

"I can see you giving up, Spike," Ranger said. "You look screwed."

"Go!"

They took off again. Despite the advice he'd given Max, when they stopped, Spike bent over double, his mouth stretched wide as if it would help him breathe better.

Lance Cull started the chant from the sidelines. "Ranger, Ranger, Ranger."

"Go!"

Spike sprinted again, doing his best to focus on the next point and nothing else. Unable to stop it, his stomach bucked and he vomited, the crowd cheering him while he threw up his breakfast.

"Go!"

But Spike wouldn't back down. He ran again, spitting some of the bitter-tasting phlegm from his mouth.

"Go!"

All five of them ran. They were so exhausted, not even Ranger had a smart comment.

"Go!"

When they got to the next point, there were only four of them left. Despite the pain in his stomach, his head spinning with his difficulty breathing, Spike looked at Matilda, Max, and Olga and smiled.

"Go!"

But Spike didn't. Instead, he let himself fall onto his back and stared up at the sky, closing his eyes as he recovered, listening to Bleach shouting, "Go!" at the others. At least he'd beaten Ranger.

"Go!"

CHAPTER 40

"Well, I for one want to say well done to Max." Spike looked across the flickering fire at his teammate and dipped a nod at him. "Thanks for the lie-in tomorrow, and well done on smashing Bleach's twisted fitness test."

Bleach threw his head back with a booming laugh. "Sorry about that one."

"I must say though, Spike," Max said, "you deserve some kind of medal for throwing up and still running to the next point."

Although Spike smiled, he couldn't rid himself of the sinking feeling in the pit of his stomach. Sure, he'd proven he could keep up with the best of them. Some days Max or Matilda won; some days he, Olga, or Ranger. But he still hadn't dealt with facing the diseased. And worst of all, Ranger saw straight through him.

When Spike refocused, he saw the others were all looking at him, waiting for some kind of response. He stared off into the darkness behind them, so pitch anything could be waiting there. They were having a small fire off to one side, the rest of the cadets in their dorms because they'd be getting up early in the morning. They were close to the hole, not that he could see the fence sectioning it off from the rest of the national service area.

The glow from the fire robbed him of his night vision. "What is the hole, Bleach?"

It turned the group's attention to their team leader, who paused for a second before shaking his head. "You don't want to know, and you should pray you never get a chance to find out." He quickly followed up with, "How did you get so fit, Max? I've never seen anyone get that far before."

"I'm from the construction district," Max said.

Olga this time: "You know that doesn't explain anything, right?"

A shake of his head, he said, "Oh, sorry. No, I don't suppose it does. Well, my parents are in charge of one of the kilns and they need someone to deliver their bricks. Every morning, I'd fill a barrow with bricks and run the deliveries for them. I didn't have to do it, but I wanted to work on my fitness because I knew I'd be coming here, and being fit is what's going to keep me alive."

Spike noticed something shift next to him. He snapped his head around to see Hugh squirming. Max's statement clearly made him uncomfortable.

Max then added, "I got a bit of insight about what national service is like because I have four older brothers."

"*Four?*" Olga said. "And all of them made it through national service?"

Max nodded. "Yeah. Every one of them." He laughed. "I suppose the law of averages says I'm screwed now, right?"

For a few seconds, the sound of the wind ran across the open field. Spike pulled his knees up to his chest and hugged them to himself. He imagined what could be in the shadows around them. He saw the pallid and wrinkled faces of the diseased. The snarling and snapping mouths. The yellow teeth.

Heidi finally broke the silence, pulling Spike away from his imaginings. "I had a brother. He was called Rufus and was four years older than me." A glaze covered her eyes, the flames reflected in her distant stare. "He didn't make it."

"I remember him." Bleach's deep voice cut through the night. "When their team was jumped by the diseased, they all ran, but Rufus tripped and fell. It was enough for the diseased to set upon him."

The constantly shifting light animated the shadows around them, flashing movement through Spike's peripheral vision.

In the entire time they'd been there, Spike hadn't spoken to Elizabeth much. She tended to watch the group, never offering her thoughts or opinions. When she spoke, her small voice was barely audible over the wind and popping fire. "I have a younger brother and sister. I'm the first in our family. Mum and Dad wouldn't tell me anything about what I'd be facing. They said they wanted to save me the nightmares. It didn't work."

Spike shifted closer to the fire to get warmer. Closer to the fire also meant farther away from the darkness surrounding them.

"Two older sisters for me," Olga said. So nonchalant in how she spoke, her next line gave Spike a jolt. "They both died during the same national service. I suppose better that than separate one twin from another."

Again Bleach spoke, recalling Olga's sisters. "Nikki and Jacqueline, right?"

Olga stared suspicion at him. She seemed comfortable talking about them, but she clearly didn't like it when someone else did.

"Strife was their team leader. The entire team fell that day."

"Like Elizabeth, I have a younger sibling. James. He's eight." Hugh lowered his brown eyes, the shadows highlighting the bags beneath them. "I don't expect I'll see him again."

Spike watched Elizabeth comfort Hugh by stroking his back before he looked at the others. They were all watching him as if waiting for him to speak. "I'm an only child, so I'm the first. My parents went before me and they don't talk about it either." He spun the skull ring on his finger. "They had good luck charms they thought got them through." He held his hand up to show off his ring. "My dad gave me this." To think about Matilda's hummingbird clip lifted a lump in his throat. His mum had been wrong about her. When they finished national service, he'd never see her or it again.

"It must have been hard for your parents to say goodbye to you," Max said. "Being an only child and all."

The thought of his dad made Spike's eyes itch from where tears spread across them. The lump in his throat swelled, and when he opened his mouth, no sound came out. A tear ran from each eye, which he quickly wiped away. But they didn't need to hear about that. About how his dad had let him down on his final morning. About how he made up for it by stopping the carriage. About how he came to national service ready to take on the world, and now he didn't know if he'd even return. About Matilda, his first and maybe only love. They couldn't reduce their relationship to sterile nights in the square. What if they got evicted like Mr. P and his boyfriend? But he had to say something, the others all staring at him. "So we all have our theories, right?"

The wind shook the flames and the fire popped, making Spike jump. A quickened pulse, he looked around at the shadows before addressing his group again. "About where the diseased come from."

"I don't go in for conspiracies," Bleach said, getting to his feet. "Well done on your efforts this week." He half turned away from them to show he intended to leave. "Don't stay up too late, make sure the fire's fully out, and keep the noise down."

When Bleach had walked out of earshot, Olga said, "Well, if that didn't just confirm there's something weird going on, I don't know what does."

Max leaned closer to her, his face illuminated by the fire. “What do you mean?”

“He has to remove himself from a conversation about the diseased. Is that because he knows something? Is he on strict orders not to talk about it?” When no one answered, Olga said, “So what’s your theory, Spike?”

Maybe Spike shouldn’t have mentioned it. Probably not the best conversation to be having in the middle of the dark field, the glow of the fire blinding them to attackers. But at least it had stopped his tears. A look over both shoulders showed him nothing, their surroundings too dark. “I dunno.”

“Of course you do. Just say it.”

He and Matilda had talked about it a lot. All the kids did. “I reckon there’s something in the air. Not where we are. Far away. Like far, far away. I think it’s turned the air poisonous, changing normal people into those *things*.”

“Why are there still new diseased all the time?”

“How do we know they’re new? What if they’re hundreds of years old? Maybe no one knows where the poisonous air is. Maybe it moves around, attacking different groups of people.”

A derisive snort, Max shook his head. “What, so it’s just a matter of time until it gets to us?”

“Maybe. Why not?”

Before Max could reply, Hugh said, “I reckon it’s an experiment. I think someone has caused it and continues to cause it. I think they’re doing this to their enemy and we’ve been caught up in the crossfire. Maybe they don’t know we’re here. Maybe they think all of this land is abandoned and think there’s no chance anyone could be living here.”

Max shook his head. “I don’t believe that. I think they know we’re here. They must have seen the protectors when they’re out on their travels.”

“Ahem,” Olga said. “Didn’t you just see how Bleach reacted?

Maybe no one else knows we're here, but I'd bet my life the protectors know more about what's going on than most people."

"Maybe they're in on it," Hugh said. "I wonder what the politicians know."

Heidi looked around her as if they were being listened to. "But why would they let it happen if they know where it's coming from?"

"Maybe we're also the enemy of the people responsible for the virus."

Like he'd just seen Heidi do, Spike looked into the shadows again. Why had he talked about the diseased in the first place? Even when he shifted closer to the fire, he felt colder than before. The familiar tightening of his lungs, his pulse quickened.

Heidi stood up first. "I'll be glad when this national service is over and forgotten about. I'm going to bed. Sleep is the only way I can make time pass quicker in this hellhole."

As they watched her walk off, Spike could have sworn he saw something again. It looked like movement over to his left. He breathed quicker than before and his palms turned slick. No one else got up as they all watched Heidi vanish into the darkness, walking back the same way Bleach had gone. The longer he left it, the more awkward it would be to follow her. He stood up. "I'm going to bed too. It's been a long week."

If the others looked at Spike, he didn't know because he turned away from them and walked off in the same direction Heidi had gone in. Despite his desire to run—to get back to the safety of their dorms—he kept his pace even and stared straight ahead. He didn't want to catch up with Heidi and he didn't want the others to see how spooked he was. He should never have brought up the conversation in the first place. But he had to do something to stop himself crying in front of them.

CHAPTER 41

"You don't have Bleach to protect you now," Ranger said as he led team Bigfoot past Spike.

Caught off guard, Spike reacted before he'd had a chance to control himself. "What's that supposed to mean?"

While most of his team walked on, Ranger held back, Lance by his side. His usual sneer—a grease stain on his smug face—he said, "Juggernaut set this one up, and he isn't going to leave the diseased out of it to protect you like Bleach did. The rest of us want to get used to them, seeing as they're going to be *everywhere* when we go outside the walls." He then nodded at a dark hole in the ground. "See that tunnel over there?"

Spike looked at it, his pulse already quickening despite him fighting to keep it slow.

"That goes through a pit of diseased. They're down there waiting for you." He cupped his ear. "Can you hear them?"

Even if his throat hadn't tightened—making it hard to get his breaths out let alone his words—Spike probably wouldn't have replied. Instead, he looked away from Magma's son, listening to him and Lance cackle while they walked off to join the rest of their team.

When Spike felt a hand on his back, he jumped, turning around to see Hugh's wonky grin staring back at him. "We'll be okay," he said.

Spike shrugged him off by turning his shoulder. "I'm fine."

Although they'd done the previous two end-of-week tasks in the apprentice's arena, this time they went past it to a patch of grass on the other side. A small obstacle course had been set up, which included the tunnel Ranger had pointed out. Juggernaut—team Bigfoot's leader—showed the cadets what they were facing. "This," he said, pointing to a wooden wall about eight feet tall, "is the first obstacle. All you need to do is get over it. I don't care how, just that you get over it."

None of the cadets spoke as they watched the leanest of all the team leaders walk over to the next obstacle. The man used to be fast, and when he started running, nothing stopped him, hence his name. Cargo netting lay on the ground, pinned down at the edges. He pointed at it. "You then need to crawl under this."

A high platform, similar to the one they had all climbed with ease in the first task. It stood about twenty feet tall. "You need to climb this rope and then you descend via the netting on the other side."

All the while Juggernaut spoke, Spike couldn't help but look at the dark entrance to the tunnel Ranger had talked about. He focused hard to see if he could hear the diseased. Nothing. Maybe there weren't any in there.

"This is the rat run." Juggernaut walked from one end of the tunnel all the way to the other side. "Once you've crawled through here, you go back to the first obstacle and start again."

If he needed to, Spike could simply refuse to go in. When he glanced at Ranger, the boy winked and pointed at the tunnel. Sweat lifted beneath Spike's shirt and he shook to think about what lay in wait for him in the hole. He'd just refuse. That was all he needed to do. There was no shame in it. Many of the cadets had done it already. He could blame it on claustrophobia.

"The idea," Juggernaut said, positioning himself so he stood in front of the cadets again, "is to keep going until the team behind you catches you. You need to get used to being chased. It'll happen a lot over the next few months."

After letting the silence hang, Juggernaut said, "But this is a team event. You'll go outside the wall as a team, so I want you to work as a team now. You all get through or none of you do. I'll stagger your starts, fifteen seconds between each team. The way you take out the team ahead of you is for the last person in your team to touch one of the people in theirs. It's not about being the fastest, it's about being the most cohesive unit."

Although Juggernaut went on to explain more of the rules, Spike didn't hear him, all of his attention on the dark holes at either end of the rat run. The day had a chill in the air, the grey clouds pregnant with the promise of rain. While he watched the holes, the temperature seemed to drop several more degrees.

Spike would fake an injury. Nothing else for it. He could come up with some reason for not being able to do it so he didn't let his team down by refusing to go into the hole. They could do the task without him. Then he looked at Ranger and his smug face, Lance beside him, also looking over. He'd never hear the end of it. It wasn't like Juggernaut would allow it either. Injury or not, the diseased would still kill you outside the walls. Maybe they'd fail before they got to the tunnel anyway. No way could Hugh climb the wooden wall or the rope. No way.

The crack of Juggernaut's hands made Spike jump, which Ranger picked up on. Nudging Lance next to him, they both laughed. "Because it's my task, my team goes first, followed by team Minotaur, who are the next closest in points."

Although Spike tried to fill his lungs, he still couldn't get his breath in. Despite every urge in his body to resist, he followed his team and lined up in front of the wooden wall behind Bigfoot.

Close enough to Ranger for the boy to lean back and say, "Me and Lance tested the tunnel out, didn't we? My tip to you is to pull your arms in. You'll still feel them pawing at you, but as long as you don't give them something to grab onto, you should be fine."

While laughing, Lance nodded. "That's a good tip. I would say close your eyes so you don't have to look at them, but it's darker than the devil's arsehole down there, so it doesn't matter."

Ranger nodded. "The devil's arsehole. I like it, Lance."

Clearly lifted by Ranger's comment, Lance stood slightly taller than he had a second ago. The boy lived for Ranger's approval.

"Look," Hugh said, butting between Spike and the two boys, "why don't you two leave him alone and focus on what you've got to do, yeah?"

Hugh probably thought he was helping, but before any of them could say anything else, Juggernaut shouted, "Go!" While counting down from fifteen, he lined the rest of the teams up one behind the other. So distracted by Ranger, Spike hadn't yet tried to look at Matilda. As always, when he finally did, she acted like he didn't exist.

Team Bigfoot—dressed from head to toe in their brown tracksuits—hit the wooden wall first. They must have had a chance to practice it because Ranger and Lance, the tallest two in the team, gave a boost to the shortest and weakest. Once they'd helped them, they jumped up and dragged themselves over the wooden wall too.

Because of the wall, when team Bigfoot had slipped over the other side, Spike couldn't see them. Now they were gone, he looked at the tunnel again. How would he avoid going through it?

Maybe he imagined it, but as a gust of wind hit him, he could have sworn he smelled the vinegar tang of the rotting diseased.

"Go," Juggernaut shouted.

It took for Hugh to shove Spike in the back to make him move. He ran for the wall to see Max reach it and wait for him. They copied team Bigfoot's strategy, Spike standing opposite Max while they boosted Olga, Hugh, Heidi, and Elizabeth over. "Come on, man," Max said to him before they jumped. "Get your head in the game. You can do this."

Fatigue already dragged on Spike's strength, his adrenaline robbing him of his athleticism, but he managed to catch the top of the wall and drag himself over.

Landing on the solid ground on the other side, Spike saw the rest of his team were already halfway through the cargo netting, and team Bigfoot were getting to the top of the platform at the end of the long rope. He heard Juggernaut shout, "*Go*," at the team behind them.

Even while he scrambled beneath the netting, Spike threw glances in the direction of the tunnel. Hopefully Hugh would hold them up on the climb.

It took for Spike to get to the rope on the next obstacle to see it had knots tied in it. Hugh had already made it halfway up.

"Go," Juggernaut shouted, and Spike saw Hugh quicken his pace. The knots made it simple for him.

The rest of his team on the rope, Spike turned to see team Yeti behind them as Suzi Swing, the last member of their team, dived under the cargo netting. Maybe he should be the one to slip on the rope. They'd catch him if he stalled just a little.

"Spike!"

Spike looked up to see Olga on the platform above. Max and Heidi were still climbing towards her.

"Hurry it up, yeah?"

He couldn't throw this task. He had a team relying on him.

Because they had Heidi in front of them, Spike caught up to Max on the rope and the two of them had to move at her pace.

When Spike reached the top and dragged himself up onto the platform, he watched his team climbing down the netting on the other side and then looked at the tunnel again. Just before he started his descent, Ranger waved up at him and smiled. Another kick of adrenaline accelerated his pulse before he backed himself onto the netting, his entire body shaking.

The net twisted and swayed on his way down. Spike could fall. That would be believable.

At the back of his team still, but off the netting, Spike looked up to see the front runners of Yeti were on the platform at the top of the rope. Hugh led Minotaur into the tunnel.

"Remember," Ranger called at Spike as he emerged from the other side of the rat run, "just get your head down and go quickly. You're a fast boy; I'm sure they won't be able to grab you."

The noises around Spike faded, the deep thud of his pounding pulse taking over. The entrance to the tunnel looked darker than before. He tried to listen for the diseased inside. How many were there? But he couldn't hear anything. He watched Elizabeth, Heidi, Olga, and Max follow Hugh into the tunnel as if it were nothing. They all vanished from sight, consumed by the darkness.

When Spike tried to move forwards, he couldn't. His heart beat at the speed of a hamster's, and every inhale dragged in less air than the last. His hands went to the skull ring on his finger and he twisted it while staring at the hole.

No matter how hard Spike gasped, he couldn't catch his breath. If he went in the tunnel, he'd have a heart attack. While shaking his head, he muttered, "No." His panic reached up and wrapped two strong hands around his throat.

Another look at Ranger showed Spike the red face of the boy as he laughed at him. Then he looked at Matilda. She looked sad.

Deeply sad and disappointed. She'd gambled on him and she'd lost.

Spike fell to his knees and shook his head. "No, I can't do it. I can't do it. I can't do it." Unable to catch his breath, stars flashed in his vision. He looked around for someone to help. Anyone. All the cadets stared at him like he was contagious.

Bleach ran over and dragged Spike to his feet. He put a protective arm around him and led him out of there.

Just before they rounded the corner out of sight, Spike looked back at the others one last time. He saw Ranger and Lance, both puce with laughter. Just before he vanished, Magma's son took one final shot at him when he said, "There wasn't any diseased in there, you fool. It's all in your head!"

Spike looked up at Bleach. "Is that true?"

Although Bleach didn't reply, he didn't need to. Instead, he released a hard sigh and focused on where they were heading.

CHAPTER 42

A bowl of vegetables in watery gravy in front of him, Spike lifted another spoonful of it into his mouth. He had no appetite, but if he didn't eat, one of the team leaders would say something. He'd also grown sick of the flavour. It had tasted novel on day one, but now they were three weeks into training with no change in their diet, he didn't know how much more of it he could eat. The once appetising smell now reminded him of feet, and the broth tasted like salt water. It didn't help that he had a nauseating rock in his stomach. Having panicked in front of everyone had ruined him. How could he be taken seriously as a contender to be the next apprentice? When he looked up, he saw at least half the room watching him like they'd done since he'd sat down.

When Bleach had taken Spike back to their dorms after his second panic, Spike had stated his intention to skip dinner, but Bleach wouldn't let him. Whether he faced the others at dinner or breakfast or the next gym session, he'd have to face them. Avoiding the dining hall would only delay the inevitable and make it an even bigger deal when he finally turned up. Besides, some of them would have panic attacks at some point during training. Some of them probably already had. Like Spike, they needed to know that although it might feel like death, it wouldn't kill you. When he'd said panicking while being chased by the diseased would, Bleach had chosen not to respond.

Spike looked up again, the attention of many of the cadets still on him save for the one that mattered most. Ranger sat close to Matilda like he always did, and he talked at her like he always did. Not for the first time, Spike imagined himself going over there and smashing Ranger's head against the table in front of him. He'd slam his face so many times against the wooden surface it would turn his nose to mush.

For the past few years Spike had wanted nothing but the chance to go for national service. Now he wanted to be anywhere but. Things were so much easier before. He and Matilda would run through the city without a care. They'd stay up late, talk until the sun rose, look into each other's eyes, and he'd dream of what their future looked like. Now she wouldn't even look at him. How could he tell her how sorry he was? How he shouldn't have made her gamble her freedom on him. Tears itched his eyes. He should have climbed the wall with her that night.

Then she looked at him and he gasped. She held him in her brown-eyed gaze. If she felt something at that moment, he couldn't read it, but at least she showed him she knew he still existed. A blink of her long eyelashes, it looked like the slightest glaze of sadness magnified her eyes, but he couldn't be sure. He looked at her hair. The hummingbird clip had gone. He looked back at her face again, but she'd already shifted her focus.

When Hugh shoved his bony elbow into his ribs, Spike tutted and spun around. "*What?*" Faced with Hugh's soft features, some of the tension left him. "Sorry," he said, glancing at the rest of his team and their slack shock. "That was uncalled for. What's up?"

Although slightly redder than before, Hugh said, "We just want you to know that you haven't let us down. We understand what happened today, and you should know we're here for you, standing shoulder to shoulder with you."

"I've nearly had a panic attack every morning I've been here," Elizabeth said.

"Me too," Hugh said.

Spike rubbed his sore eyes, his movement clumsy as his hands shook. "Thank you. And I'm sorry I've been so off tonight. I'm sorry we're not getting a lie-in tomorrow. I …" Before he could say anything else, he saw Matilda in the corner of his eye as she stood up from her seat. She appeared to be heading towards the toilets. "I … uh, I need the toilet."

Spike got to his feet, watching Matilda leave the room as he moved through the tables after her.

To get to the bathroom, Spike had to pass team Bigfoot. Ranger sat—like he always did—at the centre of his table, close to the space Matilda had now vacated. Lance sat so close to him, he was damn near perched on his lap. Spike noticed the glint in Ranger's eye and saw it coming from a mile off. So when he got close to Ranger and the boy shoved his foot out at the last minute, he simply stepped over it and hissed the word *prick* as he passed him.

Once through the door leading to the toilets, Spike saw Matilda heading for the girls' cubicle. He broke into a jog to catch up with her and grabbed her shoulder, pulling her around to face him.

After she'd glanced back down the corridor behind him, she said, "What are you doing, Spike? You know the teams aren't supposed to mix."

"It's been so hard to sit in the same room with you every day and not talk to you."

Matilda looked from one of his eyes to the next and her own glazed with tears.

"Talk to me, Tilly."

"What do you want me to say?"

"Tell me why you're behaving like I don't exist."

For a second, she just stared at him. For a second, she looked like she wouldn't reply. "You want to know? Really?"

"I can't feel any worse than I already do."

"At first, I ignored you because I could see Ranger winding you up through me. I've ignored him too. I wanted you to stay focused on the task at hand. I knew what lay in front of us wouldn't be easy. I knew you needed to keep your head. Also, we were told we couldn't have relationships in here. I didn't want to push that. And then …"

"And then?"

"I saw how you reacted to the diseased. I've witnessed your suffering and it hurts too much. Not only is this place breaking you, but it's taking away all my hope of a better future. I had some before we came in here."

"I'm sorry. I'll get better."

"You've nothing to be sorry about. I don't blame you. I blame myself. Artan and I had freedom in front of us the night before we came here, and against my better judgement I decided to give this a try. I should have taken responsibility for Artan's and my safety. To look at you reminds me I didn't. That my brother's with that man, and will be for the next six months, all for nothing."

"It's not for nothing, Tilly. Please, you've got to tr—"

"Don't, Spike! I have to trust myself and my instincts. Have you seen how you react to the diseased?" Her eyes pregnant with tears, she looked disgusted to take him in. "When was the last time we had a protector that has panic attacks when they see one of those things?"

Although Spike opened his mouth to reply, Matilda cut him

off. "I'm not angry with you, I'm angry with myself. I made a bad choice. I should have known better."

"Why don't *you* try to be the next apprentice?"

"Haven't you listened to anything I've said? I *have* to be here for these next six months. Every night I pray for Artan's safety. If I tried to be an apprentice, I'd have to leave him alone with that man for even longer. And what do you think it would do to Dad to see me trying to be the next apprentice? What do you think it would do to him if I got it? I can't put Artan in that kind of danger."

"We could make sure he's—"

"I need to make the choices that are the best for me and Artan. I need to trust myself and my own judgement. I'm not seeking counsel on it."

"But—"

"Stop, Spike. Just stop."

As Spike looked at his love, he drew a deep and stuttered breath. "What does this mean for us?"

No change in her expression, tears now ran from Matilda's eyes. "We were kids before we came in here, Spike. We dared to dream. Dreams don't come true in Edin. Ask my dad."

When a booming laugh bounced off the walls, Spike spun around to see Ranger in the corridor, Lance a step behind him. "Well, well, wasn't that a beautiful performance? I never realised you were so in *love*, William." He winked at Matilda and grinned. "All right, sweetheart?"

Spike balled his fists. "What do you want?"

While covering his chest by laying the palm of one hand against it, Ranger stepped back a pace. "My goodness, you're a feisty one, aren't you? I just wanted to use the toilet. I wasn't expecting to walk in on *this*. But now I have, I just wanted to say how sweet you two look together. You make a nice couple. That's okay, isn't it?"

When Spike looked at Matilda, she shook her head at him. But what did it matter what she wanted anymore? After national service he'd probably never see her again.

"Anyway, enjoy the rest of your evening." Ranger turned to walk off, pausing before he'd shown them his back. "Oh, and I wanted to warn you about public displays of affection. If the team leaders found out about you two, they'd crush this relationship like a bug beneath a boot heel."

A rush of blood, Spike moved forward, his shoulders squared. "It's not a relationship, you idiot."

Ranger shrugged. "I'm just going by what I saw. Whatever you guys do is your own business. It's just … it would be an awful shame for the leaders to find out about it, don't you think?"

"I know something else that would be an awful shame for everyone to find out about," Spike said.

Although Ranger turned back around to hear it, Matilda said, "Don't, Spike. That's not your story to tell."

A slight frown, Ranger looked from Spike to Matilda. "I must say, you have me quite intrigued."

When neither Spike nor Matilda replied, Ranger said, "You do know, Matilda, that when all of this is over, I can come and see you in the ceramics district. I can go wherever I want in the city because I'm the son of a protector. So whether I win the apprenticeship or not, I'll be available. I just wanted to put that out there. I'm not sure William will make it to the trials with his *condition*."

Spike pushed off from his back foot, propelling himself forward as he slammed a hard punch into Ranger's nose. His fist sank with a crunch, driving both him and Lance back several paces.

While Ranger appeared to be trying to find his bearings, Spike threw another punch, Ranger's head snapping to the side from the impact.

Ranger rallied and yelled while reaching out and grabbing

Spike by the shirt. He slammed his back against the wall, driving the air from Spike's lungs. Wild-eyed, he sprayed Spike with spittle as he shouted, "I'm Ranger Hopkins." He smashed his forehead against Spike's, the collision sending a flash through Spike's vision and giving him a tinnitus ring.

Despite the wobble in his legs, Spike remained upright. He shoved Ranger back, driving him through the boys' bathroom door, knocking it clean off its hinges to the sound of tearing wood. His teeth clenched and fists balled, Spike fell on top of Ranger and rained punches down on the protector's son. Blow after blow, he'd destroy that cocksure grin. He'd shatter his cheekbones. He'd—

A strong grip wrapped around the back of Spike's collar and dragged him off Ranger. He twisted and turned to be free of it, but the person behind him slipped him into a headlock he couldn't get out of. It took for the man to speak before he recognised Bleach's voice. "Stop, Spike. Stop now."

~

A FEW MINUTES LATER, SPIKE AND RANGER WERE STANDING NEXT to one another on the stage in the dining hall. All of the cadets were still there. The coppery taste of blood in his mouth, Spike looked at Ranger to see his red and swollen face, his shirt sodden from where he'd split his nose. As before, when Spike looked at Matilda, she refused to look back at him. If he hadn't thrown their relationship away before then, he definitely had now.

The beat of Sarge's limp moved across the front of the stage and the two boys while he addressed the room. "I won't tolerate fighting. It's hard enough outside those walls without you tearing each other apart inside them. Besides, it's a fat lot of good being able to fight each other when you can't fight them, wouldn't you say, William?"

Spike didn't reply.

"I'm taking the lie-in away from team Bigfoot and giving it to Dragon."

"But—"

Sarge cut Ranger off, and what he said next made Spike's blood run cold. "That's not the half of it. As punishment for your behaviour, you're both going to be spending a night in the hole."

CHAPTER 43

Maybe the weather turning had affected Spike more than usual, or maybe the sight in front of him made him cold to his bones. Whatever the reason, he shivered, his stomach tight as he was led towards the large fence sectioning off the hole from the rest of the national service area.

Juggernaut on one side, Ore on the other, they each held one of Spike's arms in a tight grip as they marched forward. Ranger also due the same fate, Bleach and Fright ushered him towards the fence in front of them. When they'd first mentioned the hole, Spike wondered if it had been an empty threat. A bit like the bogeyman would come to get kids who didn't behave. There seemed to be nothing empty about his current predicament.

The clouds were grey and heavy with the threat of rain. They pushed down on Spike, their oppressive weight increasing with every step forward.

When they stopped in front of the fence, Spike watched Juggernaut—who left him with Ore—walk over to the gate and free the large bolt on it with a sharp *crack.* As Juggernaut opened it, Spike tried to see inside, but from his current vantage point, he still couldn't ascertain what his punishment would be.

Bleach and Fright led Ranger through the doorway first. Following on their heels, Juggernaut and Ore took Spike through after him.

On the other side, Spike saw four more fenced-off sections. Much smaller than the one at the front, each one had a gate in it. Each gate had a long metal pin hanging from its frame so they could be locked from the outside. From what he could see, none of the smaller sections had roofs. It looked like four open-air prisons. He could cope with that. In fact, he'd take that punishment all day long and laugh in their faces the next time they tried to use it as a deterrent.

Like they'd done on the way in, Ore kept a hold of Spike while Juggernaut now closed the main gate behind them.

Bleach and Fright led Ranger off to the right. When Juggernaut had finished with the gate, he and Ore led Spike left.

The farthest left of the four gates, it opened more easily than the main one had, swinging into the cell beyond when Ore raised one of her heavy boots and kicked it. As they led Spike through, he got a closer look at the large metal pin hanging from the wall. At least a foot long and an inch thick, when it went through the metal hoop on the outside, the door would be nowhere near as compliant in granting someone access or escape.

The second he stepped through the doorway, Spike's stomach sank. A sparse ground with patchy tufts of grass, it had a hole in the centre of it. Too dark to tell how far it dropped, but it looked deep. A large beam ran above his head from one side of the cell to the other. It had a rope hanging from it. A thick rope with a chunky knot tied into it every few feet. It looked much like the rope they'd used on Juggernaut's last challenge. Easy enough to climb up and down. Access to the hole wasn't the thing they wanted to make hard here.

Although Spike had kept quiet until that point, he shook his head. "You're joking, right? The hole isn't an actual *hole*, is it?"

But neither Juggernaut nor Ore replied. Instead, Juggernaut held him while Ore grabbed the rope, which lay gathered on the ground like a large snake. She dropped it into the hole and Spike watched it unravel. It had been tied to the beam to allow it to hang down the centre of the pit like a plumb line.

Spike jumped when he heard Ranger scream from the cell he'd been taken to. "*No!* I'm not going in there."

Until that moment, Spike had managed to contain himself, but a familiar feeling came over him that he had no control over. Rising up his body, it snapped his stomach tense. His lungs restricted and his throat dried. Although he tugged on his collar with his spare hand, it did nothing to ease the constrictor's grip tightening around him.

"Now," Ore said while peering into the hole, her hands on her hips, "you have two ways down. The first one is you climb by yourself. The second is we throw you down there. Whatever happens, you're going in the hole. You get to decide how you do it."

Despite his body feeling like it was shutting down on him, Spike wouldn't give them the satisfaction of hearing him protest. They wouldn't change their minds, so there seemed little point. Besides, he had to learn to hold onto his panic if he was going to feel it so frequently. After shaking Juggernaut's grip off, he walked to the rope and grabbed it, his hands sore from punching Ranger in the dining hall. So thick, he needed to hold the rope with both hands. He peered into the darkness. Despite the daylight above, he couldn't see how far down it went.

"Climb!" Ore said to him.

Spike glared at the woman, who stuck her chin out and pulled her shoulders back. She looked like she'd be glad of the opportunity to throw him down there. He shook his head at her before climbing onto the rope.

On the way down, Spike kept his back to the two team leaders.

By the time his face got level with the ground, Spike heard Ranger again. "No, I'm not going in there. I want my dad. He needs to hear what you're trying to do to me."

Spike's arms and legs shook, struggling to support his weight as he continued his descent. When his head sank below ground level, the stench hit him. A vinegar reek of rot. He halted his climb and gripped tighter than before.

Ore shook the rope as she leaned over the hole. It didn't matter that he clung on, she could shake him free if she wanted to. "Don't stop now, William. One way or another, you're going down there. You'd be sensible to do it on your own terms. It'll hurt much less."

A deep and stuttered inhale, Spike nodded to himself to keep moving and continued to drop down into the hole.

No more than a ten-foot climb to the bottom, the second Spike stepped onto solid ground and let go of the rope, Ore whipped it away, dragging it back up to her. "Have a good time," she called down, her voice echoing in the pit. "I've heard the nights are long in the hole. It should give you plenty of time to think about your attitude."

Again, Spike didn't reply. Now he'd climbed down into the pit, the rotten vinegar tang had given way to the reek of damp earth. If he could see any farther than the beam of light surrounding him, he surely would see the walls alive with bugs. Worms, millipedes, beetles … A slow writhe twisted through his body to imagine them crawling on his skin. But as grim as it was, he'd take a night with insects over seeing any more diseased.

The gate slammed above Spike, making him jump. He looked up at the grey sky and listened to metal scraping metal as they secured the pin. Too deep in the ground to hear any more of Ranger's protests, he focused on his breaths. If they were going to keep him there for the night, he had to stand at ease before his body turned into one large spasming cramp.

Spike heard something. He fought against the shake now running through him and peered into the darkness, the weak glow from above still bright enough to make it impossible to see his much darker surroundings. He stepped forward a pace.

It sounded like movement.

As his eyes adjusted, he saw a caged wall no more than four feet from where he stood. He squinted to look at it. Why did they have a cage down there? Maybe it stopped the hole from caving in.

Then he heard footsteps. The slathering pant of a diseased. The slam of it crashing into the caged wall with a snarling hiss. Its pallid and wrinkled face twisted with fury. Its mouth opened wide and it shrieked at him as it reached through the bars.

Spike stumbled backwards and fell.

The cold damp ground soaked into his trousers as Spike sat there and stared at the horrific twist to the thing's features. It bit at the bars, yellow teeth still in its foetid mouth. It pushed its entire body up against them. The press of the metal against its face looked painful, but it seemed hell-bent on getting any extra reach it could.

It took for hands to touch Spike's back before he screamed. Another snarling hiss behind him. He got to his feet and jumped away from the beast. A caged wall on his right. More of the creatures reached through. The swell of rage rose in volume.

The noises of the diseased swirled around Spike, coming at him from every angle. It scrambled his thoughts as he spun around, every part of the caged wall showing another pair of arms desperate to get to him. His chest tight, stars in his eyes from his lack of breath, the sounds closed in. The air curdled with the stench of vinegar. The squirming hands wriggled on the end of pasty and atrophied limbs.

Like in their last training session, Spike couldn't contain himself. As his breaths grew quicker and shallower, his heart ached. He fell to the ground, but the diseased dropped down with him. Their hands reached for him, the long nails on the ends of their fingers clawing at anywhere his skin was exposed, his arms, his face … one even reached up his trouser leg, a deeper violation than any before it.

Barely able to move, Spike's lap turned warm with his own piss before he scrambled to the middle of the room into the beam of light cast from the stormy sky. He curled into a ball and hugged his knees to his chest, trembling like the sheep he'd seen in the gym.

Although utterly alone, if he had to die afraid, better he did it in the hole without an audience. He'd been a coward since he'd started national service. He deserved nothing less than to perish in the darkness. Cold, wet, and covered in his own piss.

CHAPTER 44

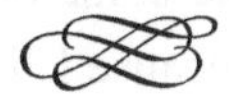

The heavy and knotted rope fell next to Spike, dead straight like when he'd climbed down it. Although he saw the light change above him from where someone peered into the hole, he didn't look up. Instead, he did what he'd done for the past few hours: he stood in the spotlight cast by the moon above, and he stared straight into the face of one of the diseased reaching out to get him. Unrelenting in its desire, the beast snapped, snarled, and hissed with the same ferocity as it had for the whole time he'd been down there.

Where Spike had seen something to be scared of, he now saw something to pity. A pathetic once-human, the man in front of him looked so decrepit, he wondered how he remained on his weak legs. But having been knocked to the ground by one and felt their strength, he wouldn't be deceived by their appearance again.

The cold in the damp hole had found a way into Spike's bones and he shivered where he stood. The wet patch on his lap remained sodden, turning as chilly as his surroundings as it bit into the front of his thighs. It served as a stinging reminder of his lowest moment. He'd pissed himself in fear of being attacked by something utterly incapable of getting to him.

"William." It sounded like Bleach's voice. "Come on, it's time to come out."

Spike continued to look at the twisted and bitter face in front of him. He continued to stare into its crimson hatred, and he continued to give it back with interest.

"William! Don't make me come down there and lift you out. It'll just cause more drama because I'll need to call for help."

Despite wanting to make it as difficult for his team leader as possible, Spike climbed the rope. The knots were as easy to scale getting out of the hole as they had been going in. When Spike got to the top, Bleach held a hand down towards him to give him assistance.

Instead of taking it, Spike pulled himself out of the hole, his eyes taking a few seconds to adjust to the bright moonlight above.

"Are you okay?" Bleach asked.

Spike stared at the door out of there, his back to Bleach, who dragged the rope from the hole.

"It was for your own good. We can't let cadets get away with fighting during national service. It's life or death outside those walls. The last thing we need is two hotheads trying to knock seven shades out of one another. You understand, right?"

A few seconds of awkward silence passed before Bleach led the way out from the small cell and then through the main exit.

The long dewy grass turned the bottom of Spike's trousers as cold and damp as his lap. The slight breeze hit him as he walked into it. The dorms looked so small now. So constricting. How could he spend another five months there? And he'd have to sleep one room away from the arsehole next to him.

Maybe Bleach saw the futility of trying to talk to Spike, because on the walk back he didn't attempt it again. Maybe he knew Spike had half a mind to swing for him. Broadsword or not, he'd get one good punch in before Bleach realised he'd have to fight back.

"Good night," Bleach said as they entered the dorm, the rich lavender scent quite a departure from the muddy vinegar reek of the hole. He walked to his bedroom.

Spike watched him move away before he looked at the entrance to his room, the sounds of Hugh and Max asleep inside.

The moonlight through the gap in their curtains gave Spike a clear enough view. Despite how small the hole had been, his bedroom felt tiny, like the walls were closing in. Maybe he saw the weeks of monotony ahead. Fighting to win an apprenticeship he had no chance of winning. Fighting for a girl who'd already given up on him. It all seemed like such a waste of time now.

Peeling the cold bite of his trousers away from his lap offered him some relief. A chilly nip in the air, he leaned down to pick up his pyjamas. They lay next to tomorrow's training gear. Could he really do another five months of this? Could he go home to the agricultural district knowing he'd ruined his chance to be with Matilda because he didn't have the stones to face the diseased?

Instead of going for his pyjamas, Spike picked up tomorrow's clothes and dressed in them. When done, he looked around the room at his two sleeping teammates. Other than the ring on his finger, he had nothing else he needed to take with him. In the quietest voice so as not to wake them, he spoke in a croaky tone. "Good luck, boys. You'll be safer without me."

Because he'd not lived in the dorm long and, until now, hadn't had a need to sneak out, Spike didn't know which floorboards creaked and which ones didn't. As a result, he walked out of the room on tiptoes, on edge with every step as he waited for a yawning alarm to give him away.

The door to Bleach's room hung open. Before looking in, Spike listened and heard the heavy breathing of sleep inside. That hadn't taken long.

Tiptoeing like before, Spike snuck across the front of Bleach's room and out into the night. There had to be a corner of the wall like the one he, Matilda, and Artan should have used to climb out a few weeks previously. How different things would be now if he'd done that. Although, he probably would have panicked on day one and got them all killed.

When a hard hand clamped on Spike's shoulder, he yelled out and spun around. Bleach stood behind him. But he didn't say anything to his team leader. He'd rather do more time in the hole than grovel for the man's forgiveness.

"Walk with me," Bleach said.

At first, Spike didn't move, watching the man's broad back as he strode away from him. When Bleach stopped and turned around, Spike shook his head, but followed this time.

Together, they walked away from the dorms in the direction of the dining hall. Neither spoke for about a minute before Spike finally gave in. "This place has been hell."

"You were expecting better?"

"Yeah. You lot are nothing but bullies."

"By *you lot* I assume you're referring to the team leaders and trainers?"

"Who else?"

"You know how many cadets we lose every year? How many cadets I've personally lost under my leadership?"

Spike stared at the wall with the large gates in and kept at Bleach's pace.

"If we went easy on you, you'd get slaughtered the *second* you stepped outside."

"Sounds like we already do."

Bleach heaved a weary sigh, his eyes pinching at the sides. "*More* slaughtered."

"So you don't want to make it too easy, but when it comes to your task, you choose not to put diseased in it like the one before?"

"You weren't ready for them."

"So you *did* do it to protect me?"

"I figured you needed a bit more time before you saw them again."

"You've heard how Ranger's gone for me about that. Talking to me like I needed the help."

Bleach let Spike's rage hang unchallenged.

"Matilda and I are in love."

"It happens a lot."

"That doesn't mean it isn't real."

"I never said that. We get a lot of cadets who have fallen in love with someone from another district. Although, I'm impressed that we haven't had to pull you two apart from one another. We usually have to watch out for that. We don't need to be sending pregnant girls home to their parents."

"Matilda's ignoring me. She could see Ranger winding me up and thought it would be better to step back while I dealt with it."

"At some point," Bleach said, "you need to realise Ranger's going to be a dick no matter what you do. The sooner you learn to ignore him, the easier your life will be." Before Spike could tell him he wasn't staying, Bleach said, "Look, it's not surprising you had a panic attack. You're coming into a stressful environment where survival isn't enough for you. You want to be the next protector, you *need* to be the next protector, and you have Magma's son standing in the way of that."

"And so many of the other cadets are better than me."

"That's a lot of pressure. But I believe in you."

Spike snorted a laugh.

"Look at what you're trying to do now."

"Run away?"

"Go out there. You're ready to face the diseased."

"I'm not afraid anymore."

"There's a reason for that."

"Are you trying to take credit for throwing me in the hole? What? You want me to thank you or something?"

A shake of his head, Bleach said, "Being a protector isn't about being fearless. We all get scared, and often those of us who shout the loudest are the most frightened. Being a protector also isn't about feeling nothing when you look at those things."

A flash of the creature in the hole came back to him. "Well, what is it, then?"

"It's about standing tall and letting yourself feel it. It's about having that panic attack and seeing there's calm on the other side. About knowing what you can take and experience and still remain standing."

Although Spike opened his mouth to reply, Bleach cut him off.

"Also, you need to measure your progress against yourself. If you're better today than you were yesterday, that's progress. I think you'll be surprised by how far you've already come. You arrived here ignorant."

"*You're* ignorant."

"But you're stronger now than you've ever been. Celebrate that and be kind to yourself. You'll get to where you need to be if you allow the process to happen."

They'd come to a halt halfway between their dorm and the dining hall.

"Come on," Bleach said. "Come back and get some sleep. Tomorrow's a new day and you have several months to get to where you need to be. You're ready to go outside those walls, so don't write anything off just yet. Not even Matilda."

"What do you know about her?"

"Not a lot, but I've seen how she looks at you when you're not watching."

Bleach turned around and walked back towards the dorm. For a second, Spike remained rooted to the spot and watched. When he saw the man had nothing more to say, he shook his head and ran after him.

CHAPTER 45

The sounds outside Spike's dorm woke him with a gasp. He sat bolt upright, his heart racing as he heard more screams. The cold bite in the air nipped through his thin pyjamas where his covers had fallen away. He scanned the room, his head still thick from sleep. It felt like only an hour or two had passed since his talk with Bleach outside. Still night-time, the moonlight shone through the gap in the curtains, penetrating the darkness with a bar of illumination.

Spike's body ached from fighting with Ranger, yet he still swung his legs from the bed before slipping down and landing on his bare feet with a slap where skin met floorboard.

Both Hugh's and Max's beds were empty. Why hadn't someone woken him? Spike ran out into the hallway to see several of the weapons had already been taken. At the sound of more cries, he picked up a broadsword, wrapping his grip around the cold metal handle.

When Olga burst from her room, Spike said, "What's happening?"

Wide eyes, she spoke with breathy panic. "I just looked out of the window. There are diseased outside!"

As the reality of her comments sank in, a high-pitched scream sent a chill down Spike's spine. Not that he didn't believe Olga, but the tormented shriek rammed home the reality of what she'd said. He charged outside.

The moon gave a silver highlight to the chaos before him. The shrill cry of the diseased filled the night as the cadets fought the monsters. Although every silhouette out there looked human, the twitching and erratic movements marked foe from friend. The wet squelches of swords hacked at flesh. Both cadets and the diseased roared with the intensity of the battle.

The same reaction he'd had every other time, Spike felt the paralysis of fear worm up through his body. Despite his experience in the hole, tension gripped his stomach. The tautness moved to his lungs, and his heart surged like it would burst. He gripped his sword's handle tighter with his sweating hands, but he still didn't move.

Then he saw her. Matilda. She stared back at him. There were no diseased around her. It gave her a moment to witness his panic. Again.

Before Spike could do anything, he heard Hugh call for help.

Three diseased surrounded the small mole of a boy. Isolated from everyone else, Spike watched him spin on the spot, trying not to turn his back on any of them. If he'd picked up a sword on his way out, he didn't have it with him now.

Another look at Matilda, he saw she continued to stare back.

Spike pushed through his fear and charged over to his friend. He brought his sword up and took the head clean off one of the diseased. They might have been deceptively strong hand to hand, but they had no defence against cold hard steel.

Hugh dropped to the ground and pulled his arms over his head. For the briefest of moments, Spike thought about himself doing that when he'd first entered the hole. Gritted teeth, he roared through them and shoved his sword into the stomach of the next diseased. It folded and fell. A swing at the third one's neck, Spike cut into it. Although he didn't decapitate the thing, it still went down.

Before Spike could check on Hugh, something crashed into his side. It sent him flying and he dropped his sword. The creature landed on top of him, winding him with its weight.

Too dark to see the creature's face, Spike gasped for breath as he reached up and grabbed its throat. A tight clench of his jaw, he squeezed with all he had, his hands still sore from punching Ranger.

The diseased made a gargling noise and its warm saliva ran over Spike's tight grip. The thing took its hands from Spike and clawed at its own throat as if seeking a release of the pressure.

After a few seconds of struggle, Spike yelled and threw the creature off him. He jumped to his feet while it gasped on the ground. His broadsword next to him, he picked it up and drove it —tip first—into the diseased's face.

While panting, his weapon stuck in the soft ground, Spike looked around the battlefield. The fighting appeared to have stopped. The diseased were done.

An adrenaline-fuelled shake running through him, Spike fought for breath while watching Max walk his way. Hugh scrambled to his feet.

Max spoke first. "You did it."

Then Hugh. "Thank you."

Spike nodded at both of them. The panic had vanished when he saw his friend in trouble. In that moment it didn't matter how he felt, just that Hugh survived.

Another scream tore across the battlefield and Spike looked to see Ranger. He twisted and turned in Juggernaut's tight grip, Lance following behind him as they headed back to their dorms. He shouted, "No more. No more. No more."

Before any of the boys spoke, the glow of a torch grabbed their attention.

Bleach—a flaming stick in his hand—walked over. "Well done, boys."

Where Max and Hugh looked at their team leader, Spike looked down at the creature he'd pinned to the ground. Now better lit, he stared at its face, its mouth spread wide. "It doesn't have any teeth."

Bleach paused for a second before nodding. "You're right. But you didn't know that at the time."

"How could we?" Hugh said.

"Exactly. It's what we wanted to happen. In less than a week you're going to be outside those walls. You need to know how to fight the diseased. We've been working on desensitising you, but nothing will test you like fighting the things. It was important you believed the threat to be real." He looked straight at Spike when he said, "You needed to prove to yourselves that you can do it."

Hugh again: "I'm not sure I did."

"Well, you now know you need to stick close to William. From what I just saw, he's capable of doing the fighting for both of you. And seeing as you need to get yourself more comfortable around the diseased, you're part of the cleanup crew. William and Max, you can go back to bed."

Judging by Hugh's pale complexion, Bleach's words had offered him zero comfort. It made Spike feel awful in contrast because they were exactly what he needed to hear.

CHAPTER 46

Very little got in the way of Spike having a good night's sleep. He could count his restless nights on one hand. The more stressed he felt, the better he slept. Anxiety made him tired, so with training over and them going outside the walls tomorrow, he should have slept like the dead. Instead, he'd suddenly snapped awake in the darkness of his room. Although he blinked, it did little to give him a clear view of his surroundings. Then he felt the reason for the disruption. The bed shook and he heard a wet sniff beneath him. Hugh had been growing ever more frantic as they got close to the end of the month. They all had. But what did he expect? That the guards would decide the wall didn't matter as much as the precious little cadets' well-being? They had to deal with it whether they liked it or not. Plenty died while building the wall; they were now responsible for whether they became one of the expired.

When Hugh's cries turned into whimpers, Spike shook his head. If he ignored him, maybe he'd go back to sleep. He didn't need to go outside the walls tired.

But Hugh's sobbing grew louder. After tutting, Spike leaned

out of his bed, his head spinning to look down on his friend in the bunk below.

The snivelling stopped with Hugh drawing a sharp intake of breath and holding it. He'd been rumbled.

"Are you okay?" Although Spike tried to keep his voice low, he heard Max stirring across the room from them.

Hugh's mewling reply told him everything he needed to know. "I'm okay."

Slipping out of bed, flinching when his bare feet hit the cold floor, Spike pulled his trousers and T-shirt on. "Come on. Let's go outside."

Another wet sniff, the hunched silhouette of Hugh stood up, put his clothes on too, and followed Spike out of the room.

JUST BEFORE HE STEPPED OUT INTO THE CORRIDOR, SPIKE TURNED to Hugh and pressed his finger to his lips. When he got the nod from his squat friend, he moved off again.

Maybe Spike made some noise with his steps, but if he did, he couldn't tell because of Hugh's slapping gait behind him. The flat-footed boy sounded like he walked with flippers. Even his breathing served as an alarm call for any light sleepers in the dorm. Hopefully Bleach didn't wake up easily.

About half the distance travelled towards the door, Spike stopped and turned to his friend again. They'd passed Bleach's room, but they still needed to be quiet. This time he pressed a more forceful finger across his lips and scowled at him. Shut the hell up! When Hugh nodded, he rolled his eyes and took off again, quicker than before. If he couldn't silence the boy, at least he could get them out of there ASAP.

Hugh followed, louder than ever.

As they passed the girls' dorm, Spike glanced in to see three still forms in the two bunk beds.

Just a few metres until they got to the dorm's exit, Spike stopped and waited for Hugh to catch up. When he looked back, he saw the boy standing still, staring into the girls' room.

Spike flapped his arms to get Hugh's attention. Bloody pervert, what was he playing at?

When Hugh finally looked over, his face sank. Spike pointed hard at the floor next to him and hissed, "Come here!"

A sharp nod, Hugh then flapped over to Spike's side.

"Why don't you just tell Elizabeth you like her?" Before Hugh responded, Spike pushed his finger to his lips again and shook his head. "Actually, don't answer that. Come on, we've got to be quiet. Bleach'll kill us if he knows we're trying to get out."

Hugh opened his mouth to reply again, but Spike silenced him with yet another finger pressed to his lips. What part of 'shut the hell up' did Hugh not understand?

Just about to lead the way out into the night, Spike stepped aside and motioned for Hugh to go first. After watching him out, he checked back one final time, holding his breath to listen for any activity. It sounded like they'd done it. He followed his friend into the darkness.

THE CHILLY NIGHT LIFTED GOOSEFLESH ON SPIKE'S SKIN AND HE hugged himself for warmth. He should have worn more than a T-shirt, but there seemed little point in going back now. Hugh waited for him to pass him again and lead the way.

The moon shone as a semicircle in the cloudless sky, putting a silver highlight on all the buildings and the open expanse of grass. A low-lying mist hung in the air.

Vulnerable in the open field, Spike led them at a jog to the back of the dining hall. Not only should he have worn a sweatshirt, but shoes would have been good too, the dewy grass turning the space between his toes cold and slick.

When they were both in the deep shadow of the large wooden building, Spike checked back the way they'd come from. It still looked clear. Mist formed on his words when he said, "So, what's going on, mate?"

Tears returned to Hugh's eyes and he shook as he said, "I dunno, I just, I dunno, I never thought this moment would come. I thought they'd realise their error and get me back in the labs, but that's not going to happen."

Spike shook his head. "No, it's not."

When Hugh looked down at his clasped hands, Spike saw how violently they shook. Hugh said, "We're going outside *tomorrow!*"

From their current spot, Spike could see the tall wall with the high wooden gates in it. While looking at it, he said, "But we've trained for it. We're ready to go."

The muscles in Hugh's face buckled. "*You're* ready to go. I was in the bottom five percent in *every* physical we did."

"I hardly did much better!"

Hugh raised an eyebrow at Spike.

"Okay, but my point is I expected to smash it when I came here, and I didn't. Did you see how I dealt with the diseased for most of training? It was only the hole that sorted me out."

"But you're sorted out now."

"And you will be too."

"By tomorrow?"

"We'll be fine."

"How many cadets go out to work on the wall thinking that? Do you know how many of us will die over the next five months?"

"I'm not psychic."

"You don't need to be. You just need to look at the evidence. Fifty percent! I'm not in the top fifty percent of this group."

"You're going to be with *us*. Bleach is a good team leader. Max and Olga are strong. We have a good chance. Besides, if you have a negative attitude, of course you're going to die. You're going to put your teammates at risk too. You need to snap out of it, if not for yourself, then for us."

"Did you know Elizabeth's cousin was a cadet a few years back?"

"No, she only talked about her siblings."

"He survived. He broke the rules and told her what it was like. Apparently he wakes up screaming most nights. He tries to kill himself every few months. He told her she'd be better taking her chances outside the city than going in national service."

It took Spike back to that night in the field with Matilda and Artan. They should have escaped when they had the chance. "But she hasn't done that, has she? She's made her choice and she has to deal with it."

Hugh backed off in the face of Spike's aggression.

"Look," Spike said.

"No, it's fine. You're right; there's no point in dwelling on something we can't change. Um, Spike, there's another reason I wanted you to come outside tonight."

When a silhouette appeared around the corner, Spike moved back a step. "What's going on, Hugh?"

CHAPTER 47

"She asked me to get you out here."

It took that moment for Spike to see his overtiredness had made him paranoid. "*She?*"

When Matilda stepped into the moonlight, the silver glow revealing the hummingbird in her hair, he said, "Tilly?"

"Were you expecting someone else?"

"I wasn't expecting anyone. Even less so you."

Before Matilda could reply, Hugh said, "I'm going back to bed." A nod at Spike. "Thank you for the talk. I'm not sure I feel any better, but thank you anyway. I'm glad I've got you around me."

Spike watched Hugh walk away. When he'd gone from sight, he shrugged at Matilda. "Well?"

"Look, I'm sorry, Spike."

She stepped close to him, but he showed her his palm to get her to keep her distance. The rejection made her wince, but he needed his space. "You can say what you need to say from there."

"I panicked. I felt overwhelmed."

"And you think I didn't?"

After a deep inhale, her cheeks puffing out when she let her breath go, Matilda stepped another pace towards him. "I felt cross with myself for expecting you to save me. I shouldn't have done that because it made me blame you when it wasn't your fault. I'm scared for Artan and I'm scared for the future. But fear doesn't get me anywhere. I need to have faith."

"What, so you finally trust me now?" Spike said.

Another pace towards him, Matilda held out her hands to Spike. He looked down at them. "It's not about trusting you. It never should have been. I've *always* trusted you. You have my heart already, Spike. You've had it for years now. You know that."

"So what's it about, then?"

"It's about having faith. About holding onto the light when the world seems so, so dark."

"What do you have faith in?"

"*Us.* I have faith that we'll find a way. No matter what happens, we'll make it work. It's my turn to make a promise to you."

Spike waited for her to continue.

"I promise to stand beside you on this journey. There are so many things out of our control, but not that. The future might look bleak, but if I don't try to find a better way for us and for Artan, then how can I expect anything to change? I should have said this years ago, and I'm sorry it's taken me so long, but I'm ready to stand beside you. If you're prepared to stand with me?"

Spike reached out and held onto her warm grip. His words caught on the lump in his throat and his eyes burned as his view of his love blurred. "I never went away, Tilly."

While biting her bottom lip, Matilda nodded at Spike. "Thank you."

They leaned towards one another and kissed. Spike tasted the salt of her tears.

When they pulled away, Spike's chest swelled with an energy he'd thought lost. "We'll find a way."

She smiled. "I know." After letting go of his hands, she stepped back a pace. "Now I'd best go before someone notices I'm not in my bed. Thank you for hearing me out."

Spike watched his love walk back around the corner she'd appeared from. Whatever happened starting tomorrow, they'd find a way.

After he'd given Matilda a minute or two to get clear of the dining hall, he walked back in the direction of his room. The moonlight gave him a clear enough view of the open field for him to see his love. It also showed him the figure in the doorway to his dorm. He stopped and stared at the thickset man. Maybe Bleach stood in the light on purpose. It showed Spike that he watched Matilda.

When Bleach returned his attention to Spike, he did something Spike hadn't seen from the stoic man before. He smiled.

After staring at Spike for a few more seconds, Bleach turned around and walked back into their dorm. Whatever happened tomorrow, Spike now had Matilda beside him. He didn't need anything else.

END OF BOOK ONE.

Thank you for reading *Protectors - Book one of Beyond These Walls.*

If you'd like to be notified when book two becomes available, you can sign up to my spam-free mailing list at www.michaelrobertson.co.uk

~

Support the Author

Dear reader, as an independent author I don't have the resources of a huge publisher. If you like my work and would like to see more from me in the future, there are two things you can do to help: leaving a review, and a word-of-mouth referral.

Releasing a book takes many hours and hundreds of dollars. I love to write, and would love to continue to do so. All I ask is that you leave an Amazon review. It shows other readers that you've enjoyed the book and will encourage them to give it a try too. The review can be just one sentence, or as long as you like.

Or save money by picking up the entire series box set at www.michaelrobertson.co.uk

THE ALPHA PLAGUE
THE COMPLETE SERIES
MICHAEL ROBERTSON
THE ALPHA PLAGUE 1
THE ALPHA PLAGUE 2
THE ALPHA PLAGUE 3
THE ALPHA PLAGUE 4
THE ALPHA PLAGUE 5
THE ALPHA PLAGUE 6
THE ALPHA PLAGUE 7
THE ALPHA PLAGUE 8

ABOUT THE AUTHOR

Like most children born in the seventies, Michael grew up with Star Wars in his life. An obsessive watcher of the films, and an avid reader from an early age, he found himself taken over with stories whenever he let his mind wander.

Those stories had to come out.

He hopes you enjoy reading his books as much as he does writing them.

Michael loves to travel when he can. He has a young family, who are his world, and when he's not reading, he enjoys walking so he can dream up more stories.

Contact

www.michaelrobertson.co.uk

subscribers@michaelrobertson.co.uk

ALSO BY MICHAEL ROBERTSON

THE SHADOW ORDER:

The Shadow Order

The First Mission - Book Two of The Shadow Order

The Crimson War - Book Three of The Shadow Order

Eradication - Book Four of The Shadow Order

Fugitive - Book Five of The Shadow Order

Enigma - Book Six of The Shadow Order

Prophecy - Book Seven of The Shadow Order

The Faradis - Book Eight of The Shadow Order

The Complete Shadow Order Box Set - Books 1 - 8

~

GALACTIC TERROR:

Galactic Terror: A Space Opera

Galactic Retribution - A Space Opera - Galactic Terror Book Two

~

NEON HORIZON:

The Blind Spot - A Cyberpunk Thriller - Neon Horizon Book One.

Prime City - A Cyberpunk Thriller - Neon Horizon Book Two.

Bounty Hunter - A Cyberpunk Thriller - Neon Horizon Book Three.

Connection - A Cyberpunk Thriller - Neon Horizon Book Four.

Reunion - A Cyberpunk Thriller - Neon Horizon Book Five.

Eight Ways to Kill a Rat - A Cyberpunk Thriller - Neon Horizon Book Six.

Neon Horizon - Books 1 - 3 Box Set - A Cyberpunk Thriller.

THE ALPHA PLAGUE:

The Alpha Plague: A Post-Apocalyptic Action Thriller

The Alpha Plague 2

The Alpha Plague 3

The Alpha Plague 4

The Alpha Plague 5

The Alpha Plague 6

The Alpha Plague 7

The Alpha Plague 8

The Complete Alpha Plague Box Set - Books 1 - 8

BEYOND THESE WALLS:

Protectors - Book one of Beyond These Walls

National Service - Book two of Beyond These Walls

Retribution - Book three of Beyond These Walls

Collapse - Book four of Beyond These Walls

After Edin - Book five of Beyond These Walls

Three Days - Book six of Beyond These Walls

The Asylum - Book seven of Beyond These Walls

Between Fury and Fear - Book eight of Beyond These Walls

Before the Dawn - Book nine of Beyond These Walls

The Wall - Book ten of Beyond These Walls

Divided - Book eleven of Beyond These Walls

Escape - Book twelve of Beyond These Walls

It Only Takes One - Book thirteen of Beyond These Walls

Trapped - Book fourteen of Beyond These Walls

This World of Corpses - Book fifteen of Beyond These Walls

Blackout - Book sixteen of Beyond These Walls

Beyond These Walls - Books 1 - 6 Box Set

Beyond These Walls - Books 7 - 9 Box Set

Beyond These Walls - Books 10 - 12 Box Set

Beyond These Walls - Books 13 - 15 Box Set

~

OFF-KILTER TALES:

The Girl in the Woods - A Ghost's Story - Off-Kilter Tales Book One

Rat Run - A Post-Apocalyptic Tale - Off-Kilter Tales Book Two

~

Masked - A Psychological Horror

~

CRASH:

Crash - A Dark Post-Apocalyptic Tale

Crash II: Highrise Hell

Crash III: There's No Place Like Home

Crash IV: Run Free

Crash V: The Final Showdown

~

NEW REALITY:

New Reality: Truth

New Reality 2: Justice

New Reality 3: Fear

~

Audiobooks:

CLICK HERE TO VIEW MY FULL AUDIOBOOK LIBRARY.